EVERY MAN IN UNIFORM DREAMED OF THE DAY HE WOULD ATTAIN THE HONOR OF THE GOLD SHIELD.

Anthony Sorrentino had won his—honestly. Joseph Sorrentino was going to make certain that no one took it away.

Here is Joseph Sorrentino's dramatic story—the true story of one man's passion to acquit his brother . . . the shocking trial that shook the New York Police Department . . . and the triumphant personal story of Joseph Sorrentino's rise from the depths of street gangdom to the top of the legal profession: the story of a street tough who made all his finest dreams come true and—in the most ironic twist of all—found the touchstone of his career defending the brother he was certain had been framed.

THE GOLD SHIELD

JOSEPH SORRENTINO

A DELL BOOK

Published by
Dell Publishing Co., Inc.
1 Dag Hammarskjold Plaza
New York, New York 10017

Copyright © 1980 by Joseph Sorrentino

All rights reserved. No part of this book may be
reproduced or transmitted in any form or by any
means, electronic or mechanical, including photocopying,
recording or by any information storage and retrieval
system, without the written permission of the
Publisher, except where permitted by law.

Dell ® TM 681510, Dell Publishing Co., Inc.

ISBN: 0-440-13097-2

Printed in the United States of America
First printing—September 1980

*To the teachers of America
who bring out the gifts in us all*

This is a true story. However, dramatic license was taken in presenting the legal events—without altering the legal merits—of the case depicted in this book. Except for Arthur Goldberg, John Lindsay, Frank Serpico, Gary Olsen, the names of teachers, Father Russo, the author's family, and celebrities, all names appearing in this book are entirely fictitious, and any resemblance to the names of living persons is wholly coincidental.

PROLOGUE

I do not believe that when an accusation is made against a police officer it should be swept under the rug no matter how spotless is the background of that officer or how unsavory his accuser. But I do believe there is a better way af airing the charges than to leave the decision of whether or not to have a trial solely up to the police department's Division of Internal Affairs. I cannot blame all the agents of Internal Affairs for the egregious action described in this book. I am sure there are good, decent, and fair men in that agency who do their job conscientiously, but in the case of *NYPD* v. *Sorrentino* one or some agents in hot thirst to come up with bodies were willing to go forward with any accusation no matter how it reeked of fraud. With the Serpico scandal in the headlines, someone in Internal Affairs, overzealous and unconscionable, got behind the accusing John Tarras and added to his lies, polished the lies, and pushed the lies to get a department conviction. I believe in the common sense and fairness of the people, and I don't think this outrage would have occurred had this matter gone to a grand jury. I think that before a dedicated police officer has his reputation, career, and financial security wiped out by a department trial, he first should have the benefit of an objective hearing by fair-minded citizens of his community.

PART 1

THE SET UP

CHAPTER ONE

It was a breezy California night; my wife Sherrill was snug under the blankets with her eyes closed, drifting into quiet sleep. I propped up a pillow, preparing to get some late-hour work done on a legal matter that required some review of code sections in civil procedure. As my eyes strained under the faint beam of light from a small reading lamp, I realized how many more hours I was putting in since I had opened my own law firm, but the independence I was enjoying and the sense of accomplishment were more than worth the extra effort. When the phone rang, Sherrill's eyes flicked open but they closed again as she saw my hand reaching over and picking up the receiver. The caller was my brother Anthony from Brooklyn, the oldest son in our large family.

"Hello, Joey. I'm sorry it's late but there's something I gotta talk to you about."

"What is it?" From his strained tone I immediately sensed it was urgent.

"I've been dismissed from the police force." His voice trailed off. "I've been found guilty of taking a bribe."

There was a strained silence. I couldn't believe it. I just couldn't believe that he had been found guilty of taking a bribe. The word had such an ugly ring to it, carrying a moral stench and criminal consequences tied unswervingly to the labels of convict and ex-con. These words and labels I could never imagine falling on my brother. He was the son who was always the model boy, and the cop who was ranked number one in virtually every precinct he served with and who had become the number-one-ranked detective in the entire Bronx Borough command.

"My God, Tony, how could this happen?"

"A syndicate operator named John Tarras, who I arrested five years ago in the The Bronx, claims he paid me money to copy the syndicate's bank data that we had confiscated from him. Then he said we had meetings for a pad, you know, regular payoffs." He spoke volatilely. "The whole story is a stinking fraud. I never took anything from anyone. I don't know why he's doing this. I gave him a fair shake."

"Wait a minute!" I interrupted. "You mean this all allegedly happened five years ago and he just came forward now to accuse you? That sounds fishy to begin with."

"It's all so phony. What he's saying makes no sense at all. He would have no reason to copy the plays."

"I'm not following you. Why would he have no reason to copy the plays?"

"Because we didn't go into his place with the warrant until two-thirty P.M. By that time all the numbers are called into the syndicate. They already had the information on the slips we confiscated. That's the way they operate. All the action is called in before two P.M."

"But the department was still willing to accept his story."

"This Serpico mess has the department in a purge fever. Internal Affairs would have run with anything."

Sherrill, awakened by my rising voice, got up and went into the bathroom. The phone was shaking in my hand. "Do Mom and Dad know yet? Did you tell them?"

"I went to see them right away." His voice caught. "You know the way the papers put things."

"It's good they didn't get it cold that way. And Theresa? She knows?"

"She found out the same afternoon. Captain Fazio called me into his office. I don't remember what I said. I just mumbled something to him, and left his office in a daze. I ended up in the bathroom with the dry heaves. All I could think about was Theresa and the family."

"How did they find you guilty of this?"

"The accusation was totally uncorroborated. It was my word against Tarras's. Not even his wife would back his story."

"And they accepted his word over yours."

"We found ten thousand plays in his apartment. He was a big banker tied to the syndicate in New Jersey."

"What about your police work all these years? Didn't the court give any weight to your record?" My anger was rising.

"The judge was tuned out to my side. He was a deputy police commissioner. The Serpico scandal has blown the roof off the police department and they're going crazy."

"That's no excuse. They can't treat you shabbily because they've got a scandal to clean up. They have to prove this guy was telling the truth."

"I was the first cop to arrest him and get him a felony conviction."

"There's a motive right there. He was looking for a chance to get back at you all these years. He saw this scandal as his chance."

"Joey, at this time Internal Affairs will swallow anything."

"Aren't they like the CIA of the police department, the cops who spy on cops?"

"Yes, but I suppose you can't blame all of them. It was a Deputy Inspector Hopper who wouldn't listen to me. He brushed off whatever I told him."

"Crusty, eh?"

"For a little publicity he threw me to the sharks."

"For a little publicity men have become whores."

"Anyway, Deputy Inspector Hopper asked why I

took this case to the grand jury. Can you imagine? This was one of my best pieces of work. We found ten thousand plays. This guy was a big syndicate banker, dealing in millions. So I took it to the grand jury and got questioned about it."

"And because you got a felony indictment against Tarras, Hopper got suspicious?"

"Right. He was thinking I was out to get the guy. Of course I was out to get him. Hell, I'm a cop. He was a big honcho. The fact that I wanted to get him badly in Hopper's mind could only be explained by a mercenary motive. It couldn't be out of a sense of duty. That's how crazy this department has become. It makes me sick."

"If you do your job too well it's suspicious. What an Alice in Wonderland moral universe."

"Can you imagine?" he said in a mocking laugh. "They even gave me trouble for reconnoitering junkyards on my day off. You know, I should have listened to the old-timer who gave me advice my first day on the job. He told me to keep my mouth shut, look the other way, and collect my pension in twenty years. He said the active men who risk their lives only get kicked in the ass. He warned me that on this job you're only a shield number. He was right."

Intuitively, I could not accept the possibility that my brother had accepted a bribe. Such behavior was too out of character, too much against his proven honesty and extraordinarily conscientious approach to his job. I was stunned and confused, believing in his innocence but not immediately blind to the other possibility that he might have been guilty. Yet deeper thought melted any hazy lingering webs of doubt, and put the truth in unshakable form for me to cling to with confidence. Tony's explanation of events was reasonable enough, but even more convincing to me was the moral sinew in his character that I had been familiar with for many years. The earnest feelings came through in his voice that trembled at times with hurt, anger, and a deep sense of disillusionment. Everything that connected me with life in all my experiences told me these were the emotions of an innocent man.

On the other end, I heard him clear his throat.

"Joey, will you take the case and be my lawyer?"

"Of course I will. I think the first step will be to try to get the matter reopened within the department. I'll have to prepare a brief. Then I'll come back to New York to argue it. Then, hopefully, I'll represent you in a new trial. Tony . . ."

"Yes, Joe?"

"Try to get some sleep. We have a fight ahead of us and I can't have you breaking down in the middle."

"I'll do my best. I can't say it'll be easy."

"And, Tony?"

"Yes, Joe?"

"That goes for Theresa and the family too."

My hand was shaking when I hung up the receiver. My God, this was unbelievable. I sat back on the bed feeling stunned by the enormity of it. I did not see how this could have happened. It shouldn't have happened. My temper was smoldering. I slammed my fist against the table, ranted a few curses, picked up my law book and threw it down, knocking over an ashtray and spilling ashes over the rug. I rambled on bitterly about Internal Affairs and the New York Police Department, where Anthony had served with brilliant dedication. Their idea of a fair trial reminded me of a back-alley butcher performing an abortion with rusty knives.

Sherrill came out of the bathroom having heard what had happened and she lifted her face up to mine, moving very close so that I could smell the shampoo scent in her hair. She gently guided me to the side of the bed. "Surely his innocence will come out in a trial," she said.

"There was a department trial the police gave him, similar to a court-martial in the military. They found him guilty solely on the word of this crook. Dammit, Sherrill, there wasn't one corroborating witness."

"Oh, my God, what a horrible thing to do to someone. His lifetime dream ruined and disgraced. Theresa must be going through so much."

"I'm sure the whole family is torn up. He was the pride of us all."

"It sounds so crazy."

I gazed into her sympathetic eyes for a moment, and then went back to looking straight ahead. "Tony has a set of principles he lives by. You grow up with somebody and you know what they're made of, and how they tick. We shined shoes together, delivered newspapers, worked in the garment center, even in the same grocery store, and he always did things the right way. He was always so conscientious. God, I couldn't even get him to steal a can of tuna fish."

"He was such an outstanding cop," she said affectionately. "He was always that way. Your mom told me over the phone how he always worked to help the family."

"Do you know why he became a cop? There was an incident we both witnessed as boys. We watched a huge man walking with the wife of a small frail guy who was chasing after them. The husband was begging his wife to return to their home and children. The larger man grabbed hold of him and pounded him in the face until the husband was bloodied and senseless. Then the hulk flung him contemptuously into the gutter. The scene was so tragic that it hurt Anthony deeply and made him cry. Later the injustice of it made him angry and he wanted to do something for the littler man. As a cop he felt he had a chance to protect people."

"Is there any way he can get his job back?"

Not answering her question right away, I shook my head in bewilderment. "If anything bad had to happen you'd figure it would be me. It would make sense that way. I was the son always in trouble." I paused and looked over at her. "He wants me to be his lawyer."

"Think this over carefully, Joe. Don't rush into a pool that has no water in it."

"What does that mean?"

"Look before you leap." She put her hand tenderly on my neck. "Maybe a New York lawyer might be better. The procedures are so complex."

"My brother means a lot to me. He knows I'll work harder than a stranger."

"Maybe in the morning you'll feel different. You're so upset now. I just don't want you to rush off on impulse and anger."

"Sherrill, I have to go. To me it's a personal war." I could feel my heart pounding at my words.

Showing concern at my eagerness, she seemed to hesitate but then expressed the real thought that worried her. "Maybe you're going back there to prove something. I was never blind to how much you cared about what your father felt about you and how it has bothered you that he shows so little interest in you."

"It has nothing to do with my father," I said rather sensitively.

"When will you leave, if you go?"

"I'm going to have to first prepare a brief and most of that I can do here from the office. It will probably be three or four weeks before I go. I'd love for you to come but I know with your master's thesis coming up that's out."

She reached up and kissed me on the cheek. "Whatever you have to do to help Anthony, I'm with you. Now get some sleep."

I got under the covers and lay there in bed, hands behind my head, staring up at the dark ceiling, still brooding. I was feeling old impulses from my street years coming back in waves. I felt the urge to drag this Tarras into a back alley and prove his lies with my fists. He had ruined everything my brother had worked so hard for so many years to accomplish. I had heard hurt in his voice although he had too much pride to reveal how deep were his worries about himself and his family. I just didn't know how he was going to manage as an expelled cop out of work to take care of a wife and three children. He had a right to be bitter at the New York Police Department. For ten years he had strived and labored to build an exemplary record as a police officer. He had racked up more than four hundred arrests, which easily doubled that of the average police officer, and his police work was so methodical and painstakingly thorough that his conviction rate was more than a hundred percent higher than the average cop's. He had given his dedicated best to the police department, and they treated him like fodder. It was clear to me that his disappointment in the department had been all the stronger because he had a stubbornly sincere faith that it was run by men of courage and integrity.

Restless, I got up from bed and paced back and forth in the room, almost sick with the desire to do something. At the window a rising moon was above the palm trees brightly dimming the flicker of distant stars. I could pick up the shadowy dance of branches casting their shapes on walls and the neon dots of a bank clock blinking on and off. The quiet of the sleeping neighborhood magnified the intruding sounds of static electricity in wires and the drone of the distant freeway and the lumbering of a truck rolling on Wilshire Boulevard. I could feel the coolness from the sea and smell the pine trees and the sharper odor of eucalyptus. How aloof nature seemed to the fragile tumults of the human spirit.

I broke out of my trance when I saw a twin-engine plane flashing its beacons as it swooped down to land at Santa Monica Airport, reminding me of the continent dividing New York and California and once again setting off my frustration and fury. Moving back to the bed, I sat on the edge looking down at Sherrill's face on the pillow. Just watching her seemed to soothe me. Her breaths were slow and gentle, her lips partly open. She never wore more than a bare touch of lipstick, so her features were the same night and day. Tonight she was wearing a bright green nightgown that accented her vivid green eyes. At twenty-eight, her hair was still a clean blond and her skin a very fair white with the delicate texture that went along with her kind of blond. I remembered how attracted I had been to those qualities of her appearance. Aside from the coloring, her features had a wholesomeness that matched the genuineness of her farm-girl upbringing. She had nice height and a good figure, and when she wore a smart dress and heels, she always drew a lot of stares. I felt proud having her for my wife. Beyond her beauty and down-home traits she had an exceptional intelligence, graduating close to or at the top of her class from every school she went to, including UCLA. Winner of a National Merit Scholarship and Phi Beta Kappa key, she was gifted with an IQ that could chew up calculus. I respected her judgment tremendously, and I was happy that she shared my strong feelings about Anthony's innocence. Her good judgment could be attributed to her intellect, but I preferred to believe that her sense of people came from growing up in the country. She had been right to point out that one of my reasons for taking on this challenge was because of my father. I was aware of the possibility that it may have all stemmed from a need to prove something to him. Maybe everything I had accomplished in my career had been to win his approval. And yet, it had never come.

CHAPTER TWO

"NYPD versus Sorrentino" was the quietly unnerving bold-printed caption on the voluminous trial transcript sitting on my desk. From the day it arrived, special delivery, I had been unable to tear myself away from it. I found myself sputtering curses as I read the legal documentation because of the unbelievable number of unfair rulings against Tony. By the time I had given the entire transcript a thorough reading, I was convinced that the court had come up with a guilty verdict on shoddy evidence and appalling legal procedures.

Going through the transcript a second time, I looked for rulings by the trial commissioner that appeared to be actions beyond judicial discretion to base my claim of reversible error. Whenever I found what appeared to be judicial error, I circled the ruling in red ink. Delving into the thicket of words, I found the transcript loaded with procedural errors dealing with the admissibility of evidence. The frequent bad rulings were carrying me to the point where I was muttering sniping criticisms. It became clear to me that the trial commissioner had not been so outrageously erroneous out of a dull legal mind. From the overwhelmingly one-sided bias of his rulings, it became crystal clear that he had made up his mind at the outset how the trial was going to come out. What had been billed as a trial was merely a sham of going through formalities to put the stamp of legitimacy on what was an expedient head-chopping to take the heat off the police brass. The presiding legal officer in the trial was himself a deputy commissioner, a member of the police hierarchy who held a top office. It seemed obvious that he was boiling with all the others in the same Serpico kettle. But why did all this have to fall on Tony?

I shifted my attention to the testimony of the prosecution's only witness, John Tarras, the syndicate banker my brother had once convicted of a felony. In page after page of his testimony, I found his words riddled with discrepancies, contradictions, and glaring inconsistencies. He often sounded like he was talking gibberish. At times his story just didn't make any sense at all. Yet I knew even with all the flagrant weaknesses in his testimony, it was going to be extremely tough to win a new trial. From time to time a little sickening ball of worry sprouted in my gut as I considered the slimness of our chances. We were up against a stacked deck. The Serpico scandal had created one of the biggest sensations in the history of the New York Police Department. For weeks without interruption stories of police corruption were carried in the media. Upheavals and shakeups in the department were headline and page-one news in *The New York Times*, the *New York Post*, the *Daily News*, and the major topic on nightly news on radio and television and picked up on national networks and followed with great interest everywhere in America. On April 25, 1970, a story was run on the front page of *The New York Times* that was shocking.

GRAFT PAID TO POLICE HERE
SAID TO RUN INTO MILLIONS

Public opinion, like a sleeping beast, was roused from its apathetic slumber and roared its indignation at the police department. Mayor Lindsay was promising the most thorough investigation in the history of the city. In this feverish climate it was going to be some task to convince police officials that they made a mistake with my brother. I had to be a candidate for *The Gong Show* to imagine my talents were going to budge this giant soulless monolith. Shouts of foul play or denial of due process were likely to have as much impact on the police department as a gnat hitting steel. It was a gravely mistaken notion to believe the abstract principles of jurisprudence so dearly embraced in a court of law had much weight in a bureaucratic universe. When I accepted this challenge, my rather naïve fantasy was that by charging into the police department on a white horse of justice, brandishing the lance of a Harvard law education, this blubbery, insensitive monolith was going to undo its wrongful action, even though politically it was in its best interest to do nothing.

Still, I couldn't give up hope on the idea that somewhere in the police department was a powerful official who was also a man with guts and integrity and a strong sense of fair play who would hear me out and grant a new trial. Ineluctably I was drawn to consider other strategies of attack to beat City Hall. Scratching my head, it occurred to me that the best way to fight politics was with politics. A sense of realism told me the logic of politics more than justice was going to be the lever to make the police department act. It was a sound conclusion as far as it went, but how was I going to muster political muscle, not being connected to any authority myself? Maybe, I thought, I could be a gadfly turning one giant against another. Every day the newspapers reveal how when one bureaucracy fouls up, another is ready to take advantage for political gain. Internal Affairs was the watchdog of the police department, the agency that went after malfeasant cops, but no one appeared to be watching how Internal Affairs conducted its own ship. The vigilance of the muckraking press curiously stopped at the watchdog's door. Never in the history of New York did the press ever scrutinize Internal Affairs.

The constant and omnipresent question in my mind was, Why was Tarras framing Tony? Revenge had probably played a part in it, but an old grudge hardly seemed a strong enough motive to take on all the risks of falsely accusing a gold shield detective. I squeezed every word of his testimony trying to find a link to his motive but not a shred came to the surface. While I had no concrete evidence, I did have intuitive notions and theories on why he might have fabricated this story. My chief assumption was that he was in need of immunity. I had to believe that Tarras had been snared in a jam and was desperately cornered, and he was looking for a way to wiggle himself clear, and it dawned on him that he could win big favors with the police department if in the midst of their Serpico scandal he offered a detective's head. With the media and public opinion raining denunciations, Tarras must have rightly surmised that the police brass would be ready to deal if he offered them something big and that they would not care how badly tattered his story was. For a man like Tarras, a street survivor, it would make no difference that the policeman he was targeting was innocent so long as it got him out of his jam. The idea of falsely accusing someone and thereby ruining his career and reputation seems a callously ugly way to protect oneself, but I had long ago witnessed the fierce ruthlessness of the survival instinct. I remember as a child I once watched a frog with its belly ripped and its torn vitals hanging out and its heart severed manage to drag itself into the cover of bushes for safety.

It was easy to feel a strong measure of fury against Tarras. I knew Anthony was a good and decent man, and I believed in his innocence. I knew how much hurt Tarras had caused him, yet I harbored even greater resentment for the Internal Affairs agents who were responsible in this case. What galled me was the consistent impression that certain agents knowingly and deliberately furthered this false story out of blind ambition. I found it hard to accept the fact that these so-called sophisticated, savvy, street-wise veterans were duped by Tarras's absurdly illogical story. I was convinced that the agents let themselves be fooled.

Yet my theories on motivation, while plausible, were too general and vague and would remain speculation until I could find the concrete facts. I needed names, places, dates, times, and hard evidence to justify a retrial.

I picked up the phone and asked my secretary to put a call through to New York. I wanted to speak to Anthony. I had questions on my mind in trying to structure the arguments of our brief but I also felt a need to talk to him. My emotions were as deeply caught up in the case as his own. It was good to hear his voice.

"Hello, Joey. Well what did you think of the transcript?"

"Makes Joe McCarthy look like Cicero," I chuckled weakly. "I want to go over certain facts with you."

"What do you want to know?"

"Tell me what happened after you arrested Tarras."

"The normal procedure. I brought him back to the station house to book him."

"You put the cuffs on him?"

"No, nothing like that. He wasn't giving me any trouble. This guy was a syndicate banker. You don't figure him being crazy or that he'd pull something violent. My partner was with me, and we were always behind him."

"In California they put the cuffs on you for any arrest, even overdue parking tickets, if it goes to warrant."

"They operate differently out there. More crazies, maybe."

"Did you talk to him?"

"Sure."

"What about?"

"Small talk. The ball scores, maybe. Nothing worth remembering."

"Tell me something. Is it possible the people in Internal Affairs were out to get you?"

"No, not me personally."

"What does that mean?"

"Well, after Serpico broke some heavy scandals in the department, Internal Affairs came out looking bad, like they hadn't been on the job. So I'm sure they were anxious to make something happen."

"Would that include making deals with hoods for evidence, even granting them immunity?"

"It could. But look, I don't say there's anything wrong with that; sometimes it's the only way they can get at a bad cop, by promising leniency to somebody in return for testimony."

"Let's go back to the first time you heard about the charges. How did it come down?"

"A lawyer for the Patrolmen's Benevolent Association came to see me. He told me he had something important to discuss with me. We went to lunch on the Grand Concourse in The Bronx. He had a manila envelope with him, said it had a list of policemen. My name was there. He told me I was going to be dismissed from the force."

"This was before any hearing or inquiry?"

"Yes." His voice rasped. "I said to him, 'What are you talking about? I haven't done anything wrong. I'm not guilty of anything.'"

"How did he answer?"

"He asked if I wanted to be represented by an attorney at an inquiry that was going to be held. I told him I didn't need an attorney. I had nothing to hide."

"Was Tarras at the inquiry?"

"No, I only saw him later at the trial. I felt so helpless sitting there, watching him lie."

"Let's assume Tarras got into trouble and someone offered to go easy if he'd hand them the head of a bad cop."

"Pretty safe assumption. Tarras did exactly that a year before."

"Did he mention you?"

"No. Nothing about me came up until this case."

"That almost fits, doesn't it?" I tapped my fingers against my forehead. "Let's suppose he couldn't bargain with them this time because he'd already told them everything he knew. He'd be forced to make up something. And who would be the logical choice? You!"

"I suppose it would be me because I was the first cop to bust him, to stick him with a felony."

"Perhaps, but I don't place much weight on revenge. I'm sure he hated your guts, but criminals don't come out of the shadows to use the legal system to hurt back. The street mentality wants to keep a distance from cops and courts. Revenge comes with a switchblade in the back."

"You rule out revenge?"

"I don't rule out anything, but I see it as ancillary. Survival was his motive. He must have been facing imminent annihilation."

"What if he wasn't up against the wall like you figure?"

I scratched my chin meditatively. "Then someone else must have put him up to it."

"Who?"

"An egomaniac in Internal Affairs."

"Deputy Inspector Hopper?"

"He did a good job going after crooked cops but maybe he got overzealous, lost his ability to be objective, got intoxicated with his kills or became sloppy, or maybe he hardened into a ruthless grandstander."

"His main concern was protecting the police department. He said he wanted to throw out the bad eggs. He wanted the department to look good."

"And that's why he joined the priesthood, because he's such an altruist. I'm sure he wanted to make himself look good, was growing heady with his own image as the great corruption slayer. With Hopper I see more probability of blind ego rather than blind ambition."

"A fine distinction."

"There are more sinister scenarios to consider."

"You mean high-ranking officials in the department behind all the corruption?"

"Serpico complained that none of the big bosses were being reached. What if someone felt the heat was getting too close to him and he wanted the investigation stopped? A frame-up helps."

"That's pretty farfetched, Joe." His voice was loaded with skepticism. "You're saying a boss put Tarras up to it."

"Maybe a police boss has stocks in the syndicate. Takes a big cut out of the street action. He orchestrates the whole galaxy of pads in the city. Someone like that would want the Serpico probe stopped. Throw out heads and get the media off the department's back."

"You're getting pretty wild for me."

"I still think survival is the key in the motive for this fraud, but if we're going to discover the truth we can't overlook any hidden corner. Let me explore one more intriguing theory of conspiracy. What if organized crime was behind the frame-up? They could have put the screws on Tarras."

"That doesn't make any sense. Why should they want me off the force? I'm only one cop."

"Didn't you crack that bulldozer and diesel truck theft ring? You closed down a business that was netting them two hundred grand a day. You cost them tens of millions of dollars. It rankled them enough to make threats on your son's life. Certainly they had a motive to be rid of you."

"What you're saying implies collusion. I can't accept the suspicion that bosses on the police job are allies with organized crime."

"I am sure that most of the top cops are honest straight shooters, but you can be sure that there have been and are now and will always be crooks in high places. Look at recent history in this country. A supreme court judge in Illinois, a crook; a senator from Connecticut, a crook; a governor of New Mexico, a crook. These men caught represent tiny hairs plucked out of a furry monster. Conspiracy buffs think the CIA had a hand in the Kennedy assassination, and they still haven't found out the truth."

"I suppose if you look at it that way then anything is possible."

"That's precisely the point. Our energies have to be focused on the probable motive, but we should not close our eyes to other ideas."

"So what do we do next?"

"First I finish the brief and then come to New York to make a motion to the commissioner's office for a new hearing. After that we persuade the judge that Tarras lied. If I only knew what kind of trouble he was in. If he'd been arrested, there'd be records, wouldn't there?"

"Assuming he made a deal with Internal Affairs?"

"Yah."

"No way. They don't exactly want it in the *Daily News* that they make deals like that, you know."

"Then that's going to be a big problem for us. Let me think further on this and I'll get back to you when I can."

I hung up the receiver and swung around in the swivel chair, comfortably rocking back while staring out at the magnificent view from the floor-to-ceiling window running the length of the wall. Stacks of legal files were waiting for my attention but I lacked the willpower at the moment to push myself up from the relaxing position. In the distance I could see the blue waves of the ocean breaking into the shore and drifting clouds of pearl fluff as the sun grew brighter and redder as it blended into the steely blue. It was a form of aesthetic therapy to watch the ocean and it always gave me a release from the tight vise of the daily grind.

After a while I got up from the desk and went to the glinting silver coffeepot on the credenza and poured myself a cup of coffee, and then moved back to the leather chair, stirring the cream into a smooth brew and scanning the surroundings. The mahogany, insulated, air-conditioned office was adorned with thick shag carpeting and furnished with leather reclining chairs and a redwood chess set and a number of tasteful antiques. Along one wall were framed certificates of admission to practice law in the federal, state, and maritime courts and some civic awards and Latin-worded degrees from Harvard Law School, UCLA, UCSB, and a special-study program at Oxford University. From the window I looked down, feeling eerily separated from the street eighteen stories below by a waferthin panel of glass. We were in the newest, sleekest high rise in Century City, the prestigious commercial wing of Beverly Hills, and our address was on the Avenue of the Stars, a string of symbols that blared success with the subtlety of an air raid siren; but that was the way things were done out here in a newcomers' society, success symbols replacing long-established reputation as the guide to one's professional abilities.

On top of one of the high-rise structures, I spotted a foursome of aging businessmen in white tennis outfits playing a relaxed set of doubles. I thought there was something symbolic about a tennis court paved on top of an office building in southern California. I could never imagine businessmen on Wall Street riding the elevator up to the roof for a game of doubles. I laughed to myself imagining a bronze sculpture of tennis players atop City Hall in Beverly Hills, which was visible for miles. I could picture future archaeologists digging up the ruins of ancient twentieth-century civilization and finding intact the bronze tennis figures and pondering how important this symbol was to Beverly Hills man. Play was certainly important to the laid-back, mellow southern-California culture.

Conveniently nearby was the enormously sprawling

Hillcrest Country Club, the verdant acreage of solid oak trees and trimmed grass looming larger than all of Watts. I could see the afternoon golfers casually strolling or rolling in their little carts, making business deals while they played. I remembered how curious I once had been about how these people lived when I was a cabdriver in this town. No longer curious, I had been to and known a lot of members of the country club and I had come to conclude that their way of life wasn't all it was cracked up to be.

There was something about all this glittery flaunting of status that was shallow and offensive and that touched old scars of when I was on the bottom, but at the same time I always felt a proud sense of accomplishment. I was a partner in a law firm with our own offices on top of a Beverly Hills high rise and I was answerable to no one in any way. I could remember reading in the newspapers as a boy about places like Harvard and Beverly Hills and thinking of them as pinnacles of success and status. I had come a long way. I had to consider myself an extremely lucky person. Only a little over ten years ago, I could see myself, sprawled on my back in the inhuman blackness of the padded cell in the Parris Island brig, then kicked out of the Marines, and coming back to the Brooklyn streets, a four-time high school dropout with a long line of job failures behind me. No one would have given a penny for my future. Yet somehow I managed to redirect the course of my life. Anger had driven me. Anger had pushed me up and out. Anger had fueled the energetic effort I had made to become somebody. And now that anger had to be channeled for Tony.

I started to think that while hard work might have paid off in realizing my career, it could mean nothing in this challenge. I knew that no matter how hard I pushed and worked, I might fail. Still, set deeply in my mind, and contradicting the tides of doubt, was an aggressive pride born out of all the bloody victories in my past, both in the streets and in the ring. Overcoming the obstacles of my youth to climb to a position of respect and dignity had created a mystical faith that somehow, inexplicably, destiny had preplanned a storybook ending. It was a cryptic belief evolved and shaped from years of droning on menial jobs and plunging into one failure after another and floundering from one blunder to another and then one day finding myself a fair-sized success. I have always suspected that there was a benevolent magic working in my behalf. Yet Sherrill always warned me that one of the biggest weaknesses of any ego was believing, after winning a lot of hard battles, that you could win in any battle. Time after time I had seen individuals arrogantly miscalculate their powers because of previous victories. History was a monument to civilizations being wiped out on the fatal logic of hubris.

I had not arrived at any decision yet on how to proceed if we won a new trial. I was going to have to meet with Anthony so that we could put our heads together and figure out the best defense strategy to pursue. I expected to bone up on New York law, but I was going to rely on fundamental concepts of due process applicable in any American legal forum. Although I would be the active attorney pleading the case, it would be under the auspices of the firm that had previously represented him. If I failed in winning a new department hearing, I could still take it up on appeal in the state courts. This was a procedure that could become dragged out and complex, and could easily take up to two years before being heard. For Tony's sake, this was a fact that I obviously dreaded, but both of us would still have to accept it nonetheless.

I resumed my study of the transcript and at six o'clock I packed my briefcase, grabbed my keys, and locked up the office. The elevator dropped me like a whiz and I found my car in the underground parking lot. The sun was dimming over the horizon when I pulled out onto the street. Up on Wilshire Boulevard the commuter rush had reached its peak and taillights blinked and gleamed as the lines of cars inched their way home with exhaust smoke puffing in the smoggy air.

It was less than a twenty-minute drive to my house in the Brentwood suburb. As I drove along San Vincente Boulevard, an island-divided thoroughfare handsomely lined with trees and covered with groomed grass, I looked out at the Brentwood Elementary School stretched out on a spacious campus, all the small buildings immaculately white and topped brightly with red adobe tiles matching the Spanish architecture of the nearby country club lodge walled in by giant eucalyptus trees. The housees on the blocks were freshly painted, with new shutters and white picket fences, and the large lawns were kept neatly trimmed and the cars were all relatively new and shining and trees were punctually pruned to enhance a general appearance of crisp neatness and cleanliness. Brentwood was an affluent suburb with spacious and comfortable homes, but there was no sense of neighborhood. Nothing could be more different from Brooklyn, where you knew everyone on the block and you could hear people yell at each other at all hours or watch them sit on the stoops talking to each other day after day. In Brooklyn, for good or for bad, the neighborhood was another family.

The first thing I did when I went into the house was to hand Sherrill a batch of flowers I had picked from the yard. She brightened warmly and threw her arms around me to give me a tender kiss. I knew she loved flowers, and appreciated hand-picked flowers far more than store-bought, even if they were only little daisies versus a florist's long-stemmed roses.

I changed into casual clothes and went out into the yard, where I got the lawn mower out of the shed and began mowing the large lawns around our house. I once had a long conversation with my neighbor about grass and lawns. That conversation made me realize what it meant to be middle class. It also made me realize that mowing lawns had become, after jogging and tennis, my main source of physical drama and action, all three of which seemed like bland mashed potatoes when compared to where I had come from.

As I mowed, my mind drifted back to my Brooklyn days when I was fighting in the ring and brawling in the streets. I conjured up old scenes of flying over tables in saloons and crashing on chairs in the bowling alley and swinging on chandeliers in the movie house. While I was pleased with middle-class success, I had to admit, introspectively, those early years had been a time of excitement and adventure. Yet, philosophically, I knew that what went down in the streets was full of sound and fury signifying the emptiness of a rolling tin can. As a teen, I was a cool fool.

After dinner I went to the UCLA law library to do more research for the brief. I sat down at a rear table with no one else near me. The steady silence gave a tranquil and timeless atmosphere to the library and helped to relax the tightness of my nerves and composed my mind in a frame of undistracted readiness to get to work. Rolling up my sleeves and concentrating on the law books and what I had to get done released all the pent-up emotion about this case. At this point work was the best form of therapy for me.

I had mapped out clearly what I needed to get done at this research session. As in almost all legal matters, I had to get myself prepared on two tracks, one side dealing with questions of fact, the other with questions of law. For the purpose of winning a rehearing, the law side was going to be more important.

I took out a pad and pencil and began outlining diagrams and charts of the numbers operation. The organizational lines took the shape of a pyramid. The lowest and most numerous employees were the runners who went from factory to factory, apartment to apartment, and candy store to candy store gathering up all the bets. At the next level there were collectors who went from runner to runner picking up their betting slips and money collected and paying them a small fee. After taking out a commission, the collectors passed on the money and betting slips to the banker. The hub of the betting flow in a given territory was the banker. Everything came in to him. The banker called in all the information on the betting slips to syndicate headquarters and it all had to be called in by two P.M.

When Anthony and his partner arrested Tarras, who was a banker, they confiscated ten thousand betting slips for that day. According to Tarras he had still not called in those betting slips when they were confiscated and thus he was amenable to a bribe arrangement whereby he would be given an opportunity to copy the slips in exchange for a certain sum of money. The obvious flaw in his story was the fact that Anthony had not arrested him until two-thirty P.M., which meant he would have called in the information on the betting slips already. Tarras had no reason to copy the slips confiscated from him.

I pored over a bunch of decisions by the New York Court of Appeals dealing with police dismissals. My eyes squinted going over the tiny print of case after case of policemen trying to get back on the force. The cases were all going against the appealing policemen. In every instance the actions of dismissal were being upheld. It was very discouraging until I came across *Crawford* v. *Monaghan,* a case that had similarities to the present one and was extremely promising, and I found myself excitedly squirming around in the chair reading it. It was a case where an ex-felon had accused a policeman of misconduct and the officer was found guilty though no one else corroborated the charge. It was a case of the word of an ex-felon against the word of a policeman, precisely the situation we were up against, and the higher court ruled that as a matter of law a disreputable person's word alone was not enough to convict. I quickly grabbed up my pen to copy the language of the opinion, feeling uplifted and sure that I had found some strong legal ammunition at last.

Here is where I would begin to develop my case.

By the time I was making my way back home, it was quite late and dark. Glancing up, I saw blackish clouds slowly drifting over the rooftops, which meant we could be in for some rain in the morning. I walked up the block going over various ideas in my mind. A rough configuration for the brief was slowly taking shape in a conceptual stage, the major planks of arguments roughly suggesting themselves along certain logical lines, leaving it only for me to reinforce them with case citations and to fill out and polish the language. All the hours of research and digging were also a period of pulling and bringing things together in a cohesive and balanced geometry. I was considering five major sections for the brief but then decided three might be easier to organize and clearer to follow for the reader. I continued to sculpt the brief in my mind, walking up blocks without a soul in sight. Everything was lonely and distant in every direction and echoed with the silence of a ball park after everyone has gone home. It was the kind of magnified silence that's great for undistractedly looking into your own mind to get some fertile activity going.

Sherrill was asleep in the house when I let myself in the rear door. I went to the refrigerator for a beer, feeling a need to unwind and unravel the grind of a long night at the library. I plopped myself down in the living room, unbuttoned my shirt, and swigged on the beer. I glanced over at a photograph of Sherrill in the hall leading to our bedroom. Her cool green eyes had in them an honesty and directness but above all a gentleness that matched the gentle timbre of her voice. Though she was soft-spoken in a very feminine way, she could be vehemently argumentative on strongly held views. She certainly had a mind of her own resistant to any attempts on my part to influence her career. With my insecurities I was pushing and prodding her to become a doctor, looking for another status feather in my cap, but she felt no inclination at all to go into medicine, even though with her top science grades she could have been admitted to just about any medical school in the nation. Her motivation was to pursue interesting, meaningful work that would leave time for her to enjoy plenty of camping trips and hiking and outdoor activities with her family. She felt no need to impress the world and poked fun at my circle of Harvard Law friends, calling us the Harvard lizards because we reminded her of the creature who has a tendency to prance and puff and strut to attract attention. I knew she was right in attacking the vanity and hollowness of status seeking but I couldn't help myself. I was like an object shot into space caught up in the momentum of the trajectory with no freedom to change course. However much I tried, I couldn't stop running.

I chuckled to myself, thinking that there were rewards in being a status seeker or compulsive achiever. Philosophically, I could put it down, but I knew that if I had not been a Harvard lizard, I would not have ended up with a beautiful wife like Sherrill. I could remember, at the age of twenty when I was a sweaty cement laborer, how the only girls I could date were those dumpy gum-chewing ladies heavy on the arm hair in Brooklyn saloons. I thought of the all-American beauty Grace Kelly, and how I used to drool over her from the seat of the Fortway Theater in Brooklyn, dreaming of that clean, fresh, silk-skinned blond beauty. Amazingly, by running, by driving and pushing myself and winning a place in a profession, I felt I had won my own Grace Kelly.

At midnight I was still in the living room scrawling out a first draft of the brief. I was so exhausted and drained that I had a hard time focusing clearly on my

THE GOLD SHIELD

own print. From a legal point of view, I was sure there was strong justice in my arguments, but I found myself reasking the question, How much weight does justice have with the New York Police Department?

CHAPTER THREE

For the character section of the brief, I had to delve into Anthony's lifetime record of employment. He started working at age eleven in Rosenbloom's Candy Store, putting in twenty-four hours a week at twenty-five cents an hour, carting soda cases, mopping up, and polishing counter fixtures. His young eyes were mesmerized by the glinting brass soda fountains and he itched to operate the polished spigots, but he obeyed the owner's orders never to touch them. School did not hold much interest for him, although his IQ scores were high. He often daydreamed in class of captaining an ocean liner on world cruises. At twelve he was able to get a street-trade badge for a delivery route with the *Brooklyn Eagle* and by diligent canvassing he ended up with the thickest ring of customer tags on the newsboy rack. By fourteen he was able to obtain working papers from the city Board of Health and his next position was in a bleach factory. His attendance at school began to fall off as he stayed home to put in more time at the factory, but Mom and Dad did not protest his absences because in their scramble to make ends meet they needed his help. He quit school when he heard that Harry Rosenthal was in need of a new man to do sales in one of his shoe stores. His action followed the usual neighborhood practice for a son to drop out at the legal age to find a full-time job. He looked upon the shoe business as a good field to enter, believing it could lead to a store of his own someday. I remember during his first day of selling shoes he had a rattling experience. A pasty-complexioned man came in for a pair of shoes. Anthony located the style requested and placed the shoe on the man's right foot and was about to put on the left shoe but the man protested, saying it was unnecessary. Anthony insisted that he had to lace on both shoes for a proper fit. As he placed his hand around the man's left ankle to slip on the other shoe, he noticed the flesh was rigid and cold, and he suddenly realized he was clutching a wooden leg.

With his inborn streak of perfectionism, he was promoted to manager of the store after a year and then became regional manager of Rosenthal's three stores. In spite of this success he found himself growing restless with discontent. At a young age he had already mastered all the horizons of the shoe business, and instead of being a challenge, selling shoes had become confining and dull for him. There were only so many angles of lacing and unlacing a shoe on a person. It wasn't too long before he realized that the shoe trade could not hold him.

The idea of joining the police department was planted in him by an Officer Brady who had his beat around the store and often came in to talk. For Tony the life of a policeman appeared to be an exciting challenge. From Brady he heard about the competition for advancement up the ranks to gold shield detective, and it was not long before he realized that the police department offered a chance to test the untested side of his potential. As a cop he would have a chance to protect decent people against thugs, and his initial undefined need to grow became a spurring and longing to realize a dream. Out of twenty-eight thousand men who took the examination for patrolman, only nine hundred were admitted to the New York Police Department. He finished in the upper ten percent and all his proud relatives could not stop talking about how well he had done. Elated by the news that he was accepted, he went out with his fiancée Theresa to celebrate. His acceptance was good news for both of them because they could proceed with plans for getting married knowing seventy-five hundred dollars a year would be coming in and he would have a pension and hospital benefits. He told her that night that he would never become a little dictator with a shield. He resented the policemen who acted bigger and superior to ordinary people. He thought that a policeman should stand for something, a public servant who did his best to make the city a safe place to live and raise children.

He was sworn in as a probationary policeman and issued a gray uniform, gun, and shield number 3437. His recruit training period lasted four months, divided among classroom instruction, pistol practice, physical training, and fieldwork. At the graduation ceremony clear skies and a golden sun looked down at the neat formation of recruits sitting outdoors in folding chairs on the parade grounds. For the first time he was in uniform in public and he sat erect down front, feeling a proud sense of accomplishment. He had absorbed a comprehensive store of knowledge preparing him for police work. Sitting in the audience in the back rows were the recruits' parents and wives and among them were Mom and Dad and Theresa, thrilled to be a part of the pomp and ceremony.

The very next morning he reported to the 90th Precinct carrying a clothes bag, his new leather gun belt squeaking and his nightstick slapping with his steps. Gusts of strong wind flapped the American flag on the dreary old stone building, but the bad weather could not dim the bright mood that infected him as he started his first day as a full-fledged member of the New York City Police Department.

Waiting in the main sitting room along with other men for squad assignments, he checked his appearance in the full-length mirror, swinging from side to side, satisfying himself that he had no unsightly bulges or creases in his trousers. He cut a handsome figure in his uniform. At six feet he was tall by first-generation

Italian-American standards, and he had fair rather than rugged good looks with his light skin, watery blue eyes, sharp-lined jaw, and profuse shock of tawny hair set naturally in rows of rolling waves. He had a firm smooth body with wide, sloping shoulders, a broad back, and tapering waist. It was the build of a good swimmer, which he was, and he spent a lot of time at it. He always held himself erect with his shoulders thrown back, his gut sucked in, and his legs straight, but without stiffness, relaxed in their movements, which balanced well with his warm, outgoing manner.

He tried to hide the delight he was feeling seeing himself in uniform but a rippling smile gave him away. He juggled the cap to get it straight on his head. He thought it should be perfectly level, not slanted the way a cabbie wears his cap. It said something about your job attitude if you let the straightness and smoothness deteriorate in your appearance.

Initially he moved to the FBI Law Enforcement Bulletin, studying three photographs of a wanted fugitive. As he carefully observed the tough facial features, he heard a voice over his shoulder.

"Busting to make a collar, heh, kid? Want to read your name in the paper? Nail a big FBI perp?" The voice thick with a Queens accent overlaid with Irish tenor belonged to Joe Leary, fifty, a veteran patrolman, beer-bellied, round-faced, and with a receding chin that sagged around the strap of his cap. "I'll bet you're full of notions." He grinned.

"Notions?" Anthony shrugged.

"Ready to be a big hero. You're green. You'll learn."

"Am I doing something wrong?"

"I was full of notions, too, my first day on the job. I was gonna be a crusader. Wipe out the thugs from the streets."

"That sounds like good thinking for a cop."

"All emotion, no wise sense behind it. You can't wipe them out. No way. You can clean out a swamp but the weeds will always grow back. Thugs are the weeds of society."

"Well, maybe the idea is to keep down their number. I don't expect to be a police messiah. I just want to get some of these bad guys off the streets."

He patrolled his post from left to right, as taught in the academy, checking the streets for potholes, stopping at stores to make sure doors were locked, scanning windows for suspicious activity, and going into vacant buildings looking for drug buys. The 90th Precinct was considered a hazardous precinct in the midst of the Williamsburg slums. His post covered a high-crime stretch of blocks known as the hell zone. Twice he came close to being killed when he was shot at by a sniper, and on another occasion when a brick was hurled down at him from a roof. By good instincts and hard effort he was able to make a lot of arrests over the first six months on duty, and what was important in terms of attaining the gold shield, he was making them stick. His conviction rate was proving much higher than the average cop's at the 90th Precinct.

As a recognition for his good work, he was assigned to a sector car. Naturally, he welcomed the chance to be out of the weather and to enjoy the comfort of riding over walking all day, and the security of a shatterproof windshield. Driving gave him a sense of speedy potential, the mobile ability to cover a wide range, and quick means to close the gap on the fleeing criminal. His eyes surveyed all the dials glowing dimly under the panel, the two-way radio, the speedometer, the siren switch. All the electronic equipment made him feel he had more power and more control. He was enthralled by the horsepower under the hood. He would always laugh at how the little boy in him got a thrill out of hearing the ripsaw roar of the special-built hot engine when he put his foot down on the floor.

It was late one evening as he was cruising the ghetto at three A.M. when a call came over the radio: "Suspicious man in car at Flushing and Bedford." Accelerating to top speed, he and his partner reached the location in a matter of minutes. They found the block silently asleep with not a soul in sight. His eyes raked the stores lining the block. There was a closed pawn shop, a secondhand furniture outlet, a mom and pop bodega market, and several liquor stores blinking with neon lights. They hopped out of the radio car and scampered to opposite sides of the street and began checking the rows of cars. They checked and rechecked all the hallways without seeing a sign of anyone. Anthony went back to the radio car and picked up the microphone. "Central, this is R.M.P. four three eight of the ninety at Flushing and Bedford. Call is unfounded." He looked down the corner where the neon signs blinked on and off, lighting up and turning dark, and he saw no one. He repeated his report. "Call is unfounded."

Suddenly, a black man the size of Bigfoot jumped out of a liquor store. For a split second Anthony got a heart-jolting glimpse of the man's huge body and abnormally large head with a grotesque scar running from his mouth to his ear. He skidded over garbage, knocking over a trash can in a scrambling attempt to go down stairs under the building to the basement. Anthony pushed open the door to get out, but his partner grabbed his arm.

"Forget it, Tony. You got nothing here. You didn't see him do anything."

"Let me see where he went."

"You're wasting your time. You got nothing here."

"Maybe he's got something on him."

"You got nothing here. No probable cause. What did you see? A guy coming out of a store. Forget it."

"There was a witness who saw him."

"What she gonna say she saw a black man at night?"

"This one was like a standing handball wall." He jerked his arm free. "I'm going down." He sprinted across the street to the stairs leading to the basement. He hurried down, and as he entered the pitch-black quarters, he took his flashlight from his hip pocket and slipped his gun from his holster. He made sure the safety was off and a bullet was sitting in the chamber. He could see only a slender beam of light from his flashlight in the darkness. He listened for sounds of movement. The tension and fear brought adrenaline flooding into his veins and he could feel his skin begin to prickle. His heart was pounding and he knew he had to be prepared to kill the suspect. His brain filled with a playback of this man's frightening appearance. What a monster he was in size. He had to be over six six.

Anthony held a finger over the switch on the flashlight as he moved forward warily, flicking the beam up and down and to the sides. The narrow stream of light moved like a glowing crystal ball on the objects it hit, bringing shape to stacks of beer and whiskey crates and plumbing pipes and an old roller washing machine. Everything the light scanned seemed to be given a sole life as it was sculpted out of the darkness. There wasn't a sound. His shoulders scraped against the narrowly stacked beer crates in the basement, and he knew that he could easily be ambushed down here in the dark. He was giving the suspect a big edge and an easy target walking in the basement with his flashlight advertising his location. There was no doubt that the man would have the first shot if he had a gun. Subconsciously, he was hoping what they said at the academy about criminals being terrible shots was correct. At the firing range the instructor had told them that few hoods can hit a man at twelve feet. Evidently this was why bank robbers out west switched to tommy guns; they could then spray the bullets from rapid-firing automatic weapons without aiming. New York gunmen rarely could handle a pistol accurately as they tended to aim for the head, which is an elusively small target. All policemen were trained to aim at the belly. But in a dark basement, clutching a small flashlight and looking for a man the size of a standing wall, suddenly all of the lecturing on marksmanship seemed intensely irrelevant.

He smelled the air as he had been taught to do and he kept his ears perked. His scent and his hearing were his most important and vital senses in the darkness, and he focused on them intently. A slight brushing sound raced into his ears and shot around inside the skin of his skull and he whirled around with gun and searchlight. He was breathing in fast spurts that almost matched the loud racing thumping of his heart. He could feel the sticky wetness on the gun handle from his sweating hand. Suddenly from behind a tier of boxes the enormous man came out and headed for him like an oncoming train.

"Freeze or I'll blow your brains out!" he roared. "Another step and you're dead." He trained the searchlight in the man's face, holding his gun near the lens so that it could be seen by one looking into the light.

"I cop out. Don't shoot." The man's voice trembled.

"Come forward slowly or I'll kill you." Anthony's tone was truculent. In broad daylight he might have spoken more calmly, but not at three in the morning in a dark basement facing this giant. He wanted to absolutely terrorize this man into docile submission. Force had to be uppermost in the suspect's attention. It was a life-or-death game. Does he fear you or do you fear him? Anthony backpedaled slowly until he felt his back up against the door and then he shoved the gun into the suspect's belly and they both moved back out to the street. He made sure the man felt the steel jabbed into his flesh. At the academy they had taught him not to treat a prisoner gently. If you made a mistake by being nice, you could end up in the grave. Protect number one. Frighten the hell out of the other guy. For any cop in this situation, life is on the line.

"Turn around and lean against the wall," he snapped.

The enormous figure went through the motion of stretching his arms out facing the wall but his hands were touching lightly. He was casually stanced so that he could easily turn and run. Anthony noticed that the suspect was shifting his shoulders, slowly tensing his body for the right moment to whip around and punch him.

"I said lean." Anthony was not going to give him any leeway. He latched his foot around the man's thick ankle and pulled it back and at the same time he shoved hard with his free hand.

With the big man stretched off balance against the wall, Anthony frisked him and found a barber razor in his pocket. "Do you use this for styling your hair? Have you ever sliced anyone?" The man did not respond. Also in his pockets were checks made out to the liquor store as well as rolls of coins marked with the store name. Anthony handcuffed the prisoner and marched him out to the radio car. A black couple on in years came out to the street in bathrobes and the husband identified himself as the owner of the store. The couple lived above the store. Anthony took their names and telephone numbers and told them he would be needing them as witnesses.

Anthony sat in the back with the handcuffed prisoner while his partner drove them back to the station house. His voice distraught, the big black man pleaded with Anthony. "Don't book me on this. I got a wife and kids."

"So did the guy back there who owned the store."

"I needed the money. I needed the money."

"So why don't you go out and work for a living."

"I'm jammed up. I have bills and things to pay."

"So does the man who owned the store."

After earning the rank of number one patrolman at the 90th Precinct, and then also at the 68th Precinct, after only four years, Anthony got the peachy assignment that other cops longed for and waited for as long as ten years. He was promoted to plainclothes. He was sent to plainclothes school, where he attended class eight hours a day in a program of training that would last four weeks. He got to meet and know other students who had been handpicked from all over the city, presumably the best cops in the city, cops who were being moved along. The selection to plainclothes was the first step to the detective division. The classes focused on problem solving, using unorthodox methods that were totally new in the thinking of police officers. Instead of being told that his uniform must be crisp and military sharp, Anthony was being told the sloppier he appeared the better; the object was to be casual.

He was extremely happy with his promotion to plainclothes because it could help him win the gold shield. He could never emphasize enough what the gold shield meant to him and to all cops in New York City. It was raised to a cult status in police circles. When cops talked in the locker room or at a coffee shop or in a radio car, what they talked about most was the gold shield. Every man in uniform fervently dreamed of the day he would attain the honor of gold shield detective.

His first plainclothes assignment was the prostitution detail, attached to the Manhattan Task Force, which was known more familiarly among cops as the pussy posse. Chasing hookers and trollops was not his idea of an investigative challenge, but he was pleased to be doing something new and different in his police career, and he was anticipating a colorful education. His life had been pretty straightlaced. In his short tour on the vice squad, he could expect to see and hear more about the kinky side of sex than most people know about in a lifetime. He did not have a morbidly eager curiosity—awaiting him were repellingly bizarre encounters—but he did have a clinical openness to all forms of learning, and the vice world would add to his growing knowledge of people from all walks of life.

He did not go about the task of arresting prostitutes

with any great zeal, but he did lock up a good number
in the course of doing his job conscientiously. He felt a
sympathy for the girls caught up in this desperate life.
A number of women he arrested were very lovely and
sometimes showed high intelligence and the promise of
a much loftier and dignified career. He found his emotions getting pulled into his work, developing a growing bitterness and anger toward the pimps whom he
perceived as the real evil in the flesh trade. It infuriated him to see the way young girls so slavishly and
self-degradingly crawled before these satin-laced sadists. It frustrated him not being able to free one girl
from the brutal grip of this exploitation. By the time
he was moved out of vice he had grown to despise the
pimps.

Transferred to the South Bronx in the fall of 1967,
the next phase of his police career put him into the
drug war. In his efforts to crack down on the pushers,
he felt that he was fighting the mainsprings of all
crime. Behind the batterings, burglaries, and bloody
bludgeonings was usually a crazed addict thirsting for
a fix. He knew that by putting some of the pushers in
prison he would be protecting a lot of people from
injury and death. Probably his greatest satisfaction in
this campaign on the drug front was his pursuit of a
pusher named Tito Rings, who presided over a big operation in the South Bronx. Dealing in Burmese heroin, a purer and stronger variety, Rings was preying on
a lot of young people including high school and junior
high school students. After several weeks of searching
and tracking down leads, he learned that Tito made
his drops on the roof of a certain building on Kane
Street. One afternoon he went up on that roof and positioned himself behind a furnace duct out of sight,
waiting for the pusher to come to make a sale.

He heard footsteps coming up the stairs. He
crouched silently behind the duct where his eyes had a
crack through a metal loop to watch who was going to

step through the roof doorway. The steps grew louder, until the door flung open and out stepped a lone Puerto Rican boy no older than fourteen. The boy was neatly dressed in school clothes, with a clean white shirt and crisp knotted tie of dark blue and closely matching pair of blue trousers. He looked clean-cut with a fresh haircut that was short for this neighborhood. He was carrying a lunch box colorfully sketched with Walt Disney cartoon characters. Still watching him Anthony felt his heart jump when the boy removed a needle and candle from the lunch box.

The boy rolled up his sleeve and made ready with the needle to inject the drug, but before he could do it, Anthony sprung out of hiding and roughly grabbed the boy while knocking the needle from his hand. The boy began wildly thrashing and punching, cursing him as a junkie trying to rip off his stuff. Blocking the blows, Anthony grabbed the boy by the shirt and rocked him in his shoes. "Cut the shit. I'm a cop. Who gave you this stuff?"

"Tito sold me on the sidewalk. In front of the cuccifritos place. He just made a move. He turned his back and took out his hankie. He had the stuff in his hankie."

After dropping the boy off to his mother and arranging immediate medical treatment for him, Anthony and his partner headed for the cuccifritos place. They parked down the block and moved on foot hurriedly, catching sight of Tito Rings standing out front, appearing even more sinister-looking than in his mug shots. He sashayed on the sidewalk, letting the sun warm his swarthy skin while gyrating his hips to a Latin beat from a transistor radio in a tenement window. Rings was acting casually cheery, but tightly tense underneath, as his small eyes were jumping beans of alertness. He was preened as nattily as a pimp, wearing a flashy sharkskin suit that was too warm for the weather, and his wrist glittered with the expensive gold of a jeweled watch. More glitter came from diamond chips in his gold tie clasp and a gaudy pair of full-carat diamond rings flaunted on each hand. His teeth were white floss clean and unmarked, and one of his canines stuck out like an angry dog's. His facial skin had the sweet-smelling fragrant sheen of a mud-pack massage. From time to time he wiped the sweat from his face with a silken handkerchief and then took out a pack of jujube candy and poured out a little pinch on the palm of his hand and sucked down the juices, bringing a smack to his lips and satisfied gleam in his eyes, as if his thirst were temporarily quenched by the melted sugar. His brows gathered into a scowl as he gazed at the two plainclothes officers approaching him. He instinctively shot them a look of hate.

Anthony moved him back to the cuccifritos window hanging with stalks of pygmy bananas still unripely green. "We'd like you to step in the hallway."

"I'm not going noplace, man. I ain't done nothing. You got nothing on me."

"You're coming with us into that hallway." Anthony nodded at the adjacent tenement building. "We're going in there for a few minutes."

"You got something to say, say it out here."

"We want to talk to you in private." He studied the face from all angles, noting every line for future reference. No matter what feature he studied or what ripple of expression, the face was a mask of shallow deceit. But one thing Anthony knew for certain. This creep saw a good dentist, pampered himself with massages, and obviously ate well. "Let's go in there."

"Hey, you're loco." Rings frowned with bunched lips. "I ain't moving from this place. I'm staying near cuccifritos. Man, I ain't done a damn thing. I ain't going noplace." His tone was defiant.

"C'mon." Anthony shoved him.

"Hey, get your pig hands off."

"I'll pig you." Anthony clenched his fist and raised it.

"Hey, why don't you guys bug off and go find some bank robbers." Rings nervously rubbed a sweat bead from his nose. "I'm taking some sun. Sunbathing's no crime. I got my clothes on."

Anthony tried to get a grip on his arm. "I want to pat you down."

Rings yanked his arm free. "Go get a warrant. You got no warrant that I can see, so take a walk."

"We have cause to search you on the spot. You creep, preying on kids so you can wear diamonds." Anthony's face flushed, and he grabbed the pusher's right wrist, yanking it behind his back with a brutal tug. He then scooped up a handful of greasy hair with his free hand and slammed Rings into the hallway. There was a cursing yell of pain.

"Take it easy, Tony. What's the matter with you?" His partner looked concerned. "I've never seen you like this before."

"I can't stand this skel. I wish to God that I had the power to be judge and jury right here. I'm sick of seeing young kids take heroin out of their lunch boxes so that this scumbag can buy another diamond."

So they went through Rings's clothes and sniffed all over his silken handkerchief but he was clean. As Rings sauntered away, he turned back to Anthony and smirked.

"So long, there. I hope next time I see you you'll be directing traffic, that's where you belong, with a whistle in your mouth, blowing it out your ass."

The images of the boy and the pusher remained with Anthony for the rest of the day. He came in the side door of his house quietly giving Theresa a kiss on the cheek as she prepared a meatloaf for dinner. After putting his gun on a shelf in the closet, he washed up in the bathroom. His mind was preoccupied when he sat down at the kitchen table, and picked lightly at the meatloaf on his plate, staring intently at it and not saying anything to the children. He couldn't shake off the bad currents in his mood. He looked at the face of his son Nicholas and found he couldn't taste the food he was chewing. He dropped the fork on the table realizing he was too upset to eat.

"What is it, Tony?" Theresa asked worriedly, picking up his mood.

"Nothing. I just had one of those days."

"Go in the living room and have your dessert there," she said, sending the children away.

"Terry, we came across a pusher today, a real bad character. He sells heroin to kids. One boy was fourteen, just Nicky's age." Theresa went over and hugged him.

"Oh, Tony, it's awful, I know. But you can't let it haunt you. If you let it haunt you, you get angry. If you get angry, you get killed." She shuddered and held him closer, pulling his head down to hers in quiet comfort.

Somewhere in the deep of that night, he had sensations of little dots dancing by the millions in his mind. He became aware in a blurry surreal dream of seeing himself climbing down the side of a tenement on a ladder. At the base of the building he saw Tito Rings laughing up arrogantly at him with his white floss teeth. Somehow the ladder continued inside Tito's dark eye, and he was moving down into the inner walls of the pink-colored stomach, taking notice that the anatomy was barren of familiar organs. Inside the internal space, smelling thickly of old blood, he saw no kidney, no liver, no lungs, no intestines, and no heart. At the bottom was a smoky, eerie miasma floating with the corpses of young boys. Descending lower among the young faces, he saw the fourteen-year-old Puerto Rican boy he had caught on the roof. The boy's eyes were closed and his lips were gently sealed. He was wearing his school clothes which somehow remained unmoistened and unmessed, and slowly, gradually, to Anthony's horror, he saw the boy's face reshape like malleable putty into his own son's face. The eyes came open but the pupils constricted and the face flushed, and his son Nicholas began showing all the symptoms of a heroin addict. He suddenly sat up screaming, "No! No!"

His movements immediately woke Terry, who went for the light switch. "My God, Tony, what is it?"

He let out a heavy breath. "Nothing. A bad dream. I'll be all right." He could feel his heart pounding. The ominous fear he was feeling persisted. His whole body was covered with sweat and he was burning up.

"Let me get you an aspirin. You look as if you have a fever."

"No, I don't need any aspirin."

"Let me get a glass of water. Maybe that will help."

He rubbed the St. Christopher medal around his neck nervously. He clenched his jaw resolutely. He was not going to let this job get to him. Terry was right. He couldn't get himself involved personally. He couldn't allow it. It would eat him up alive. There was too much twisted cruelty in this city. Too much to let it touch you.

Terry came back in with the water and rubbed her hand over the soaking sheet where his body had been rolling and twisting, and she wondered about the content of his nightmare. She knew some terrible fear had been crawling in his brain and eating at his peace. He took the glass from her and sat up sipping the water, hoping to shed the horror of the nightmare.

"What was it, honey?" Terry stroked his hair, squeezing with her knees behind him. "Tell me. Maybe sharing it with me will relax you."

"It made no sense."

"But it was hurting you."

"Maybe it was the food, the pepper or vinegar. It's cramps."

"You hardly touched your food. How could it be

cramps?" She ran her hand tenderly down his neck. "Tell me, hon? What was it you dreamed?"

"It's the job, the damn job. I'm all worked up about these drugs. They make me scared for Nicky and all those young kids like him. It worries me to know men like this Tito walk the streets freely and could go after our son. But I think I'm over it. I had to get it out of my system. Maybe I sweated the dreadful bug out like in a fever."

After an intensive effort of surveillance Anthony discovered all he needed to know to make the arrest of Tito Rings. By dressing up as a postman and trailing junkies, he was led to the heroin cutting and packaging factory, located on the fifth floor of a tenement. From the sixth floor landing he watched unseen as sales transactions took place at the door. He was ready to move in. When the next junkie came up to make a purchase, he crouched, slowly making his way down to the fifth floor, moving stealthily on silent toes, keeping his gun trained on the back of the man's head waiting at the door. Mike followed him down. At close range Anthony leaped forward, instantly grabbing the junkie with a choke hold and ramming the gun into his back. "Make a peep and I'll shoot your insides out. We're cops." He whisked him to his partner who moved to the side with him, gagging him and holding him at gunpoint. Tensely, with his gun tightly in his sweating hand, Anthony waited for the door to reopen. Having witnessed sales at the door, he could enter without a search warrant.

His thoughts were vengeance-minded as he waited to seize the moment. He wanted Tito so bad he could taste him. Hearing voices murmuring in the apartment, he had to figure there were at least three men inside. It was hell not knowing what was waiting for him. His mind was racing with moves and countermoves he could make if he encountered several men armed with guns. When the door opened, he had to fly in on reflexes without any interference from the slower reactions of thinking. As he heard footsteps returning to the door, he crouched to make himself a smaller target, figuring that if any shots were fired they would be high. The moment the doorknob twisted and the latch was undone, he rammed his shoulder into the wood and crashed into the apartment, banging into a dark, burly man and sending him backward on the floor. He saw another man standing over a table who let out a yell and mumbled curses about cops and with widened, startled eyes threw his hands in the air when he saw the gun moving at him.

Almost instantly Anthony's eyes swept in the sight of the rather barren front room, zeroing in on the objects of legal relevance. A table set up with measuring spoons, scales, razors, scissors, glassine bags, a large plastic bag nearly filled with a white narcotic powder. Before he even registered the full scope of the first room, he was racing into a narrow hallway leading to another room, following the sound of commotion and shoes hurriedly scuffing and tempers yelling. His eyes caught the back of another man and Tito opening the window and preparing to climb down the fire escape. He ordered them to freeze. The first man wheeled around with a .38-caliber gun shaking in his hand.

"Drop it!" Anthony screamed. "Or I'll blow your head off."

Frightened, the man meekly let go of the weapon and remained in his tracks, almost shivering with terror. Tito jumped through the window and began scrambling down the ladder, and Anthony bolted after him. Dropping from a good height, Tito landed off balance, crashing into and knocking over garbage cans but quickly righted himself and raced out of the alley. Anthony sprinted after him, catching up with him around the corner and tackling him hard around the waist and yanking him down to the pavement. His voice was shaking. "We got you, you skel. You're my collar."

Anthony knew that he had Tito not only physically in his hands but also legally with sufficient evidence to nail him on several heavy felony counts. Out of breath, he dragged Tito back up to the apartment, where he found Mike in control of the other prisoners. He took a closer look at the plastic bag with the white powder, and spreading the substance in his hand, he saw that it was a high-quality heroin that was coming into the South Bronx from Burma. Opening the refrigerator, he found three kilos of heroin, enough to supply the whole neighborhood.

He turned and watched Mike handcuff Tito and lead him to the waiting squad car.

"That one's for you, Nicky," he said quietly under his breath.

CHAPTER FOUR

It was a clear, bright morning with warm sunlight splashing in the window when I opened my eyes in bed and remembered that it was the day of my flight to New York. I was booked on an early-afternoon flight with a comfortable margin of four hours before check-in time at the airport. I got into my robe and went out into the hall to get my traveling bags down from the closet. I snapped them open on the bed and began to pack. I did it slowly at first, neatly folding the clothes in square bundles and fitting them side by side and smoothing them down. With an eye on the clock I grew increasingly less calm and less methodical and picked up my pace until I was going about it with an air of hurry and bustle. I had made a checklist the night before of all the lawbooks and legal materials and personal articles that I needed for the trip, but even with the list I had nibbling doubts and worries about overlooking an important item. I felt more assured having Sherrill act as my fail-safe reminder of things that I would need. Her memory was infallible. The departure time kept rushing up on me as I went through a bunch of phone calls I had to make before leaving. Sherrill helped by bringing out my new three-piece suit from Alondales, never worn before, an elegant blue velvet fabric styled by the impressive sounding Ermenegildo Zegna of Italy. It was my best suit and I was saving it for a special occasion like this one, my return to my family in New York after three years. I began moving the suitcases to the trunk of the car while Sherrill got in on the driver's side to do the driving.

She drove me to LAX airport, and we hurried on foot from the parking lot under clear blue skies, good flying weather, to the terminal. On the move I could feel the slap of the two suitcases against my hips. Sherrill was carrying my leather briefcase, which bulged at the seams from the cumbrous trial transcript. After checking the luggage with a sidewalk porter, we scampered through the long corridor up to the gate, hearing a loudspeaker announce the first call for American's Flight 147 to New York. People were just beginning to board. I got my seating assignment and then paused at the jetway facing Sherrill feeling a confluence of tense emotions over leaving my wife for an indefinite period of time, having gotten myself into the role of rescuer for my family in New York with a high risk of failure.

"Give my love to everybody." She put her hand on my arm.

"I will."

"And don't forget to call when you get in. Don't make me worry."

"As soon as I get off the plane." I dropped my briefcase on a chair to take her hand.

"I know you're going to do what you've set out to do. You'll clear up this mess. I have faith in you."

"That makes me feel good to hear you say it."

"I'm gonna miss you." Her eyes moistened. "Don't be too long."

I smiled and kissed her and swung around for the boarding ramp. I waved back to her before stepping in the plane, and my thoughts were still with her as I automatically reached down to fasten the seat belt. The big plane jerked briefly before beginning a smooth roll back from the gate. I then closed my eyes and let my thoughts drift toward the case and the family that would be waiting for me in New York.

I kept thinking and wondering how I got myself

hooked into this thing. Maybe it did have something to do with proving something to my father. Sherrill had a valid point about a New York lawyer being better qualified to know his way around that city's legal system. And frankly, I was afraid that my own feelings could become a stumbling block against effective advocacy. I had to be afraid of losing my temper in a proceeding where my brother was being denigrated and attacked. I knew this was going to be the toughest battle of my career. What an illusion it was to have thought when I quit boxing that I had given up fighting. For a trial lawyer the courtroom was a similar arena with all the same stresses on nerves, stamina, and adrenaline but with the main burden on the mind instead of the body. I began wondering why I had chosen to be a trial lawyer instead of going into more tranquil tax work. A connection had to exist between my careers in boxing and trial practice. My thoughts drifted back to my boxing days. I had gone into the sport because of Tony Bavimo. I was so full of hero worship for him I would have followed him into anything. I used to act like a puppy dog to win his approval which he freely gave when I followed his teachings. As I had never gotten that kind of approval from my father, I became a boxer to become like Tony Bavimo.

Dad rarely came to my boxing matches or paid much attention to them, but he was going to scrutinize my efforts in this battle. I glanced out of the window at the undefined stretches of brown earth below, feeling a twinge of worry about losing. My confidence was being infected by the recurring fear that I was going to fail. If there was a bad outcome, I could easily see Dad blaming it on me, saying I wasn't a good enough lawyer, downgrading the worth of my efforts. Maybe I should have listened to Sherrill's advice about not jumping in the middle to take on this awful responsibility.

* * *

The Fasten Seat Belt sign blipped on as the 747 jet gradually began its descent into the New York area. The No Smoking sign came on as the pilot lined up the plane with the gleaming infrared lights of the runway on final approach, and with seeming ease the jumbo touched down softly. Rolling toward the terminal, we passed the American Airlines hangar where maintenance crews were crawling on the silver skin of a DC-10 jet. Waiting for me inside the crowded gate area, and bobbing his head over other people while waving wildly, was my twenty-four-year-old brother Ernie. He was dressed in white biscuit shoes, a white turtleneck sweater, white bell bottoms, and a knee-length black leather jacket. Lean, dark, and sinewy, he was looking more boyish with his glossy black hair cut long. A rock singer, he was the only son to pursue Dad's love for music, although to Dad's ears his twists and shouts and acid tempo were as musical as a Roto-Rooter coughing in a clogged pipe. I sieved through the bunches of happily reunited people feeling groggy from the jet lag with the whining engines still aching in my ears. Ernie came over in bouncy steps to meet me, threw his arms around my shoulders, and grinning from ear to ear, gave me a kiss. This made me feel slightly uncomfortable underneath the warmth it gave out from him. Of everyone in the family, he was the most uninhibited, volatile, and expressive with his feelings, strongly shaped by his Italian roots and urban New York. He was also of the sixties generation, being for a time a fringe flower child. For him kissing and hugging another man was a way of showing that men had feelings too, breaking away from the stiff steely macho tradition that our family had been raised with.

Sprung from three cultural currents, Italian, inner city, and hip, Ernie was trying to meld them into a single unique style in his singing career, and he went about it with the aggressiveness of a hungry street kid. In his first attempt to gain bookings as a singer, he staged the bold ploy of renting a sound truck and riding up and down Broadway, performing for the streams of pedestrians, hoping that some important producer might book him into one of the theaters. He managed to get himself a spot in a Brooklyn nightclub, adopting the flamboyant stage name of Adonis, coming out onstage in a wild shimmering suit, his hair bleached a flaming platinum, believing that this kind of sensational gimmickry would pay off in big crowds and big popularity. He dropped the name and outfit quickly when he saw males in the audience blowing kisses at him. He had a habit of being unpredictable, acting wild and funky in one moment with a rebel's distaste for everything conventional, but then he would turn around and start talking like a hard hat pillar of the great silent majority. He had the gift of a nice singing voice, but I thought he was a more talented composer writing songs that I could listen to over and over. He also had a wonderful talent for dancing. Blessed with rubbery bones, he could erupt in an electric orgy of nonstop full splits. I dropped my mouth in dumbfounded amazement every time I watched him dance onstage. When he wasn't singing or dancing, Ernie worked in the basement of NYU, taking care of the school's boilers, a trade he learned while serving four years in the Navy.

I found pleasure in being around him because he was such an upbeat person. It was nice to hear him talk with vigorous enthusiasm about his dreams in music, the big things he had planned, the stars he was going to challenge. He walked and talked with a frisky bounce, full of life, full of humor, always a bright smile in his eyes and on his lips, ebulliently overflowing with an excitement for the things he was going to do. He loved to go fishing for bluefish in New York Harbor and he talked excitedly about the little outboard motor boat he had just purchased. He talked about buying a little piece of land up in the Pennsylvania mountains to get away from the push and hustle of the city. He swaggered about his "dynamite sexiness" to ladies—"Elvis wishes he had my looks," he would say (which infuriated our three sisters)—but behind his boasting he was a put-on and tease, not taking himself all that seriously. He drove in the fun lane of life.

Down in the baggage claim area, Ernie picked up my two suitcases and carried them out to the street. It was a freezing day, or so it felt to my sunny-California-acclimated tissue. Ice on the sidewalk chilled through my shoes and a cold blast penetrated my clothes, and I hooked the top button of my coat and raised the collar over my ears, finding the season nastily biting. I found myself recongratulating myself on deciding to move out west. To Californians it was utterly insane to want to live in a place like wintry New York whose only cultural advantage in the cold weather was an ice rink at Rockefeller Center. My teeth chattered as we sprinted through a cluster of honking cabs to get across the street to the parking lot. A slight uneasy feeling came over me finding that Ernie was driving a Corvette. I was in no mood for a speed binge after the cross-country flight. Another one of Ernie's loves was drag racing. Twinkling under a lamppost, the super-juiced "Vet" had a glazed skin of violet, heavily frilled doors with chrome trim, spidery spoked hubcaps, swooshing aerials, and dual mufflers the girth of Phantom jet afterburners. The car was also loaded with locks and alarms—the life expectancy of a Corvette on the New York streets being only thirty days. I slumped down into the low seat, folding my legs, and I scanned the dials, meters, and switches glinting in the glow of dash lights.

Scooting in on the driver's side, Ernie rolled up his window and flipped on the heater and the warm air came rushing out, feeling good over my knees. He revved the engine, mumbling something that I couldn't catch over the roar and then nodded at me with a smile, switching on the radio. The small quarters were soon steaming with hot air and hot rock. His foot pressed down on the high horsepower, unleashing a loud rumble, and we pulled out to the barrier gate. He handed the attendant a dollar, and then he headed for a banking ramp that fed into the highway, ramming the gear into drive, pedal kicked down, tires screeching as the sports car accelerated around the curve. As we sped, I could feel the centrifugal force whip us out and whirl our blood and snake the rear wheels until the road straightened out. Riding free of traffic on the parkway, he let it out more, sending the speedometer needle plunging, glancing over at me from time to time with a grin, clearly proud of the powerfully smooth performance of his machine. I found myself enjoying the tranquil speed, finding it soothing to listen to the motor purring in my ears and feel the wheels sailing over the pavement. From a distance I caught a glimpse of New York's awesomely rising silhouette, radiantly flickering in the night, and by force of its dominant presence I found my eyes drawn to the Empire State Building, and nostalgically I felt an allegiance to it as the king of the skyline even though the new Trade Center had deposed it on sheer height. Along the ocean, I opened the car window for a breath of fresh air, the heater becoming unbearable, and I gazed out at the mist-shrouded waters and ocean liners silently steaming into the harbor and gulls wheeling over swells under fast-moving gray clouds. We sped on, passing the Flatlands marsh, Brooklyn's last patch of natural frontier, a stretch of high hair grass fields, the tall blades rustling and rippling in the wind, the grass running for acres before stopping at the bank of a catfish creek but regrowing on the other side, scarcely interrupted by the scattered driftwood-shacks and God-forsaken truck-body homes of hardy squatters. I was reminded of how much life was a struggle for existence for some people. I was hit with the realization that being out in the Brentwood suburbs, I had become out of touch with the harsh reality of so many Americans. At the end of the marsh we drove through the Brownsville ghetto, originally the settling place for southern European Jewish immigrants, but now a melting pot of all disadvantaged minorities. Over the years the creeping germs of decay had gained a savage momentum and the slum seemed to be growing and spreading and threatening all of Brooklyn. Wind stung my eyes and my hair blew wildly, but I stuck my head out of the window, feeling the tragedy of the people trapped here and feeling a sense of amazing providence that I had been able to get so far away by living in California.

I rolled up the window and turned to my younger brother. "Ernie, I don't believe it. No matter how much I remind myself that you're grown up, I still always expect you to be a little kid."

"A kid! I got my Teamsters card already."

"What's with a Teamsters card? I thought you were going to cut gold records for a living!"

His voice revved up enthusiastically. "The Teamsters card is my insurance policy until the record-buying public discovers me. Hey, the group cut a demo last week that will blow your mind."

"That's an improvement. The last one you sent me blew my amplifier. Who's the demo for?"

"Anybody who'll listen. We paid for it ourselves so we can send it around. Dad says he thinks it's got a real shot."

"I thought Dad hated this kind of music."

"He can't stand the acid stuff. This is plain rock."

"What does Dad know about rock?"

"You'd be surprised. He knows about all kinds of music. He amazes me."

"I guess music was once his entire life."

"You're gonna be staying at the house. I don't know whether Tony told you."

I felt a stab of tension. "I thought I'd be staying at Tony's place."

"Mom insisted. She said she's got more room. Which is true with Madeline, Camille, and Nicky all married and with places of their own."

"I see. Well, I guess that makes sense. Say Ernie, are you still doing a lot of fishing?"

"I like to go out on the ocean when I'm feeling uptight about something. Being out there by myself is calming. You can think about things better. The ocean makes your personal troubles seem puny. It makes me feel peaceful when I'm waiting for a fish to bite. It mellows me out. So how are things going out there for you, Brother Joe?"

"Pretty good. How about this jerk in The Bronx pulling this shit on Tony." I twisted my lips. "My first impulse was to come here and splatter him over a two-block wall."

He feigned shock. "Hey, man. You're a Harvard lawyer."

"That was my second thought. So I'll splatter him with inductive and deductive logic and syllogisms and empiricism."

"I love it." Ernie snapped his fingers excitedly.

"Has this thing caused you any problems?" I asked.

He kept his eye on the road, steering with one hand and holding a cigarette in the other, and answered after taking a deep drag. "It ain't caused me no problems. Sure I had some words with friends. When it hit the papers, I tried to defend Tony. Underneath I knew my friends didn't believe me. They figured I was full of shit. If you didn't know him, how could you understand?"

"Listen, Tony's no Jekyll and Hyde. There's no secret side to him, no hidden vices, everyone knew his job and his family were everything."

"Christ, he got a screwing." Ernie blew out smoke hard. "I resent what they did to him. He was a dedicated cop. He wouldn't go near a bribe. This goddamn punk Tarras lied on the stand in the eyes of God. Those were Mom's words. She says he will have no peace of mind. He has to live with himself. He swore before the Almighty."

"I just blew up when I heard." I folded my arms pensively. "That's why I wanted to punch this guy Tarras out."

"That wouldn't be too cool."

"Of course I would never do it, but there is a satisfaction you get in hitting with your fists that you don't get in submitting a brief. At Harvard I was with all these Brahmins—Rockefellers, Roosevelts, Cabots, Lodges—and I felt an inner confidence knowing that man-to-man physically I could beat their asses. I knew they had blue blood and wealth, but like Hemingway once said, there is an inner comfort in knowing you can knock anybody down who gets snooty with you."

"In Anthony's case you better submit a brief and keep your hands in your pocket or hold your wing-ding, but don't hit anybody."

"Don't be ridiculous. I'm not going to lay a finger on Tarras. I'm going to get him on the witness stand and cut him up in bloodless pieces. Fighting with fists is puny street shit. But you still need killer instinct. I've learned that. The straight world has its manners and white gloves but it's a jungle, too. Tony's been a cop a long time but he's still naïve in ways. He doesn't know about the predators out there who are ruthless in the straight world."

"Right on!" Ernie raised his fist. "Like the ones who got us in Vietnam."

"I thought you were a Vietnam veteran."

"I am, but it was a lousy war." Ernie slowly blew out wispy puffs of smoke from his shrunken cigarette. "You have any idea how hard it was for Tony to call you?"

"Why, he should have known I'd want to help."

"You're the one he always had to make excuses for.

He was a cop, when you were doing a week in jail or getting busted outa the Marines or getting fired from your job. He was the one we all looked up to, remember?"

"Sure."

"So now all of a sudden, here he is with his tail between his legs and he has to come to you for help. I'm telling you, Joe, it hurt him something awful to pick up that phone."

"I'm glad he did."

He smiled. "Me, too."

"How's the family taking it?"

"Naturally Mom felt terrible but I'm not worried about her. She's got unknown resources in her. She says God made you come from California." He grinned. "Did you know you're a soldier from God?" His words made me suddenly feel nervous. He changed his expression, sensing that I was not comfortable in hearing Mom putting heavenly expectations on my shoulders. "Mom has been helping Theresa. It has been a big strain for her."

I swallowed nervously. "How is Dad doing?"

"You can imagine, it's been eating him up." His brows furrowed, raising his eyes up to a mental screen. "This thing has been a sore on his health. Dad has a special love for Tony. I don't have to tell you."

"How does he feel about my coming to help?"

"He's skeptical. You've come a long way but Dad begrudges it or doesn't see it. You have to remember that he's a third-grade dropout. He doesn't know from Harvard. To him you're the son never listening, never holding a job, always embarrassing him. He's afraid to trust you."

"But those things happened years ago."

"He's never left Brooklyn. He's never been to California to see you in a new life. The years you went off he can't see. All he remembers about you is from Brooklyn and going down to the police station at a late hour to get you out or having the cops bang at the door at three o'clock in the morning that time with Tony Bavimo."

A feeling of guilt came over me thinking back to that terrible night, one I would never forget the rest of my life. I could only now imagine what fear and pain it must have brought my parents. "Hey, Ernie, before you take me over to the folks' place, why don't you drop me off at Anthony's. I want to see him first."

After an hour's ride which went fast with all the talking we did, we arrived in Anthony's neighborhood in Brooklyn. His small house sat in a row of wood frame houses with peaked shingled roofs joined together and looking indistinguishably alike, like house models on a Monopoly board. Conscientious about upkeep, Tony kept the place in good shape. I leaned into a strong wind going into the backyard where I thought I might catch Anthony with his pigeons. I paused to look over a Sears bathing tank that had been assembled from curved plastic sections with a plastic sliding pond jutting over the now empty tank. Dad had been impressed with the bathing tank, seeing it as a symbol of status to be able to swim in your own backyard. To him this meant his son had really moved up in class. Since Dad had never left Brooklyn, he didn't know anything about the black-marble lagoons people swam in amid three-acre backyards in Beverly Hills.

I stepped into the unlocked side door and looked down into the basement room covered with posters of Elvis, the Beatles, Frank Sinatra, and other pop superstars. My nephew Nicholas was down there and I was struck by his likeness to his father at the same age. A high school student, he had a curly shock of sandy hair, good height with more growing to do, a compact chest tapering to a slim waist, and dark brows that heightened the brightness of his green eyes. He had a striking blend, in the Travolta mold, of dark Italian and light Irish ancestry. Nick worked part-time after school taking orders for prescriptions at Klein's Pharmacy, but inheriting his grandfather's love of music, he spent most of his after-class hours playing the drums. Looking at his set of drums swallowing up half the room, I realized for the first time what a marvelous outlet for aggression or pent-up energy this instrument represented. Though he loved the drums, Nick, idolizing his father, intended to become a cop after graduation.

When he saw me on the landing, he did not run over exuberantly to greet me the way he had done on other visits. Visibly stricken by his father's misfortune, he came over to me barely able to give me a rueful smile.

"Hello, Uncle Joey. Nobody's home now. My mom went to the store to buy food. I think she's expecting you to have dinner with us. Why don't you go into the house and make yourself at home."

I moved upstairs where the rooms were small and boxlike and opened to each other without doors except for the master bedroom. Everywhere in sight, overrunning the apartment, on top of shelves, cluttering dressers, consuming bookcases, were dozens of chrome-plated trophies topped by a barrel-chested pigeon staring majestically like an aquiline Man o' War. I wondered how many wives would allow a house to be converted into a sanctuary for chrome pigeons. Theresa's toleration of this clutter was a measure of how deeply she loved Anthony. On one table was a scrapbook she had filled in herself containing cut-out articles from the *Daily News* on outstanding arrests made by him. Turning my eyes toward the kitchen, I could picture her standing behind his chair during our conversations, stroking his hair and listening with girlish fascination to his police adventures.

I took off my coat and placed it on the back of a chair and moved around the house looking at new and familiar sights. What grabbed your eyes after the pigeon trophies was a two-foot-high plaster of paris icon of the Christ Child swaddled in a red satin robe, crowned with a gold-foiled tiara, and grasping a rhinestone-studded scepter. This was a religious family and evidence of their faith was tangible in many other holy figures and painted saints and plaster crucifixes interspersed among the rooms. I walked into the girls' bedroom, which was done in soft colors of pink and pale white and filled with fleecy pillows. I picked up a stuffed teddy bear with a jingling collar and I wondered why teddy bears were so favored by children. Leaving the girls' room, I moved back into the living room, stopping to scan the photographs on the dresser. A potted plant served as a support for snapshots of the full family, showing Anthony and Theresa and the three kids in leaf-dappled light on picnic grass. Another showed them all full of mirth at Disney World in Florida, and a third caught Anthony and Theresa on the garage roof working as a team during a pigeon race. Tucked on the right corner was a framed photo of Anthony proudly posing in his first police uniform, his expression a bit stiff and self-conscious, his chin tucked in a bit too tightly into his neck, but his blue eyes and blue uniform fusing in a dashing way. I thought the photo captured the core of his character, his look solemn and reverent for the privilege of wearing a cop's uniform, his eyes revealing a simple sincerity that still believed in the old-fashioned truths of God, family, and country.

Another photograph showed Anthony in a tuxedo and Theresa in her bridal gown at their wedding party. She looked flushed and slightly out of breath from dancing while he was looking at her affectionately with his lips cast in a wide smile. She was a stunning sight in her wedding gown, her dark bright eyes in dazzling contrast to the whiteness of her veil, her dimpled cheeks and ripe skin rippling smoothly under stage lights, her burnished black hair tumbling down and around her slender neck. She was wearing a gown of white lace over satin with long frilly sleeves that billowed around her delicate hands.

They had met when he was working as a shoe salesman at Harry's Shoe Store in Canarsie. The instant they met there was an electric attraction between them. He saw her every day of that week, and the first time he brought her home to meet the family, they were unmistakably in love and planning to get married. She sat on the Castro sofa in the living room that night, her legs firmly and properly together, her hands clasped on her lap, smiling and trying to be friendly, but acting a bit stiff and hinting at the shy fright she felt surrounded by his many brothers and sisters, swarming closer to get a better look at her. All the males in the family agreed that she was quite a beauty. No one really cared that she was Irish, though she worried about not knowing how to cook any Italian dishes, and she feared that Mom might be upset over her boy eating bland cabbage meals. But for Mom the important thing was that she was a good home girl, and for Dad the important consideration was that she was Catholic.

Theresa was from a poor family, having grown up one of ten children in five rooms that were barely furnished. The atmosphere of her house was raucous and overcrowded, and her mother, long suffering from tuberculosis, had died when she was only nine.

Her father was an immigrant from County Cork, Ireland, a plain humble man who worked hard as a tinsmith for the BMT subway. When his wife died, he had to learn by necessity how to cook, and he prepared most of the meals for his ten children. At sixteen Theresa quit school to help with the cooking and cleaning because her older sisters had taken jobs with the phone company. As she got older, she felt a sense of being crowded by the others in her family, and it instilled a yearning for the day when she would have her own place and her own space. She had visions of a better life, a simple version of the American Dream, moving into not a house but an apartment of her own, marrying a good workingman, having a few children, and owning a few nice possessions. With Anthony, there was no doubt that she had found it.

The side door opened and Theresa, carrying two bags of groceries, came up the steps followed by her two daughters. She still had a shy, sheltered look, and her features remained strikingly attractive. Her high cheekbones were a bit blurred, and her chin line a touch softer with an unneeded five or ten pounds spreading her hips. The demands of raising three children and the straining stress of the last few months were taking their physical toll. Hovering around the side of her leg was her dimpled, doe-eyed four-year-old daughter, Bobbie, wearing a pretty yellow dress and glowing with wholesome health. Her fair complexion and sweeping blue-black hair made her a miniature of her mother. Close by was Angela, a totally sweet, helpful, and unmischievous child, bright and serious in her manner, and currently an honor student at Meyer Levin Junior High School. Angela's figure, which had been a straight stalk the last time I saw her, had filled out roundly, and her thick honey-blond hair fell over her shoulders, flowing with the smoothness of her skin and touched by dimples around her mouth, which was now set in a perky smile as she saw me. "It's Uncle Joey from California."

Theresa plopped the groceries on the kitchen table and rushed over and warmly threw her arms around me. Her face brightened with a shine of welcome and she quickly seemed out of breath, beaming with all the charisma of her younger days. She had always been warm in greeting me, but this appeared to be a nervous overreaction, tied underneath, I guessed, to some kind of desperate hope. Angela scampered over eagerly and I kissed her on the cheek. Bobbie, the youngest child, hardly knew me, but following her sister's example, she too scooted over to my leg and tilted her head up inviting a kiss.

"You look fine, Joey," Theresa said. "When did you get in?"

"Last night."

"How was your flight?"

"It was pretty nice. A bit choppy over the western states but smooth the rest of the way."

"Let me make you some lunch. I can cook you some peppers and eggs. I know how you must miss them." She moved toward the refrigerator.

"Oh, you don't have to go the trouble, Terry." I stroked the soft hair of my youngest niece as we followed her into the kitchen.

"I remember how you liked peppers and eggs. It's tasty and filling, not like the bland skimpy meal you probably got on the plane." She opened the refrigerator and pulled out a tub of butter and a cellophane bag of peppers and balanced three eggs on her arm snugged into her body.

"You have beautiful children," I said, taking a chair at the table and lifting Bobbie onto my lap. Angela wriggled into a space between my knee and arm and I cradled her gently around the waist. Propping up Bobbie's face, I peered into her big dreamy eyes. "You're gonna be a heartbreaker, you know that?"

Her eyes turned away from me self-consciously bringing a shy reddening to her cheeks. A barely audible sigh came out of her. "Mommy," she said, looking over at Theresa.

"Your mother knows you're pretty, doesn't she? She knows you're a darling and are going to be a heartbreaker."

A little giggle came out of her mouth as the corners of her lips creased into an impish grin and her forehead puckered knowingly as if she understood my flattery.

"How's Sherrill?" Theresa said, spreading butter over a frying pan, letting the fatty lumps melt with a crackle, and then whipping in a batch of peppers and eggs.

"She sends her love. She wanted to come but she's working on her master's thesis."

"I thought she had that degree." She stirred the omelette, sprinkling in salt, garlic, basil, and oregano. The tangy aroma filling the air was inviting.

"She's going to have two master's degrees now. This will be in biology. The other one is in psychology."

"I wish I had all that education. How stupid I was not to stay in high school." She brought the omelette over to the table, and pulled out a chair to sit opposite me. Though it was present in both our minds, neither of us said anything about Anthony's case while she forked out a generous helping of peppers and eggs onto my dish. We both sat silently eating for a few minutes with a growing tension in the air as if we could read each other's mind. After poking at the food and finishing a few mouthfuls, I stopped eating and got to what we both wanted to talk about. "How is Tony feeling being off the job?"

Her cheeks turned red and her expression went blank for a moment and her voice carried a note of strain. "He's trying to act as if it no longer bothers him." She paused to collect her calm. "He has done a good job of hiding his real feelings from the children. He doesn't want to show how much this is affecting him, but inside I know it's bothering him. Your mother has been helpful. She tries to get his mind off it, but all these strangers won't let us alone."

"What strangers?"

"Cranks who saw him on TV." She spoke with an uneasy edge. "They hear an Italian name and right away they think he's with the Mafia. The letters have been vicious. They ramble on, accusing him of being crooked. All the hate and filthy language in them you wouldn't believe. What kind of people are in this world? God help us!" Her eyes flicked over to the plaster of paris Jesus on the drawer. "You can picture these people, and how sick they must be, but how could they hate a man they don't know? How could they, Joey?"

"I guess because they hate themselves and in their twisted way they take it out on him. It's always the wretched self-hater who wants to vent his spleen. Why does Tony even bother to read them?"

"He only skims them now looking for threats. He says you can never tell when one of these maniacs is gonna carry out his threat. If he knows what to expect he can be ready."

I shook my head in disgust. "The man doesn't have enough trouble. He has to deal with demented haters."

"They want to lynch him, burn down the house, throw bombs in the car." Her hands trembled. "It frightens me. The police department should protect us, but Tony doesn't want to go to them. He says it will pass. An oddity I notice is the handwriting."

"You think it was all written by the same person?"

"No, but they all had strangeness, either scrawly like a child or perfectly straight, like a stencil, each letter pressed down hard and rigid."

"My God, what wackos out there."

"He even got surrounded by some people who said they wanted to puke or spit in his pig face."

"I'm surprised they knew about him."

"It was on all the radio stations and on the news on television. No one above detective was dismissed. Tony was the highest rank to be brought out in this whole Serpico mess. They dismissed only patrolmen before him. He was a gold shield, the highest, so that's why all the publicity and attacks."

"I remember Serpico complaining about none of the big shots being reached in this scandal. They used Tony as a lightning rod. Let him take all the heat. They didn't care that he was innocent. If you're a big shot crook, you avoid trouble. Your whole career is usually spent finding scapegoats."

"After the hearing the reporters swarmed him,

shouting at him. One lady reporter screamed at him and tore his shirt. They had no respect for his feelings. I don't know when they're going to leave him alone. The expense of the lawyers took every cent we had in our savings, so he had to sell his best pigeons. He put an ad in the *Daily News* and some crank recognized the name and called. 'Got any crooked police birds for sale?' he asked."

"The bitching vultures."

"Joey, he was a good cop, the top cop in his command. He loved the job. It was always on his mind. Even with the family on Sundays when we were on our way to a picnic he would stop to check a place when he saw loiterers and he memorized license numbers of stolen cars and was always on the lookout for them." She threw her head back suddenly and her eyes had a bewildered look. "How could they listen to that mealy-mouthed crook Tarras? How could they take his word over Tony's?"

"They don't care about Tony. To the police department he is just a shield number. To Internal Affairs he's fodder."

"Joey, he wouldn't touch a penny. He's so honest. Once one of his partners came out of a store with a bag of free cakes and said, 'Here, Tony, take home some cakes.' He couldn't eat them. He was so upset that night. He had pride in the uniform. He despised the cops who went into a restaurant and ordered coffee and sandwiches and walked out without paying. He considered them worse than slackers. He called them leeches and disgraces to the uniform. He said they cheapened the uniform. Tony has integrity. He was what a cop should be. He had ability and he wanted to help and protect people. The only ones gaining by this are the muggers, the rapists, and the criminal element."

"There must be some high-ranking police officers gaining in some way, too, and this guy Tarras must be somehow better off."

"The department should have backed him. I think they were afraid of what the papers would say. They didn't have the courage to stand by him so they took the word of this crook Tarras. They made our Christmas unforgettable hell." She sighed audibly while her head sagged in despair. She hesitated and then her speech continued in a rush. "This all happened at Christmas, you know. We found out about the verdict two weeks before the holiday. You can imagine what that did to our spirits. We went ahead and got a Christmas tree not to spoil it for the kids. Tony had bought the presents months before. That's the way he always does it. He asks the kids months before what they want and then he hides them all over the house. I remember we got up Christmas morning and we watched the kids opening their presents around the tree. It was Christmas but Tony wasn't feeling it. It had all gone sour. He knew what was ahead, and how drastic things might get. He was caring about the kids and me and it was eating him up. He tossed and turned all Christmas night. But he didn't lose heart, Joey. He has never lost heart. He never moped around and felt sorry for himself or said anything about being beaten by it all. His pride was still there even when they humiliated him. I'll never forget that day when they came to the house. That was the worst. Two police cars pulled up in front of the house, and all the neighbors saw it."

"They brought it to his home!" I was startled and appalled.

"The sergeant came in and demanded his gold shield and his guns." Her facial muscles rippled. "Oh God, Joey, it was awful."

"Why couldn't they let him bring them in? He could have brought the guns and badge up to the precinct. He could have done that himself."

"I don't know. Maybe they didn't trust him anymore or they wanted to make an example. The sergeant was a hard, gruff man. He treated Tony as if he was seedy. His tone of voice was brusque and insulting. 'Where is your helmet?' 'Where's your manual?' He barked at him and talked down to him." She looked at me pleadingly, her eyes moistening. "Tony didn't deserve that indecency. He didn't deserve to be disgraced in front of his children. They humiliated him, and there was nothing we could do."

"All this in front of his children." I felt a knot in my stomach.

"When he handed over his shield and gun he was as white as a sheet." Tears were rolling down her cheeks. "He stuttered a little to the sergeant. He just couldn't find the words." Her head turned away, and I reached over to hold her hand in mine. "I've never heard him stutter, Joey. He was so humiliated." She swung her hands up to her face, rubbing away the tears, and I could see the redness in her eyes spreading to the rest of her face. "Nicholas broke down crying, and I thought that, more than his own pain, would kill him."

Rain was lightly falling outside as I headed down the block for the main shopping stretch on Church Avenue. Patches of clouds, grizzly gray and blackish, drifted slowly across the night sky. The darkening streets were deserted except for a pack of stray cats nipping at scraps in trash cans, and a big tomcat greedily baring his teeth and hissing the others away. The wind slanting down from the buildings flapped up tin covers on the sidewalk. The air came into my lungs cold and wet and the rain, growing heavier, became a steady pelting downpour whipping across the street. I could feel the drops soaking my hair, but I was so caught up in an intense haze of thought that I felt almost unbothered by the soaking chill. The one reality that stuck in my mind was how alone my brother seemed to be in this trouble. A man of strong emotions, he was keeping it all buried inside himself so as not to hurt anyone else. Unconsciously, I was almost running. I had felt humiliation before in my life. Pain was not strange to me. I knew what it was to feel the world collapse inside of your gut. Images flashed in my mind in brisk succession—the demeaning news stories, the threats from cranks, the dismissal, the degrading ritual of being stripped of badge and gun. All these scenes were heavy burdens Anthony was carrying alone. I recalled how deeply disillusioned his voice sounded over the phone, how injured he felt by injustice, and how I had reacted with tantrums of belligerent rage. It was strange how my mind went, blowing fuses and wasting time and energy instead of concentrating in a cool, collected way on how to effectively deal with the problem.

I crossed over the cracks in the sidewalks and around little puddles and turned down East New York Avenue. The downpour made little rivulets along the curb, sweeping up cellophane cigar wrappers and crumpled cigarette packs, chugging them down into the open mouth of a manhole. I was uncertain of what I was going to say to my brother when I saw him. My temples were throbbing thinking about what Ernie had said, about how hard it must have been for Tony to call me. I was the one he always had to make excuses for; I was the one he always had to counsel, and guide, and cheer up; I was the one always in trouble and in jams. He was the oldest brother, the cop, the one we all looked up to and respected. Now he was forced to come to his kid brother for help. I broke into a trot.

The rain was drumming down on the cars parked along Church Avenue, the main thoroughfare of the neighborhood, which conspicuously showed the change from an overwhelmingly Jewish population to an unmelting pot of races. The Latin names on stores and spicy, exotic foods on display and strange bongo drum sounds loudly blaring out of windows dominated the new cultural flavor of the community. The darkening weather caused a number of stores to put on their lights and wavering neon signs, and looking up, I could see in the bright incandescence the rain broken down into tiny drops. My face dripped water as I passed a pizza parlor where inside a group of long-haired, hard-eyed Puerto Rican teens were gyrating around a jukebox which was amplified loud enough to shut out the thunderclaps. I pumped my fists up and down running along the avenue breathing in choppy breaths. I could smell the fumes from gas in the moving traffic. Sooty buses being washed down by the rain belched gray smoke rolling along the tracks of an old trolley line. I looked up at the apartment buildings, stained from age, four and five stories high, griddled with fire escapes. Diagonally across from Kelly's Saloon was the laundromat, the walls of which were galvanized sheet metal. Totally out of breath I sprinted the rest of the way. I paused in the rain for a moment before entering the laundromat. The front door, painted black around the glass pane, was splintered and flaking, and through the chalked windows, announcing rates, I could see the wood-beamed floor supporting two lines of Bendix washers. In the rear I could see my brother in gray khakis kneeling over a wash sink squeezing the grime out of the spaghetti strands of a mop. A heavyset black lady trudged by him carrying a basket of wash. He dabbed the mop in a bucket and splattered the floor with sudsy water and began swabbing up the area. I was saddened seeing him in this dingy place mopping up floors.

When he saw me enter, he put down the mop and strode to meet me, wiping his hands with a rag. At thirty-seven he still had the looks of his late twenties, the blue eyes were still friendly, the tawny hair held its color and rolling waves and the chin line was firm. Water was dripping from my hair and running down my face, bringing me soberly back to what I was doing here. Tony almost looked hesitant. Up close I could see his clothes were rumpled and smeared with dust and his eyes were darkly shadowed with drain and fatigue. He started to say something but it didn't come. Suddenly there were tears in his eyes. He tried to turn away from me so that I could not see the depth of his humiliation, but I went to him, grabbed him, and held him tightly in my arms, my own eyes filling.

PART 2

THE FIGHTER

CHAPTER FIVE

When the rain stopped, I asked Anthony to drive me to our parents' place. As we drove along Church Avenue, apartment buildings four and five stories high lined many of the blocks, but going down the side streets, we passed rows of small wood frame houses topped by peaked roofs, a number of them looking neglected and run-down. Many of the windows were filled with cardboard, because vandals were continually breaking them. The character of the neighborhood had changed rapidly in a short time. Originally, when we first moved here, it was a very safe and tranquil, predominantly Jewish neighborhood. Dad had moved the family there thinking he was removing his sons from the tough influences of the Little Italy streets. Unfortunately with unforeseen massive relocation, the community had grown poor and blighted and full of migrants from Haiti, the West Indies, Puerto Rico, and tough slum sections all over the city.

My parents' small frame house was made of ordinary wood still in decent shape but revealing peeling shingles and in need of a new roof. The wind whistled across the little patch of dirt that Mom used to call the front garden. I watched Anthony pull away from the curb feeling a strong cord of love between us. The chill air put billows of smoke on my breath as I walked around to the side door. Tilting my head up, I looked up at the window of my old bedroom, wondering how it was going to look to me now and what it would feel like to sleep in the same bed I had slept in as a boy. At the door my eyes moved over the buzzer, which had a loose wire curling out of a red stem like a firecracker.

We had moved into this house when I was seventeen. I had only lived here with my family a few years before moving out on my own to California. Over a decade I had not been back much, and my last visit had been more than three years ago. My family had yet to meet my wife. Our marriage had been a very quiet private affair. By moving to the West Coast, I had put a lot of space between normal family traditions and ties.

Under my fatigue from the long flight, I felt an enthusiasm to see Mom and Dad, but I also felt a wave of unease, not really knowing what to expect from Dad, whom I had not talked to on the phone or written in more than three years. Mom and Sherrill carried on all the correspondence for us. I pushed back the front of my hair with my hands and glanced inspectingly at my elegant suit, wanting to look successful, hoping that my parents would be proud.

I peered through a crack in the venetian blinds, able to make out only the blurred shimmer of the television screen and its noise. I knocked on the door and then bent over to grab up my trench coat and when I looked up, Dad was there, looking at me with a concentrated gaze, his mouth set in a tight line, not unfriendly or unwelcoming but not heartily cheerful. His neck had grown smaller inside his loosely swaddling collar, the horseshoes of gray around his ears had spread to cover all his wavy hair, his tightly built long body stooped and sagged a bit now but still looked hard, and his dark brown, volatile eyes moved with less animation and showed signs of the brooding strain he was undergoing because of this ordeal.

"Since when do you knock on the door at this house," he said cordially.

"It just seemed natural."

"Come in." He extended a handshake.

I strolled into the kitchen, feeling Dad's presence behind me.

"How are you?"

"I'm fine." I looked around. "How's everyone at home?"

"They're all good except for this thing that happened to Tony."

"That was a rotten deal."

"How come it took you weeks to come after your brother called?" Dad asked with a hint of reproach.

"Well, I had things to do."

"Shouldn't you put your brother first?"

"He does come first." I listened to my tone. I was trying to be nice. I wanted to avoid any quarrelsome friction my first minute in the house. "I had to work on his brief. I could do it better from my office."

"You want some coffee." Dad moved to the stove to turn on a flame under a coffeepot.

"No, thanks, Dad. Where's Mom?"

"She's upstairs. She'll be right down." He looked over his shoulder at me. "You know your brother had a lawyer at his hearing."

"I know," I said in a voice bent as matter-of-factly as possible.

"You figure you're a better lawyer than he was?"

Impatiently, I swiveled my eyes around at him. "I hope I get better results."

"This lawyer who represented him, he was a former police captain, retired."

I sighed and shrugged my shoulders, hearing irate words rising in me. I knew Dad had only the haziest notion of what I had been doing in my life for the past ten years. I also knew that the strain between us predated this visit and had been silently festering for years. There were things antagonistically weighing between us that neither of us understood.

"It doesn't mean much that his lawyer had been a police captain. He may have been great at civil service exams."

"But you have to be real smart to make captain."

"I'm not looking to argue with you, Dad."

"Who's arguing? I ask questions about how you're gonna save your brother's life and that's arguing? I just want to bring out doubts." He spoke in that toneless, indefinably underclass sense of futility.

"Maybe it hurt him more having a police captain for a lawyer." I stroked my chin between my fingers, my mind working, back in the groove of the case, wondering if the connection was more of a hindrance in dealing with the police department. I was about to ask Dad another question when I saw Mom coming down the stairs. From a distance I could see that she was dyeing her hair black, but it was weaker, unsmooth, grainy black, not like the velvet color of her young womanhood, and it carried the unnatural scent of chemicals imitating blossoms. Her face showed no wrinkles but the skin was tighter and stretched with angles and signs of strain from aging, but the smile was widely earnest and gracious, and it jumped to brighter happiness as she moved quickly toward me. She reached out with her arms, which had gotten heavier like the rest of her, and enfolded me in a warm embrace.

"Oh, Joey," she cried, rushing over with a big hug.

"Hi, Mom." I hugged her back, feeling a kind of glow knowing that through all the years, no matter what the troubles I had brought home, I was always her boy.

"Tell me how have you been?"

"I've been good."

"Is everything okay? How's your health? Are you eating the right food? I hope you're not eating any greasy fried potatoes. Stay away from grease. It rots your stomach."

"Mom, I don't eat fried foods."

"Not even bacon. It's all porky grease."

"I eat very little meat. Once in a while Sherrill will make a stew. We both like fresh vegetables."

"Why didn't you bring her? I thought you were

going to bring her. We're all so eager to meet her. She sounds like a wonderful girl over the phone. She's got such a sweet voice."

"She's got assignments at college. There's a chance she may join me later."

"I think it's such a wonderful thing you coming to help your brother in this mess. Isn't it a shame what happened to that boy. It's not right. With my prayers to God I know you're going to clear up this mess. You have the talent God gave you to win for him."

"I hope you're right."

"It would be wonderful if you could get your brother his respect back." Her eyes gazed wistfully.

"What about his job?"

"That's not as important as his respect. He's a hard worker. He'll always manage a living."

"I'm going to give it my all."

"I don't think you would have gone to all those places, way out to California and Massachusetts and Oxford unless you had a gift of the mind. No one else in the neighborhood could have done those things."

"I'm not that smart, Mom. I just work hard. Anybody who works hard can be smart."

"What are you saying?"

"I'm an intellectual coal miner. I go down and scrape up and dig out what's buried inside of me. Everybody has a lot deep inside them. The mind of man is like the mind of God."

"I believe God is guiding you in this case."

The next morning I was awakened by a howling jangle from the alarm overhead. I reached up with groping fingers to press the lever back in place. My grit-stuck eyes oozed open slowly. Instead of my wife's fair body, I found my hairy-chested brother Ernie stretched lazily next to me, not stirring at the early hour because it was his day off. For a moment I lay staring up at the ceiling, feeling the effects of a mini-lobotomy from the disorienting transcontinental flight. I stretched lazily and moved to a sitting position and slowly pushed back the covers. The room was a bit nippy from the cold air that had seeped in during the night, but the steam was hissing off the radiator and warming up the place. Pulling up the blinds, I watched the wind strumming the telephone wires and people below trudging down the block, heading for the subway and their jobs in Manhattan. From cloudy skies a pale sun peeked out with only a glimmer of faint rays. I traced the path of a soup can swept up in the wind and sent clattering erratically down the street.

I got up and crossed the room in my robe and headed for the bathroom, while Sugar, the family dog, yawned and got up to follow me. The door of the bathroom opened and Dad came out in his robe dabbing a towel on a shaving nick on his chin. He nodded a self-contained greeting of good morning before returning to his bedroom. Washing up, I started to feel inspired to get working on the case. I showered and dried quickly. I crossed paths with my youngest sister Sally as I stepped out of the bathroom. She was a beautiful eighteen-year-old girl with an hourglass figure, tall and light-eyed, moving with a graceful walk, her shiny brown hair bobbing back and forth with her movements. Not only was she very pretty but she also had a good intelligence and was doing extremely well in high school. Like my other two sisters she had no interest in college or a career and was already making plans for her marriage and a life of raising kids.

Later that day I went over to see Anthony. Sauntering into the backyard, I spotted him in a familiar scene on top of his garage roof, whistling and stirring a long pole in the air to prod his pigeon flock overhead to fly longer. His gray clothes which looked like his old rookie uniform blended with the darkening light of the early evening. A slight wind was rustling the leaves of the old fig tree bending over the garage. I climbed up the creaky wooden ladder up to the garage roof without saying anything while my nose crinkled and adjusted to the smells that were steeped in the walls and floor of the large cottage-size pigeon coop, the scent reminding me of that first step into an animal house at the Bronx Zoo. From the top rung of the ladder, I could make out Anthony's shoes, looking like a Jackson Pollack painting splattered with dry pigeon droppings from the many hours he spent with his pigeons. All his birds were robustly muscular like fullbacks of their species, bred for their brawny endurance and flying power. At one time he owned sixty racing pigeons, but because of the costs of the hobby he had to sell off half of that number. The inchoate jigsaw of feathery movement partially obscured his hands sprinkling corn seeds in one of the compartments.

He grinned a greeting and we exchanged a few words as I followed him into the coop to watch him examine a sick bird's droppings under a microscope. I was eager to ask him what he thought about the brief that I had given him to read. I felt a sense of satisfaction that it was a finely crafted legal document in the best Harvard Law tradition with all its syllogisms in crisply tight organization. He put his hand over the delicate glass slide lining it up with a fine touch. I could see the tendons and muscles in his hand contract with a control that was much better than my own.

"Did you finish the brief?" I asked.

He looked up from the microscope. "Some of the language was hard to understand, but . . ."

"Legal briefs have their own language. It's like learning Latin. Anyway what did you think?"

"It was impressive. All those cases you cited and the wording looked like quite an effort."

I raised my voice to penetrate the cooing and buzzing of pigeons flapping their wings to get at the corn seeds. "Were you fully satisfied with it?"

"This bird has some kind of ringworm," he said, nodding for me to take a look in the microscope. "The one thing I notice throughout the brief is you base it all on legal error. You're asking for a new hearing because of legal error." I could tell it bothered him. He wanted it on innocence.

I bent over the microscope closing one eye. "We have to demonstrate prejudicial error to get a new hearing."

"You really think there were enough errors?"

"Just about on any page of the transcript, I'll show you at least two legal errors. It comes off like a real railroad job. They were going to find you guilty no matter what."

"What chance do you think we have of winning a new trial?"

"I think a good one!"

"How do you figure?" He dropped down to one knee in the next compartment to scrape up encrusted droppings. "I mean, the commissioner's office approved the results of the original trial. Now you have to go back and ask them to say it was all unfair."

"That's right."

"And you think they will do it just because of unfairness or legal error."

"The answer is, I'm going to have to put some additional pressure on them this time."

"What kind of pressure?" His eyebrows rolled up quizzing and questing.

"Something that will make them look over their shoulder."

"Do you know what that will be?"

"No, but I will."

Going inside the house together, we had dinner with the family.

Anthony shot his eyes at the clock on the wall and then pushed his chair back and got up. "Time for *Columbo*." Going into the living room, he flicked on the TV and moved backward, with his eyes on the jumbling gray and white lines and he eased into the big brown sofa. The squawking scramble of electronic lines and shadows folded into focus on the image of Peter Falk in his trademark raincoat. Anthony glanced over at me, simultaneously grabbing a handful of peanuts from a dish on the coffee table. "I get a kick out of Columbo. He comes off like a schlemiel but he's shrewd. The smooth big-time operators think he's a jerk but he outsmarts them. They can't fool him. He always ends up putting two and two together. I like seeing the little guy show the big crook."

"Yeah, I like him, too," I said, sitting at the end of the sofa. "He represents substance. If you don't look and speak like an anchorman these days, you can't have brains. Kennedy started it, exalting form over substance, the age of cosmetic values, the mediagenic candidate."

"Maybe Kennedy came into it. Was suited to it."

"I see what you mean." I winked at Bobbie as she walked by me. "Columbo certainly doesn't put a stress on appearances."

"He's got his own way of doing things. Doesn't care about what's in style. Doesn't care how the world looks at him. He gets results." Anthony scooped up Bobbie in his arms and pulled her back onto his lap. She sat with her head leaned against his shoulder while he stroked her hair and neatened the straggly strands. Angela sat on the rug watching silently, seeming to be hypnotized by the images on the screen.

We continued to watch television, talking in broken sentences and spurts the way viewers often do when distracted by dramatic action. When the late news came on, there was a story of a youth with forty arrests in Harlem who had been picked up on a mugging.

"Forty arrests!" Anthony jerked his head forward with a touch of peevishness. "Can you believe this guy is out in the street?"

"What do you think should be done?"

"He should be locked up for good so he can't mug anybody else, this punk."

"In the long run force is not going to solve the problem. These minorities need decent housing, decent schools, and jobs."

"That's no excuse. I don't want to hear poverty," he yelled.

I was surprised by his explosive response. "But it's there."

"Bullshit. I don't want to hear that someone killed because he couldn't pay his bills. Mom and Dad struggled and suffered without going out with a gun. The decent hardworking people don't rob."

"Nothing excuses it. I'm not condoning any guy's crime no matter where he is born, but you gotta get rid of those slum conditions, get at the social causes. Force has shown it doesn't work."

"What are you talking about?" He grit his lips in a frown. "These criminals got no fear of the law. Force has never been tried. The courts are too lax, permissive, indulgent. The judges have their heads up in the abstract liberal clouds, worrying about nice refined technicalities. Meanwhile people are being mutilated on the streets. We had one judge here who let some rapist off because he said the jails don't rehabilitate. I wrote him a letter, signed my name and my shield number, and told him he was out of his mind. He needed to be rehabilitated. He put this rapist back on the street. Jesus, what an asshole.

"Then you look at the way they let these drug pushers off." He spoke these words in the deepest disgust. "I see them get off with thirty days or a suspended sentence and they go right back to putting poison in kids. I worked the South Bronx for drugs. Thirty thousand addicts live there, according to the federal narcs. Heroin there is like a white plague."

I listened with intense interest while he talked on about his tour of duty fighting drug pushers in the

South Bronx. He believed that most of the crime in the ghetto was committed by drug addicts. Behind the smashing of mailboxes for welfare checks, and the dismantling of cars, and the bloody muggings and store robberies, there was usually a crazed addict thirsting for a heroin fix. The real triggerman behind the shootings and the real pimp behind the girl selling her flesh was the pusher.

He said that if he was out to make an arrest for illegal drug use, he could have made one every hour in the South Bronx. At times the streets were littered with bodies, walking and stumbling, floundering with glazed eyes, drooping into wilted human weeds, crumpling into numb heaps, sprawling out in the gutter, drifting in a dead oblivion. No matter how many addicts he pulled off the streets, he felt his efforts did little to change the surging wave of the problem. The big czars overseeing the heroin trade operated too far from the dirty work to be touched. They were in distant, opulent penthouses or regal country estates in the upper-crust sections of Westchester or Long Island showing the world fur-lined and gold finished facades of social respectability.

When I got back to the house, Dad was sitting at the kitchen table in his Department of Sanitation khakis, a cup of coffee steaming in front of him, bitter and black the way he liked it. I sat down at the table across from him.

"You look so nice in your suit." Mom came over. "Did you have a good sleep? I put extra blankets on the bed for you. I know you're not used to this weather. What will you be doing in Anthony's case?"

"I'm going to make a motion for a new trial. I will get Anthony's record in open court so they can see what he's made of."

Dad swiped the air irritatedly. "Don't you think

they know his record? They're no dummies. It was there in black and white for them to see. Is that your plan? Sounds like nothing to me."

"I just mentioned his record because it has relevance. I know more is needed. I'm going to the law library to dig up more legal ammunition."

"Legal ammunition." His eyes rolled skeptically. "Fancy language. You think your brother is going to be reinstated because of legal ammunition?"

"Why do you question him?" Mom chided. "He knows what he's doing. He's the lawyer, not you. You're a garbage man. Why do you act as if you know more?"

"I know more about New York City and how things get done here. I've been in civil service for over thirty years. To get action in this city you need political clout, connections. You get nowhere with legal ammunition."

I felt anger welling up in my throat. "You may have been in civil service but you know nothing about the courts."

"I know about the courts. I've been to the courts," he said in an oblique slight.

"Look, Dad, I got my own law practice. I have my own law offices—"

"That's what your letters say," he interrupted.

I froze for a moment, and gulped. "You doubt my letters?"

"Who knows what kind of offices they are?"

"What is that supposed to mean?"

"Are you representing the people with big money? Are those big movie people coming to you? Are they gonna go with a Brooklyn boy? They go to their own. They stick with their own kind. They go with the high-class law firms that have been around for years. What kind of clients do you get? The tomato pickers out there."

"I don't need to listen to this silly talk. I don't have

to get into my law practice with you. I'm gonna beat this thing for Tony."

"That's what you say." His eyes stared. "You always were a big talker. Always words, but never deeds."

The words hung abrasively in the air. I heaved myself up from the table and went outside. I was bothered by Dad's belittling slights, but not deeply shaken. There was a time when any discouraging word from him would have been crushing. When I was a boy, it was easy for adults to brand their cutting putdowns into my feelings. Now I had been on my own long enough and had enough concrete achievements in my life to feel an independent sense of worth. I could be stronger and more detached but it still was troubling to be treated without respect or regard from my own father.

I had the keys to my brother Ernie's car. I jumped behind the wheel and started the motor which turned over with a hot roar. I pulled out of the space and rolled down to the stop sign at the corner, still dwelling on Dad's negative attitude and words. I threaded my way through the congested traffic district, giving minimal attention to the needs of driving while most of my mental energy churned in agitation. I got caught in a traffic delay, escaped it briefly but then got snared again, waiting behind a long line of cars and buses belching smoky exhausts. Dad seemed to be caught in the feeling of hopelessness. He was ready to throw his hands down before the fight even began.

It was shown that Anthony's dismissal was having a terrible effect on Dad. It was a cloud on the whole family. Yet it was Anthony, underneath the stoic facade, who was being hurt the most. I was sure he was innocent, but I knew that he might never be a cop again. I knew he had already recognized that dreadful possibility. All his beliefs, everything he put his faith in, was breaking apart, shattering, and falling down on him. It was a shame and a loss to have a cop of his abilities wasting his dreams and wasting his time mopping up floors in a laundromat. Anthony had committed his life to being a cop and it was nearly impossible for him to accept the idea that he might never wear the gold shield again. The fact that he was innocent made him believe that he had to be returned to the police force, but there was simply no guarantee that he was going to be exonerated. I was under a terrible psychological crunch feeling this thing could forever stain and taint him and the family.

By the time I returned to my room later that night, Mom had made the bed, smoothing the covers with a neatness born of her years of working in hospitals. I put in another burst of effort on the brief, which was nearly completed. It was two in the morning and my arms and legs and chest were pumping with drive and stamina to keep going. My whole body was full of tireless enthusiasm, but I could feel my eyes stiffening and biting and growing weary. Drowsiness was closing my eyes while the rest of my body was chugging like a locomotive. I hated to acknowledge the cliché that a man is as strong as his weakest link but I was beginning to feel a need to surrender to the pleas of my wiped-out eyes.

I was still poring over papers when Mom came into the room carrying a tray with a pot of coffee and a cup and a spicy-smelling salami sandwich on French bread.

"I thought if you're going to be working much later, this might help."

"Thanks, Mom." I flashed a smile.

"How are things coming?"

"I'm nearly finished."

"Good." She started to move for the door, but paused and swung around. "Your father doesn't mean all those things he says to you."

"Doesn't he?"

"He's very confused and hurt by all of this. He's afraid to trust you, that's all."

"And we both know I've given him plenty of reason. Still, you'd think . . ."

"I'm not even talking about that, Joe. I'm not sure he'd let himself trust anybody right now. Anthony was always Dad's proof that good things can happen. So now he just doesn't want to get his hopes up. You see, there are things about your father and the way he feels about things that you don't understand." She seemed on the verge of sharing something important. "It's nothing to talk about now. I'll get out of here so you can do your work."

"Thanks, Mom, for coming up."

"Don't tire yourself too much." She tenderly stroked my hair before turning for the door.

I sat there alone and gazed out at the night. I felt warm and comforted by Mom's words. It seemed that's the way things had often gone in my dealings with Mom and Dad. He would cut me down and then she would come in and soothe my wounds. I couldn't help but wonder what I would have become if she hadn't believed in me during those early tough years.

CHAPTER SIX

I failed almost every subject my first term in high school. I'd start out for school in the morning but would usually stray to the poolroom or sneak into a movie. On the days I did go to school, I'd often get into a fight. Before the second term was over, I dropped out, at the age of sixteen. I started making regular trips to agency row on Forty-second Street, trying to find a job. Every place I was sent they told me that my age or my lack of experience or a diploma disqualified me. A friend of mine told me they were hiring men wringing necks at his chicken market, but it made me nauseous to look at the birds flapping around in the barrel without heads. I scoured the Classified section of *The New York Times* looking for openings available to a sixteen-year-old dropout. The only jobs were a few stock boy positions in scattered parts of the city. After waiting hours to be interviewed, I was politely told at each place that my application would be considered and that if they decided on me I would be called. Sometimes I could sense the person rejecting me as soon as he saw my manner or heard my speech. No calls came.

I tried shaping up at a paper mill one morning but couldn't get on. It had been two months since leaving school; I was still without a job and I was worried about what Dad was going to say when I got home. Entering the dingy three-room apartment, I tossed my coat on a chair in the kitchen. Mom was fixing supper over a kettle of boiling salty water furiously whirlpooling with foam, hot drops of water from the steam moistening her face and dripping from the loose hair straggled in front of her eyes. She kept one eye on the baby in the nearby crib while she went about her cooking chores. Her wrinkled dress was buttoned out of order and seemed tight around her good round figure, growing broader and plumper each year. Mom was kind of a house prisoner, always busy with chores, scrubbing floors, washing dishes, nursing babies, cooking meals, washing clothes. Her face skin was smooth, and her coal-black hair was lustrous in color and untouched by gray, but her lips often seemed twisted in worry. Not a week went by when she wasn't racing into the closet, baby in arms, to hide from a bill collector, making sure he had the impression no one was home.

Mom had a pretty tough life. One of a large immigrant family, she lost her father at a young age and was put to work knitting booties in a basement factory. By fourteen she was working long hours in a sweatshop in the garment center. She married very young and had her third child die inside of her at three months. Then she gave birth to five more healthy children. One would think she had enough of children for a lifetime, but she said that after the job of raising all of us was over, she wanted to adopt a couple of orphans. To her the idea of just taking care of two orphans was a luxury. As a testimony of her strong religion, Mom had the walls and bureau tops of our apartment blessed by over six dozen sacred objects. Catholic missions from as far as Alaska had her on their mailing lists for donations. She sacrificed in any way possible so as to send money to them. "Have God in your heart," she was always saying, "that's the most important thing in life."

The crying outburst of the baby set Mom turning around with my three-year-old sister Camille tagging along onto her skirt and sucking a thumb. Lifting the baby out of the crib and burping her, she gently rocked back and forth, occasionally caressing and kissing the milk-white skin. I couldn't understand that surge of feeling that took hold of her face when she was holding a baby in her arms.

I was practicing throwing uppercut punches when my little brother Ernie came over to me. I had been taught how to throw them by Tony Bavimo, my neighborhood idol, the toughest gang leader around and a sensational pro boxer.

"Show me." Ernie's eyes brightened.

"You dip your shoulder this way." I demonstrated.

Mom wheeled around from the stove. "What are you teaching him how to hit for? This neighborhood's got enough who only know how to raise a fist to hurt and not a finger to help."

"I'm only showing him for self-defense."

"I heard you bragging about Tony Bavimo. He's no self-defense character, that one."

"It's good for him to know how to handle himself."

"Show your brother how to help not hurt others. That Bavimo wants to put his chest over everyone else's."

"Son of a bitch, Mom, you know nuttin' about Bavimo to knock him."

She turned to me. "Watch the low-class way you talk around here. I can see what a wonderful influence this Tony Bavimo is on you. I don't want you filling your younger brother's head with his wild ideas. He reminds me of Al Capone when he was a boy."

"You knew Al Capone?"

"He lived around the corner from us in South Brooklyn."

"That's a tough section. The Gallo brothers live there."

"We were frightened to go outside," she recalled. "Dead bodies would be in the gutter next to dead horses. Capone was no big shot then, just a crazy roly-poly making trouble. Why do you want to know about him?" Her lips puckered chidingly at me.

"I'm curious. They made a movie about him."

"He was a big gangster. A disgrace to the Italian people. He brought shame on all the decent hardworking Italians. With his guns and *cafoni*, shooting all those men on St. Valentine's Day." She curled her brows distastefully. "My God, nothing decent, no refinement, not even common, a vulgar animal with that scar down his face."

"Why did they make a movie about him?" Ernie asked.

"Because those moviemakers were as greedy as him. Imagine glorifying the likes of the devil. I don't want any of you going near the mobsters. Those people got an ugly streak. What do they stand for? They're only out for themselves. They have no love in them for other people. You should only admire people who do for others, not just themselves."

"Tony Bavimo is a boxer, Mom, he's not like Capone. He's a fighter in the ring."

"But he wants to be tough."

"When you were young, Mom, would Grandma let you date a mob guy?"

"She would have wrung my neck." A musical tone of laughter suddenly broke out of the corners of her smile. "I once got myself in trouble with those people. When I was a little girl, I saw these ritzy ladies get out of a limousine, real highfalutin types in fancy furs, and they went into a stove store on the avenue. Out of curiosity me and my sisters went snooping through the stoves left on the sidewalk. We found three big bags of white powder. We tasted it and it was tart. We knew it wasn't sugar so we threw the bags down the sewer. Had they seen us they would have killed us. Those bags all had cocaine."

"Did they come to the apartment?"

"No, Grandma wouldn't let him set foot in our place." Mom shook her head recalling. "My father died when we were young but she filled his shoes. That woman wasn't afraid of nobody. I don't know where she found the nerve. A big barrel of a man, a pervert, once tried to molest my sister Marie. My mother went right into his place and grabbed my sister off his lap and let him have a punch right in the face."

"She was something." I grinned. "I treaded very lightly around Grandma, knowing the robust storm of her fury, but I was proud of her scrappy grit."

"Did she beat up a mugger once, too?" Ernie asked.

"It was three tough women who jumped and ganged her and took her money. The next day she went back with rocks in her purse and she beat the daylights out of those women who robbed her, hitting them with the purse. My mother worked hard for her money. She was in a factory from seven to seven and she had eight children to feed. She was not going to let those thieves get away with it."

Suddenly Mom's eyebrows bunched together. "Did you find a job today? Your father will be home soon."

"No, I didn't."

"He's not going to be pleased." She shook her head. "Go wash for dinner. And comb your hair down." She jabbed my high pompadour wave. "That looks like one of those big water things in Hawaii."

"This is 'in,' Mom."

"You got nice features. You ruin them with that ugly hairstack. Comb it straight back. You'll look like Valentino."

"I'll look like a wimp."

"Listen to your mother. You'll break the girls' hearts. You'll be another Rudy."

"C'mon, Mom, stop talking like a dizzy mother. I got a girl."

"How does Dutchy feel about that gawky stalk? Does she like it?"

"Dutchy likes what makes me happy."

I went into the bathroom and stood in front of the mirror, parting my hair one way and then another, halting with the comb resting half-drawn through the pile of black hair and smiling slyly at myself wondering about Mom's crazy remark that I could look like Valentino. The only similarities were that we had dark skin and black hair, but I had blue eyes. I began posing like Valentino, narrowing my eyes and crushing the brows down and glinting fiercely and throwing my head up to blip the whites of my eyeballs and flashing a lusty maniac smile.

I walked back into the kitchen waiting for Mom to catch my Valentino slick. A smile blossomed over her face when she noticed. "Oh, you look so much better this way, so handsome." She put her arm around my waist and put a motherly kiss on my cheek.

"Cut that out. I'm no kid nomore."

"So what's wrong with your mother showing she loves you?"

The door opened and all the kids thundered to Dad coming home from work. I didn't move with them, feeling ill at ease and worried about facing him. I dreaded telling him that I again wasted the fifty cents he gave me for the subway. He was wearing the khaki uniform of the Department of Sanitation. The shirt was soiled with food stains and splotched with grease and his face had streaks of dirt, while vegetable particles were trapped in his hair from handling garbage all day. He wiped his feet on the rubber mat in the little hallway before coming inside. He looked tired and sleepy around the eyes. His ears were puffed and red with cold. His nose was shining and swollen. He was carrying a heavy brown overcoat over his arm and a pair of rubber boots, and when he put them down to take off his gloves, his hands were cracked and stiff with the chill. He affectionately kissed the four kids around him and mumbled something, wearing a tight-lipped smile. He dropped his boots and the cold came off him like a sheet. Trudging into the kitchen, he unbuttoned the half-dollar buttons on his jacket and worked his hands together and blew into them. His handsome looks were hidden by the dirt smudging his face. He seemed in a good mood but he muttered a complaint about the people loading their ash barrels to the brim. It was breaking the men's backs.

After washing up and getting out of his uniform, Dad came back into the kitchen looking fresher and cleaner in a checkered wool shirt and slacks, the dark color of the shirt heightening the vivid blackness in his naturally wavy hair, which was parted ruler-straight down the side. He was tall, lean, and taut, his body solid and strong from his work. Around his ears his black hair shaded into a rim of premature gray giving him a distinguished look in a suit. His chin line flowed sharply and went well with his well-formed nose and his volatile brown eyes. He grew a jot of beard below his mouth, a sign of a horn man, which he claimed strengthened his playing lip for his weekend gigs. Standing up straight, he wrinkled his cheeks cheerfully at everyone. I watched in mildly stunned surprise as he winked boyishly at Mom and widened his smiling lips into an open circle, showing the even teeth in his cold, reddened face. He moved over to her in front of the children and half suavely and half affectionately hugged her into him, while she curled the corners of her mouth up almost blushingly. He seemed to be in an unusually romantic mood. The fatigue he had showed initially was gone and he moved with light, springy steps to his chair at the kitchen table. Calling my younger sister Madeline over to him, he cuddled her in his arms and gently rocked her, kissing her on top of the head. "How's my little girl?" His lips smacked wetly on the side of her cheek.

Happily barking and wagging his tail at Dad's feet was Tiny, the little black and white fox terrier who was the family dog. Dad had raised Tiny from a puppy after having raised his mother Jenny from a puppy. Everyone played with and petted the two dogs, but Dad was like a parent to them. When Jenny got cancer, he was often getting up in the middle of the night to give her medicine to help lessen her pain, and he even borrowed money to pay for an operation to make her live a little longer. It turned out only to prolong the suffering, and you could see Dad with reddened eyes feeling the dog's pain. I didn't know where he found the time to take care of the dog working two jobs and raising seven children, but he managed to find it or make it.

The family sat down at the kitchen table, and Mom put down a bowl of pasta intertwined with broccoli, sprinkled with buttery oil sauce and sweetly spiced with lemon basil. It was steaming up a delicious aroma. This was a cheap dish to prepare and was filling, nourishing, and tasteful, but I was growing tired of it because we had it about every other day. After Dad said grace, all the little arms and hands began moving in and out of the pasta, making the platter shrink quickly.

Home from work late, Anthony came into the kitchen looking for a place to sit. His knees bumped against mine taking a chair next to me. Dad's eyes brightened glancing over at him. Dad often said he was blessed to have such a good son. Not only was Anthony a good worker and high on the list to become a cop, he also had a great feel and touch on the clarinet, one of the instruments Dad played.

When he was done with his meal, Dad lit up a twenty-five-cent cigar, waving the cigar wandlike in front of his nose, savoring the smell, acting with a sense of luxury. His face was beaming. "I had shaker-outer duty today."

"What's shaker outer, Daddy?" Madeline asked.

"That's when your daddy gets to ride on the truck instead of walking all day."

"But why do they call it that?" twelve-year-old Ernie asked.

Dad slowly rolled the smoke in his mouth. "Because that's what you do. You shake out the cans. The men walking behind the truck hand up the cans."

"You mean you're in the truck section where all the garbage is?" Ernie's lips creased uncomfortably.

Dad was unfazed. "The thing is, you don't have to walk. You ride. And you don't lift the heavy cans. You tip 'em over. Shake 'em out."

I felt something tensing in me as I listened to him. His talk was bothering me. The way he made it sound like an enviable role standing in garbage for a living. I would never say it to him, but I was ashamed of Dad's being a garbage collector. It was a feeling that had been hammered into me at a younger age by all the slurs and mockings of other kids calling him dirty names.

On the floor at Dad's feet was a labelless gallon of heavy-bodied homemade red wine. He pulled the cork out and dipped the heavy gallon with a strong grip and filled up his glass. I was thinking and hoping that he was going to forget about asking me what happened today, but he finally got around to it. "Did you get a job today?"

"No."

"What happened?" A frown broke on his face.

"The foreman said to come back in a month."

"In a month. Dammit, you better be working before then." His mood was swiftly changing. He flattened the head of his cigar in the ashtray. "It's been two months."

"I been trying."

"That's what you keep telling me." He perked up his upper lip in an expression of irritation. "How hard have you been looking?" I could see only suspicion, no trust, and his anger was rising. Dad had a hot temper that came out like a blast of steam when it blew.

"I went to agency row every day last week. I spent all morning in those agencies. I went wherever they sent me. No one hired me."

"You said you were going to B. Altman's department store. They got a good class of people who shop there. Ya got Park Avenue people going in there."

"The personnel manager gave me a rag handshake. I think he looked down at me. He wouldn't hire me."

"There are snobs in that kind of fancy store." Anthony took my side.

"What about the ship chandler job? My God, you told me about all these prospects, and God Almighty, you couldn't get one. For all I know you been going to those peep shows on Forty-second Street watching them bare-ass *putannas* in them machines."

"I been going for jobs. Every place I've been says my age or lack of experience or no diploma disqualifies me. You can't get a decent job without a diploma."

"Jesus, Mary, and Joesph!" He slammed his fist on the table. "Nobody on this block has a diploma, and they all got jobs. Excuses, alibis, anything to shirk."

"Give him a chance, Dad," Anthony said.

"He's only been out of school two months," Mom added.

"You stay out of this." He looked at her irately. "I'm the one who has to worry about the bills around here."

"I get sick in the heart worrying about bills," Mom said.

"But you don't have the loan companies breathing down your neck and taking you to court and making the judge garnishee your salary. This one's been leeching off his father."

"He's only a boy."

"He's sixteen, out of school, got a big body on him, and eats like a horse." He turned scowling at me. "There's no excuse. I know where you can get a job for sure. Over at Kings County Hospital they're always looking for orderlies. You work indoors. You don't have to be murdered by the cold like me."

I looked around the table at everyone looking at me, my sister Madeline showing worry in her eyes. "I don't want that shit job. Cleaning up after those sick dying people messing up the bed. That's a shit job." The idea sickened me of going inside patients' underclothes and wiping them up and cleaning off the smelly bed. I knew it made Dad furious when I acted too good for such work because he had to go to his garbage hauling every day, a job he hated.

His face grew redder. "It's not for you to be choosy."

"That's a zilch job. I'm the one who has to face my girl and friends and tell them I'm cleaning other people up for a living. What kind of job is that to respect yourself? That's a zilch job."

"You take it until something better comes along. You don't sit on your ass waiting."

"Who's sitting? I've been going all over the city."

"Go for that orderly job." His teeth were contorting his face out of shape.

"Screw it. I'm not going. I'm gonna look for a decent job."

"You're no damn good."

"Because I won't take a degrading job."

"Because you're only for yourself, a selfish bum. You have no feelings for your family." His rage was pulsing on his forehead. "I have nine mouths to feed and you won't help out. You got a streak in you, you're a bum."

"Whadda ya mean, bum, I've been working every summer since I was twelve. I put ten hours a day in that goddamn bleach factory those summers. None of my friends had to work summers. I worked after school all those years with Visco's Market."

"You're still a bum."

I wasn't going to cry. I wasn't going to give him the satisfaction. I pressed my teeth together forcing down the lumps of tears coming up. My body flushed with heat as I looked around at the staring and upset eyes of my little brothers and sisters around the table. I wanted to get up and run out the door and keep running. I wanted to say something else but no more talk would come out of my lips. I could hear the words stuck in my throat. Why was he always trying to find something wrong with me? Nothing I ever did was right or good for him. I know it looked bad failing to find a job in two months but I was earnestly trying and I didn't think it was wrong to want something a little decent. I knew that he resented that I refused to do messy work at the hospital when he had to earn a living by hauling garbage. Anthony had a decent job at the shoe store and was preparing to become a policeman, why should I have to take the dregs. My tongue and mouth lumped together with my feelings. I wanted to tell him, "Hey, Dad, why don't you give me a chance? Why don't you cheer me on, too, the way you do Anthony? Why don't you encourage me the way you once did when you taught me how to swim? I tried my hardest and did my best when you cheered me on. It only makes me feel down about myself when you pounce on me and call me a bum. It would make me do a lot better if you gave me a piece of confidence to take out there in the world."

Dad couldn't see what I was feeling inside. He always jumped into a hotheaded inquisition that ended with him sputtering and spraying slurs through his teeth. There was never any understanding passing between us. Even Mom could see it and she would scold him for jumping overboard with his temper and becoming "the mad dog," and using his fists on me. All of the worries eating at him, the milk bill, the rent, the money he owed to Shylocks, the money owed to his sister, the money he owed to Mr. Foreman, the grocer, and most of all his frustrated anger at becoming a garbage man instead of a musician, exploded on me.

I went into the bathroom and unbuttoned my shirt and tossed it to the ground, and then I stuck my head under the shower nozzle in the tub and turned on the water full blast and let the cold spray drum and dance on my hair and soak and splash on my face, and I felt comforted from the flow, and cooled down inside. I walked past the kitchen into the front room and sat on the sofa, staring silently at the walls. Sadness crept over me. Why couldn't Dad be proud of me the way he was of Anthony? Why did he have to see me as a good-for-nothing? Why didn't he give me a chance?

Mom came into the room sensing what I was feeling. I could tell she felt for me. She didn't say anything; she just gently rubbed her hand on the back of my still-damp head. She knew I was feeling sad, and why I was in this mood, and she was offering her understanding. I thought how warm and kindly she was to take the time to come in for one of her big sons when she had all the little ones in need of her. I felt good that she cared enough to want to pick up my spirits.

I went to the closet to get my jacket, and headed for the front door. "I'm going out."

"Where you going?" Mom asked worriedly.

"To see my friends in the pool hall."

"You should stay away from that bunch."

"They're my friends."

Dad had gone into his bedroom, closed the door behind him, and had begun blowing jazz on his saxophone. He was left in a tense nervous mood by our conversation. Playing the sax was one way he could lose himself in a dreamy, faraway refuge. He did it to improve his skills, but there was too much emotion in his sound for it to simply be practice. When he got that saxophone rolling, building up to hot notes, blowing out furious tones, throwing his head up and down, it was like he was working something out of his system, burning it out like getting rid of a demon. His hands shook around that horn like he was handling a wildly jumping bronco. He was in the grip of a powerful melancholy force. His whole life was racing inside the splash and dazzle of jazz. The intense speeding and hot flying of sounds did come down to a richer, warmer, and beautifully sensitive mood as Dad continued to play out his heart, and it seemed like his whole life. His music must have taken him back introspectively to his boyhood, to the days he lived with his immigrant parents.

At the turn of the century my father's parents had

come together from Naples in the steerage section of a steamship, all their personal belongings wrapped in a woolen blanket, and they moved into a cold-water flat shared by two other families in the Red Hook section of Brooklyn. Here a million Italian immigrants lived crammed together tier on tier in a train of red tenements, breathing air that was sooty from the smoke-belching tire factories and bacteria-infested streets. It was the worst slum at that time in New York City. Dad's father, a onetime peasant farmer, had become a bartender in the new country, and after years of saving he was able to buy his own saloon, moving his family of three boys and one girl into a rear apartment.

The men who came in for a drink at the end of the day were a hard bunch, laborers who toiled on construction gangs, emerging from work that was strenuous and even dangerous, and they were crude, loud, free-cussing, hard-drinking, and easily ignited into brawls. From his bedroom as a boy Dad would hear fights break out, with shouting and heads slamming into walls, bottles shattering, and bodies crashing to the floor, and he became frightened that his parents were going to be hurt. His mother hated the saloon because of the lawless men, the bloody brawls, the messy drunks, the prostitutes loitering out front, and the health inspectors harassing them. The bright times were when wedding parties were held at the saloon and his father, gifted with a marvelous tenor voice, got up to sing Italian folk songs. Over the years his father became popularly known locally as the Cantantore ("the Singer") and he was often invited to sing at weddings.

Inheriting his father's love for music, Dad as a boy would spend hours listening to the RCA Symphonic, an enormous mahogany console. It was the big-band sounds that appealed to him. His fancy blossomed into lessons on the clarinet at Our Lady of Peach Church. By this time, because a man had been shot to death in the saloon, his mother had persuaded his father to sell the business and move the family into a tenement and take a job with the telephone company doing janitorial work.

Though now out of the saloon, the family was still in Red Hook, the tough neighborhood that produced Al Capone, Joe Adonis, and Joe Bonnano, and around the corner from the church rectory where Dad practiced was the hangout for the South Brooklyn boys. Standing out front, the young toughs would size up a passerby, looking for targets to con, bluff, and rob, and sometimes when a music student left the church, he was spit upon and cursed or thrown to the ground and kicked.

At fourteen, Dad learned how to play the scale and a few simple compositions under Father Negri, the director of the church band; but then, with his own savings from a newspaper route, he signed up for musical tutoring with Michael Casille, a florid man with an overpowering voice considered at that time and place "the best reed man in the business." Casille emphasized the importance of learning the science of music from books. Dad loved to study, learn, and memorize music, and there were times when he remained up all night studying and his mother would find him in the morning fast asleep with the open music book on his chest. After a year he was matching his teacher note for note, the tempo leading to fast sixteenths and thirty-seconds and the strenuously difficult "Flight of the Bumble Bee."

He found that he had a fine ear and an ability to internalize notes, so that he could play an entire song after a short time without looking at the sheet music. By the age of seventeen he was playing two instruments, adding the saxophone, and he was putting together orchestrations for his own group and playing at Red Hook dances. He gained a lot of experience playing at the local church functions and he was confidently prepared when he got a booking for a social gala at the Prospect Circle Dance Hall. The people liked his sound and it led to bookings in small nightclubs and weddings and lounge gigs at the better hotels downtown like the Hampshire and St. George. On his twenty-first birthday he joined the 14th Regiment of the National Guard. The doughboy uniform appealed to him, added a masculine touch, he thought, as he struck poses with his buddies for photos tilting the wide-brim campaign hat. It was through a member of his troop that he met Mom's brother, which led to an introduction to Mom, and he knew rather quickly that he was in love with her. His courting was supervised very strictly by Grandma, who sat behind the young couple at movie theaters and refused to allow them any close dancing. Grandma gave them six months and then told Dad if he wanted to see Mom again, he better set the marriage. As a boy rummaging through my parents' room, I had found old photographs and letters and even Valentine's Day cards neatly saved in a bundle. One of the wedding photos showed them gazing dreamily into each other's eyes, another embraced in a kiss. Dad looked like a sleepy-eyed Don Juan in a tuxedo, his smooth Latin profile dramatized by rolling waves of velvety black hair, and Mom looked blushingly pretty in the satin bridal gown. The letters were from when Dad was away in the training maneuvers of the National Guard.

The wording was nothing fancily poetic, ringing simple and sincere, trying to share with Mom the nicer things he was seeing, describing the trees and singing birds and clear brook soldiers bathed in the Adirondack woods, and telling her how much he missed her and how she was his one and only love for this lifetime.

During this period Dad's musical ambitions were climbing up to brilliant promise. His bookings at social events resulted in a long-term contract for his orchestra at the fabulous Luna Park Ballroom in Coney Island. He could boast that he was the leader of a "big sound." He had organized a band of fourteen pieces including four saxophones, three trumpets, two trombones, one piano, one bass fiddle, one flute, and one set of drums. The spacious ballroom at Luna Park was adorned with gold-framed mirrors crowned by curlicues, the wood floor shimmered from a glassy coat of wax, the ceiling sparkled with harlequin globes that rotated, the bar was ornately chromed and leathered and ran a locomotive's length. More than four hundred young adults swarmed in every weekend to dance the peabody, Charleston, jitterbug, fox-trot, and rumba. Up on the stage in the blaze of footlights, the band members were dressed in tuxedos or beige sports coats and bow ties, depending on the night, slightly crouched playing their instruments behind the black cardboard stands which held their sheet music and were inscribed with glitter-crusted musical bars over the name Nick Sorrentino. The two singers sat up front ready to go to the microphone. Slickly groomed with cream hair lotion, Dad waved his baton, directing the band, and glanced over his shoulder from time to time to smile at the girls shimmying out on the dance floor; or sometimes he picked up his saxophone or clarinet to do solo flourishes in the spotlight.

A scintillating bright tide of good luck was gushing his way. Nothing but great promise loomed on the horizon. Suddenly the stock market crashed and the Depression fell upon the nation like a dark plague and his dreams began nightmarishly to shred apart with devastating speed until there was nothing left but a gloom of shadowy pieces. Overnight, it seemed, attendance at Luna Park dramatically declined as the ballroom craze evaporated in the crunch of hard times. The band was out on the street without a booking in sight. Along with hordes of other people feeling vulnerable, he was stampeded into a frantic search for security. His dreams were no longer crucial. A lot of his boyhood friends were joining the Department of Sanitation. The civil service bulletins announced sizable new hirings collecting garbage. It was an honest job, offering security, a regular salary, hospitalization, and a pension. The drop was steep from a ballroom stage in a tuxedo before the footlights and admiring crowds to the back of a garbage truck.

His first day he had to report for work at six in the morning to clear snow from an intersection. Heavily bundled in sweaters and long johns under his uniform and wearing high rubber boots, he gave his name to a foreman directing a small crew and several plow trucks at the crosswalk. It was no morning to be outside. From the gray, dark skies the snow was raging down in thick flakes, and the icy winds were knifing through his clothes, and the stinging cold was nipping at his ears. Each time he took a breath his mouth exhaled a flume of smoke. The streets were depressingly barren except for an occasional car with high beams on, slowly making its way through the treacherously frozen road. All morning he shoveled snow with a pan scraper, moving from intersection to intersection on foot, clearing the crosswalks, and resumed the same hard work after lunch until night. When he came home, every inch of his clothes was soaked with melted snow, lumps of ice were caked in his hair, his boots dripped a puddle of dirty water, his face was feeling numb and shiny red from churning blood, his nose was running, his eyes were exhausted, his back and shoulders ached from the continuous stooping and strain, his palms were calloused from the pan scraper, and his fingers were swollen and stiff. Slowly he removed his boots and socks and placed his damp and puffed feet in a tub of hot water, and he felt the soreness throb throughout his body. It was a day he hated and one he was to repeat every winter for the next forty years.

Dad continued with his music part-time, doing weekend gigs at Murphy's Tavern, one of a good number of saloons in the neighborhood. Dark, brawny men stood along the dimly lit bar jabbering about their jobs, unions, horse bets, broads, and the Yankees, draining up hard amounts of whiskey. Nobody in

Murphy's Bar paid much attention to Dad and his four-piece combo. Anyone who watched him at Murphy's could tell he was hurting inside, playing his heart out, straining himself red in the face, without anyone caring to listen. The only time the men gave their attention to the band was at midnight when the stripper came out. If the stripper was a brazen teaser, she would shimmy and shake inches from a man's crotch drawing sweat beads down his cheeks and roars of wild cheers from the other men, drowning out Dad's playing. As much as he was ignored in Murphy's, Dad still looked forward to doing his gigs. Even if others weren't appreciating his playing, he seemed to find a deep and satisfying mood in pouring himself into his horn and getting back to his own senses, the rich stream of music revitalizing and healing his spirit. The opportunity to touch music was a soul-nourishing break from his regular hard routine.

CHAPTER SEVEN

Pop's Pool Hall was located on the street level of a narrow four-story tenement. Sun shining down swirled off the chrome and mirrors of motorcycles parked out front and came in the glass front, throwing a bright pond of light over the first playing table in the hall. Deeper in the shadows, kettle lamps hanging from long chains poured smoky light over the playing tables, the sturdy, old-fashioned, hippo-legged variety, and illuminated green felt cushions tattered with rips patched over with black tape. Gagging clouds of cigarette smoke hung stagnant in the air because there were no windows and the vents in the transom were dammed by dust and fortified by grease. An open door in one corner revealed a cracked toilet with cigarette butts littering the sloshy floor around it. Fast rhythms and beats spinning out of the jukebox mingled with the loud clatter of break shots and the boisterous babble of the players and onlookers filling up the benches and milk crates along the walls. A huddle of four or five guys stood in front, guys in their late teens or early twenties, dipping around in the hip Coxsackie shuffle, cockily bragging about banging broads, looking out at the cars passing, identifying them by make and model, swooning admiringly when a Buick Roadmaster came in view, tossing insults at straight-looking men in suit and tie, flirting crudely with the girl daring enough to walk in range. Half the front window was painted black to block out the curious eyes of kids, and a big sign was posted over the door, No Minors Allowed, and even bigger graffiti scrawled over the entrance read Work Stinks.

I scooped up the glistening multicolored balls and then with the flair of a juggler flicked them on the green cushion inside the wood triangle. At the other end of the table, Tony Bavimo was stroking his cue stick, taking aim for the break shot. With a whiplike action he drove the cue stick into the white ball, sending it spinning into the pyramid of balls and cleaving them apart with a chain of crackles, the balls wildly swishing and careening around the table, the ten ball rolling into an end pocket. Tony smiled, moving around the table, surveying his next shot. His mind seemed distracted by a fresh red and black poster from Madison Square Garden with one of the bouts circled in crayon, a six-rounder between middleweight Artie Chuback, a hard-punching crowd pleaser from Hoboken, and Tony Bavimo, the pride of South Brooklyn. He seemed intoxicated with his own name on a Madison Square Garden poster. He brought his eyes back to the table and rifled the one ball into the side pocket with a thud.

He missed his next shot and sputtered a curse and thumped his heel against the floor, but behind the outburst was an unruffled calm. Tony didn't take a pool game too seriously. He didn't have the outlook that he had to win in everything. Shooting pool to him was a light form of recreation. He did not care if he was not among the top pool shooters in the gang. The required skills of hand steadiness and keen eye concentration were not important enough for him to develop. What mattered to him was his reputation in the streets, and what counted in the streets was fierce fighting ability or being a real bad tough. Tony could easily laugh off losing a pool game but his lip quivered ferociously when he was confronting someone before a fight. It looked like every nerve ending in his body was about to explode when his "rep" was on the line. The same will to win was carried into the boxing ring with him. Becoming the middleweight champion of the world mattered fanatically to him. He was going to put on a savage display when he met Artie Chuback in the Garden ring. He knew the big-timers were going to be watching him from ringside, sizing up his punching power, his heart, his stamina, seeing if he truly possessed the all-around attributes of a champion. Confident he had it all, he was eager for this chance to prove himself. The Polack, as he called Chuback, was supposed to be rugged, undefeated like himself in ten matches with nearly all knockout victories, but Tony cockily told us that he was going to knock him out in the first round.

More than anyone else in my life, Tony Bavimo was leading my destiny. I first heard of him when I was in the fifth grade. Even before I met him, he had become my idol because of the legendary stories I heard about him from older boys on my block. Huddled in a hallway with them, I listened over and over to tales of his battles and feats: how he "dropped" Blubberhead, the toughest guy on Thirteenth Avenue, and the time he flattened three guys who bothered his steady, and how he could lift hundred-pound potato sacks over his head, one in each hand.

One of the biggest thrills of my boyhood was once delivering a bottle of bleach to an apartment and finding Tony at the door. I was fifteen and he was twenty on that day of our first meeting. He quickly took a liking to me and invited me to accompany him when he worked out at the Fourteenth Street Gym. It was exciting for me to mingle among the glamorous big-name boxers and to hold Tony's towel during his sparring. After his workout, Tony still was a powder keg of energy, and at times walking with him, he would unleash hard punches into my chest and shoulders, really hurting me, but I absorbed the blows unflinchingly, eager to show him that I could take it. This eventually won favor with him and soon he started to take me under his wing, treating me like his protégé.

I had attended every one of Tony's matches, from his first electrifying Golden Gloves knockout to his impressive AAU wins at St. Nicholas Arena through his consecutive string of ten straight spectacular pro victories, following him to Ridgewood Grove, Sunnyside Arena, Eastern Parkway Arena, and other auditoriums in distant unfamiliar parts of the city, usually sitting on someone's lap in one of a caravan of cars stuffed with his Brooklyn rooters, streaming over the bridges, moving closer, uptown, to Madison Square Garden nestled among the skyscrapers, everyone nervously excited feeling a part of himself climb with Tony into the ring. Under the blazing ring lights, when he removed his black satinet robe and he was stripped down to his black trunks, he revealed a powerfully muscular physique that stirred a wave of awed oohs and aahs swelling up to the bleachers. He had huge, perfect biceps, broadly thick shoulders, rippling snakes for abdominal muscles, bulging, rock-solid thighs, and thick cables of tendon girding a bullish neck. The bright lights brought out his vivid black hair and traced the sharp line of his jaw, encased in heavy bone, and caught the expression of his dark eyes which flinted with a hard gaze during the referee's instructions and then gradually during the match smoldered to a hot rage. The bleachers were jammed with his rooters who loved his recklessly bold style of charging forward and standing toe to toe with his opponents and unleashing punches with the force of a bear trap.

During the bloody heat of battle, Tony's fans were roaring and yelling out his name, cheering him on, whistling and stomping their shoes on the benches. Ecstatic over his victories, they made the arena thunder to its foundation and surged up wildly to him to scoop him up on a throne of shoulders. Among the rooters were swarms of pretty girls, pressing closer for a look or touch of his glossy muscular body. To my young eyes it was dazzlingly heroic and almost noble for Tony to fight through such brutally bloody battles to raise his name out of the streets. To follow in his footsteps, I signed up with the Trinity Club Gym to begin boxing in the amateurs.

When we finished playing pool, we stepped outside and crossed the street, heading for Tony's house to pick up trunks and hand bandages he was going to give me for my first match. The sun was going down and long, angular shadows were slicing off buildings and the air felt brisk and breezy. I was thrilled to be at Tony's side walking down the avenue. The aura of his "rep" rubbed off on me in the eyes of everyone who saw us together. All along the avenue Tony was greeted and praised enthusiastically, his name ringing down from the windows and stoops and the shops, proving him to be the most popular local hero, far eclipsing in glory the powerful don of the neighborhood. He responded to his admirers with a nod of his head and a wave in the air. He had an amazing memory for the first names of just about everyone. We turned down New Utrecht Avenue where the sun, an oval flame, became visible behind the steeple crucifix of St. Rosalie's Church, creating an odd mystical omen of fire glowing brightly around the holy cross as Tony walked underneath.

The hum of traffic played off the rumble of el trains and staticky radios playing music on windowsills. Tony walked with a bounce, the energy highly juiced in his body. At his side, I formed my steps and swung my shoulders exactly like him. How he talked with his eyes down and in a tough tone and lingo I also copied, and it was happening without conscious effort. I just found myself doing it, becoming more like him, wanting to become someone like him. He was king of the pool hall, leader of all the street gangs, toughest of the tough, holder of the biggest "rep" in South Brooklyn, and an undefeated professional boxer. On the move he taught me the correct way to execute a left hook. Awkwardly but with force I executed the same punch.

He chomped into the white meat of an apple, and tilted a glance at me. "You're gonna be a mean banger. You got bricks in your forearms." He continued to hold show-and-tell boxing shop on the move, pricking curious eyes from some people looking down from their windows. I listened carefully, treating every word he uttered as momentous.

On Fifty-ninth Street young boys playing stickball in the twilight stopped their game when they spotted Tony and excitedly ran up and swarmed him. He tousled the frizzy hair of a freckled boy. Further on we were mobbed by shopkeepers and vendors interested in getting tickets for Tony's Garden bout. In introducing me, he thumbed a finger in my chest. "This is my boy, Joe Sarry. This kid is gonna be fighting in the amateurs next month. I want you to go see him, too. He's gonna be some fighter."

"I got a long way to go." I half blushed.

"You go see him." He playfully popped a jab at my shoulder. "This is my boy."

I grinned and blushed again in front of the men, not saying anything but feeling good inside about him calling me his boy.

As we moved on, Tony threw an arm around my shoulder. "Don't ever forget the people in your neighborhood. Don't ever forget where you came from."

"I won't forget, Tony," I said, embarrassed. "But I ain't done nothing yet. It don't make sense to say these things to me."

"You're my boy. I don't pick anybody to be my boy. I can tell you got something for the ring."

"If you want, Tony, I'll come tomorrow night for the trouble with those Eight Avenue guys."

"I expect you to be there. We're gonna need the whole neighborhood crew. This is gonna be a big rumble; there won't be a brick left on top of a brick when it's over."

Fluorescent brilliance dropped down on the sidewalk from the staggered street-lamp. I was feeling light and exhilarated, a kind of glow warming inside me hearing Tony calling me his "boy" and saying such flattering things about my boxing promise. I knew I had heavy bones in my arms and fast hands and that it was a good combination for a sport like fighting, but it never occurred to me that someone as great as Tony would take notice.

The next night seventy-five members of the Fort Hamilton boys were gathered in front of Pop's Pool Hall. Tense energy bristled in the air as we readied to go rumble with the Norwegian Eighth Avenue gang.

Not many of us really knew what had triggered the confrontation between the two gangs. Someone said it was because one of our guys caught his sister necking with one of the Eighth Avenue Norwegian boys, and so he hit his sister for going out with a Norwegian. Her boyfriend then retaliated against him, and now the necking incident had escalated into a war between the Italians and the Norwegians.

Tony moved through us with his teeth mashing and his fist in the air, muttering about jacking in heads. We began following him in a knotty file as he crossed the street, heading for a parking lot behind the Fortway Theater. The gang marching stirred a lot of attention in the neighborhood. People were quickly appearing in doorways, heads popped out of windows, bartenders came outside, and kids climbed out on fire escapes to watch. The flurry of eyes equaled the stir caused by the St. Rosalie's parade with the huge banner of Christ's face stuck with dollar bills.

I was marching in the middle of the pack. Here and there around me I could see a baseball bat or car jack or cue stick and other crude clubs raised in the air. Since it was considered more manly to fight with your fists, to rely on your own strength, Tony would never use a weapon, and since he was my idol, I wasn't going to use one either. I watched him at the front of the march, drawing inspiration from the power his presence radiated. Our bodies crashed through the street like a storm gathering fury. I could feel warm blood rush up my legs and arms and pour into my face. I was conscious of my body screeching with adrenaline. My eyeballs flicked around at the people gawking at us, and I wondered if my girl Dutchy was watching. Our red gang-jackets inscribed in black with the gang name shimmered under the street lamps. The posts flew past us as our shoes thudded over the cracked sidewalk. We reached the Fortway Theater, passing under a long boxcar-size fire escape. We tramped into the dirt parking lot, kicking up swirls of dust under our steps. There were scattered cars parked around the spacious field that was rimmed by alleys and a stretch of lovers' lane and Bob's Mechanic and Body Repair Shop. The moon danced down in pale shimmers over the no-man's-land. From a distance, under the trees of the park, I could see a shadowy swarm of bodies coming to meet us. Quickly, someone next to me fished out a lead pipe from his jacket, and I could picture it slopped with bloody hair splinters and it sent a shiver through me. The tension was igniting around me in bursts of snarls and teeth jagging against each other and low mumblings of "wipeouts" and "busting skulls." Inside my gut a fear was tugging and ripping at my breath and I could hear my heart pounding. I tightened my gut muscles, trying to keep all the fear down inside me. This was my first rumble. Whatever I imagined in daydreams, I was dreading the bloody collision about to erupt.

There was no way I could get out of it. I couldn't let Tony or the neighborhood down. I wanted to belong, and belonging meant doing whatever the gang said had to be done. I had to show I had the heart for real man action. The faces charging had wild-eyed, goofy stares, and mouths were hung open, grumbling and raving. Wading into the front ranks with his fists whipping in a blur, Tony sprang the first blow into a husky guy's face. His bare knuckles smacked loudly from the force and tore the man's legs out from under him. All around me I could hear the sounds of fists whacking flesh and the duller thuds of pipe crunching bone, unleashing horrible shrieks of pain. I found myself facing a tall lanky guy who rushed at me wildly with his fist ramming into my mouth. I was pushed off balance, and in an instant I could feel my lip had been split and blood was dribbling down my chin. He was on top of me again, crashing his other fist against the side of my ear making it sting. Before he could come around with his arm pulled back, I drove a hard solid shot into the pit of his gut, bending him to the waist, and I followed up with one, two, three more solid smashes to the side of his head. I could hear a voice inside me frantically wishing for him to cave. His legs staggered in a forward lunge and he awkwardly collapsed onto the dirt. I turned in a circle looking around to see which one of our boys needed help. Suddenly a body landed against my chest and knocked me against a car, the sharp metal cutting into my back, and I clenched my teeth to quash the pain. Whoever banged into me was as quickly gone as he had surfaced. Someone else punched me from my blind side, hurting me, but when he came at me, I counterpunched with a hard right cross. Someone cracked a beer bottle over a guy's head, drenching him with foam and blood, and sending him reeling, with blood trailing after him. The sight was sickening to me. The onslaught continued, with fists windmilling and voices shouting curses and bats slamming against arms raised to fend off weapons. The wounded from both gangs were strewn all over the field, screaming in agony and calling for help.

The police sirens came low at first, like a whining cat in one of the alleys, but as the squad cars sliced

through the streets and speedily gained ground, the
sound grew to a flood of screaming wails. The first
wave of green and white police cars headed for us at
the edge of the Fortway lot. Darting in and squealing
to a halt, the car doors opened, with nightsticks clanking against metal and handcuffs jangling against moving legs. More sirens were shrilly sounding in the back
streets. Two police precincts were closing in on us.

The appearance of cops caused a panicked stampede.
Everybody stopped fighting and scrambled to get away.
Guys on the ground picked themselves up, dazed and
bleeding, and made themselves run. My heart leaped
at the sound of a shot fired in the air. With my hands
pumping in front of me, I raced up the street, weaving
from side to side, and crushing my head into its socket,
all the time thinking a bullet was going to be flaming
over my shoulder. I swung myself over the bumpers of
two parked cars, hit the sidewalk, and made an all-out
dash for an alley. I could feel the sweat pouring over
my forehead. I looked back and caught the sight of cops
throwing guys against a building and spreading their
legs apart and thumbing a paddy wagon up to load up.
Blood was spilling out of my nose as I hit a low fence
and flew over it, kicking a garbage can with my foot
and crashing it over.

I stayed there, hidden in a corner, waiting for the
danger to pass, while my hand went up to brush the
blood on my mouth. I could feel a little flap of skin
torn out by a skull ring, and other bruises and lumps
on the side of my head. Oddly, I was pleased that I
had received some wounds in battle. It was all part of
becoming a man. It was like getting your first wallet
and driver's license and being allowed to buy a drink
in a bar. It was moving from the position of looking
up from the shoeshine stand and doing the shoes to
the position of sitting and looking down and tossing
the tip. Getting scars was part of the price or dues you
paid for the right to feel like a man. I wondered how
many of the guys saw what I had done in the rumble.

I wondered if Tony had seen me throw those punches just the way he taught me. I couldn't wait to go tell him how I had done. I knew he would be proud of me. As I headed home, I was floating in a warm glow of pride.

I fumbled inside my pocket to get the key to the house and then let myself inside the darkened building, moving on tiptoes up the creaky stairs, not daring to wake Grandma. Upstairs, I let myself in the apartment and gently closed the door in slow motion. The apartment was dark and quiet except for the old radiator clanking steam. Light leaking into the venetian blinds from the street lamp and passing cars made it visible enough to make out the time on the wall clock in the kitchen. It was 1 A.M. I listened for a moment to hear if Mom and Dad were whispering in bed or if Mom was sitting up in her room waiting for me. Since I was out of school, I was pretty much on the loose, but I could not blow in free whenever I pleased. Usually, if I stayed out past midnight on a weekday, Mom would be worrying and wondering and snap all over me when I got in.

I removed my shoes and carried them, passing my parents' bedroom going to the front room. All of a sudden I felt very exhausted and ached all over. My eyelids felt heavy and droopy and kept trying to fall shut. Undressing in the dark, I stared at the odd swirls of shadow on the ceiling, created by deflected light from the street. I could hear in the distance the warble of a police siren. Nobody stirred under the blankets, even though the screaming sound pierced the room louder than the alarm buzzer in the little clock. The gray light from the fusing moon and streetlights traced the bumpy forms of my brothers Ernie and Anthony sleeping in the open sofa bed. I was so tired that I don't even remember falling asleep that night.

The following night, to my shock and horror, Dad,

who had learned about the rumble, came stepping up the pool hall block with long fast strides and a mean look on his face. He was going to teach me a lesson I would never forget. He was going to beat the crap out of me in front of the whole neighborhood. He was going to show me that his word was to be obeyed, that I was to stay away from this place. It was clear and light in the early evening and his angry face attracted a lot of notice. Soon everyone was out on the street knowing that a fight was brewing between father and son. Dragging me out of the pool hall, he muttered a stream of curses and furiously grabbed for my shirt. "You no-good bum. I told you to stay out of this place." He dug his hands into my shirt, ripping and tearing off buttons, and swung me against the building, half of my back banging into the brick column, the other shoulder blade whipping thunderously against and nearly shattering the glass front. Breathing hard, he mauled and shook me, wrenching me down the block, shoving me toward home. Breaking away, I sprinted ahead of him, raced to the apartment, and galloped upstairs.

"Why did he do that to me?" I yelled, banging the door open to the apartment. "Why did he make me look like an asshole in front of everybody? Why did he make me lose face that way? Nobody else's father would pull that. Only him. Why does he do these things to me?"

Standing silently by the stove, Mom's eyes waited a moment before turning to me. "Maybe because your father cares."

CHAPTER EIGHT

The first time I saw Dutchy, the sight of her was like a roller coaster drop, bringing bodily sensations rippling and heaving through me. On that day she was only fourteen, but already ripe and in the full figure of womanhood, with saucily popping breasts and softly round and enticing curves to her hips and rear. Without makeup she had scrubbed cheeks and downy jet-black hair and doe eyes naturally shaded by long lashes and dimples that deepened with her smile and a delicate nose that made me think of the lovely profile on Camay soap.

It was high-fashion time when I took her dancing. For the third time I checked myself in the mirror from head to toe, satisfied that nothing could touch the panache of my creamsicle-orange suit. My needle-nose shoes were spit-polished to the flash of new silver dollars, and my only regret was that I could not afford those cool shoes with little aquariums in the heels for goldfish. The black handkerchief I had jammed into my front pocket could have been used for a parachute, it was so big. In the streets you wanted to be seen and the outcome was blinding gaudiness.

As I stood in front of the bathroom mirror combing my hair, her lovely face flashed into my mind. Something about her, the way she looked, the way she moved, the way she talked, knocked me over. Smoothing down my hair, I followed Mom's advice about brushing it Valentino-style, hoping a little of his magic might rub off. A mother's love can become a circus mirror, flatteringly bending her son's features to meet her own wishes and one's own gullible vanity knows no bounds of self-deception. With a little coaxing I could be led to believe almost anything flattering about myself.

Dutchy's father, a garage mechanic, let me in the apartment. She was waiting for me in the living room, wearing a lightweight pullover, snug over her breasts, and a short skirt. She sat down, crossing her legs, the bare calves pressing together and spreading rousingly, bringing my eyes up to the white softness of her thighs and I could feel my senses heighten. Her enthusiasm to see me showed in a sweet smile breezing through her white teeth. She lowered her lashes teasingly, slipping her hand into mine and squeezing. Out on the street she broke into a little laugh. It was a thrill to feel the attraction we felt for each other. My insides were telling me there wasn't another girl around who could make me feel this good.

She wrapped two hands around my upper arm as we strolled down her block. Nothing more than being beside her put me in good spirits. When I was with her, all the edges and unease were buried in the back of my mind. I knew it all started with her looks and infatuation, but it had grown to something deeper. Being with her, just walking beside her, filled me up inside.

"Frankie Daggy wants me to join the Marines with him." I turned to her on the move.

"The Marines. What got into his head? That Aldo Ray movie bite you guys crazy?"

"I think the Marine uniform is the coolest. It's got the colors of the American flag and gold, too. The Marines' Hymn is the best, too, better than 'Anchors Aweigh.' I like the part 'You'll find the shores of heaven are guarded by the United States Marines.'"

"God doesn't need Marines to protect him. Nobody's gonna mug God."

"Maybe the devil. But it's just the idea. God would pick the Marines because they're the toughest."

"You guys wanna be glory heroes. It would scare me.

My father says the Marines make a professional killer out of you. How can they help you?"

"The Marine Corps straightens out a lot of guys; you see guys come out who were on drugs or couldn't hold a job before. The Marines make you a man. But I don't need to join. I'm gonna be a boxer like Tony Bavimo."

"I know, you don't have to remind me." Her face showed concern.

"Tony thinks I'm gonna do good." I pulled my arm away from her, and went into a boxer's position. "Bam! Bam! Bam! Look at those left hooks."

"Why do you have to do it because he does it?"

"Because I think he's right. I can be good. Bam! Bam! Bam!" I executed a flurry of punches for her.

"I hope you don't go through with it."

"Whaddaya mean, in two weeks I'm on the card for the amateurs. You gotta come. I want you to be there. I'm doing it for you, too."

"Don't say for me. I think it's crazy to see two guys bashing each other."

"I want you to be proud of me. Tony thinks I can be Golden Gloves champion next year. Wouldn't that make you proud." I dipped my shoulder, and threw more punches, breathing choppily through my nose. "Bam! Bam! Bam!"

We strolled down to the ferry pier, we stopped in front of the guard rail and gazed out at the glassy water and listened to the waves slap and splash against the pylons, occasionally joined by lingering blasts of foghorns on ships at the edge of the harbor. The city lights across the bay were flaring like a raging forest fire. The smell of the ocean was in the air but I could smell Dutchy's skin and hair as she stood in front of me, with my arms clasped around her and her head tilted on my chest. Someone on a park bench clicked on a portable radio and the music drifted to us pure and clear and sailed out on the breeze for the open sea. I could hear her gently breathing from her lightly opened lips. I touched her hair with my fingertips, not saying anything, lowering my eyes to the ground. Her breasts were warm under her sweater and I felt shudders down my back. I longed to touch her bare skin. Excited but a little hesitant, I slipped my fingers inside, feeling the smooth skin of her navel and then moved to feel her breasts but she reached down and pulled my hands away. She stretched up on her toes and we kissed for a long time, letting out all the emotion that had built up.

CHAPTER
NINE

My first amateur fight was held at Eastern Parkway Arena. I made my way down the ramp to the dressing rooms under the bleachers. In the central room unshaded electric bulbs threw dim light on the bare cinder walls as a jowly official chewing on a cigar sat at a desk recording the weights of fighters stepping up to a Toledo scale. Trainers were nervously milling around at the desk to learn the matchups for the evening.

I had my gloves laced on and joined the other fighters in the small waiting compartment, a drab tile room resembling a bomb shelter, the muscular-physiqued fighters sitting opposite each other on long benches, draping their arms listlessly out from glimmering satin robes over their shoulders and staring blankly ahead with shiny, Vaseline-smeared faces. I squirmed on the bench, sitting in one position for a moment and then changing to another, and a third, until at last I was bent forward with my elbows on my knees and my gloves resting against my cheeks. Cool sweat trickling down from my armpits was rerouted by the elastic band of my trunks and collected in a warm pool around my navel. My new leather shoes squeaked as I balled my toes in them, nervously looking across at the rippling abdomens and bulging biceps of the fighters across from me. I knew I would be fighting one of them. We looked quietly at each other, reacting with our eyes to the sounds overhead, hearing the reverberating noises of the crowd, knowing from the uproars and howling that someone was hurt in the ring.

All during the waiting period various people trooped in and out of the room to see the fighters. For the most part they were managers, trainers, and handlers, but friends and relatives also came in to give an encouraging word. My brother Anthony stepped inside wearing a warm smile and raised his two fingers to me in the victory sign. As he crouched down to talk to me, I kept my hands hanging limply, concentrating on conserving stamina. He talked in a whisper. "I see Tony Bavimo's gonna be in your corner."

"That makes me feel good." I dipped my head thoughtfully and looked at the concrete floor. "I'm really lucky to have him for my first fight."

"All the uncles are out there. We're all rooting for you."

"Did Dutchy come?"

"I didn't see her. Maybe she'll be here later."

I hesitated before asking the next question. "How about Dad? Is he out there?"

"No, he couldn't make it." His eyes slanted away.

I felt my spirit sag, feeling that Dad did not care enough to want to see me in my first boxing match. The disappointment I felt over his absence was soon lost in the excited inspiration I felt when Tony jaunted over to guide me up to the ring. He held my shoulder in his strong hand, moving up the cheering aisles. He told me he got the whole neighborhood to turn out for his boy's debut. The sea of faces in the bleachers were blurred shadows in the arena, which was darkened except for the blazing light pouring from saucer flood lamps above the ring and creating an illuminated cage.

Up close the sight of the ring made a wave of tension flash in my gut and roll up my throat. I stepped up the three wooden steps to the ring apron while Tony spread the bottom and middle ropes for me to climb through. I immediately began springing up and down in my corner. My opponent, who had left the dressing room a minute after me, came bounding down the aisle with his manager and trainers around him, his head buried in a towel stuffed in his robe, his gloves pressed on his chest. His handlers took the robe from his brawny shoulders showing his glistening brown torso, rowed with striated bumps down his abdomen, and tapering to a small waist. His dark eyes enhanced his belligerent look.

Removing my robe, I felt the warmth of the lights flush on my skin, giving tone and highlights to my muscles. Limbering up in the corner, I caught the eyes of a woman staring up and down my body, leering the same way a man stares at a shapely behind. The referee called the fighters to the center of the ring. Harold Sloan, my opponent, snarled behind his mouthpiece and stared flintily into my eyes, trying to psych me out. I stared back, with a thick growth of beard around my cheeks that I had left unshaven for a fiercer expression. Back at my corner, Tony shoved a mouthpiece into place and gave me an encouraging pat on the head before I left at the bell. I moved warily, more concerned about warming up than landing punches, knowing the body is dangerously cold in the opening moments. Sloan came forward with his hands high and leaning away and cocked a fist under his chin. He shot a left jab briskly that rocked my head back and I could feel the power that flowed in his long arm. I forged into him knowing that simply going after him could earn me points.

As I waded into him, I got caught a punch, doubling the impact of his blow by my own forward motion, and I felt my neck whip around painfully and sweat fly off my face. I leaped at him in a frustrated rush, my head low, pushing my head under his chin, driving him into the ropes, but he pivoted quickly to reverse our positions and began raking my eyes with harsh hooks and pounded my midsection, using his body as leverage, punching with both fists to the ribs,

belly, and kidney. The punches whacked loudly on
the skin, leaving splotches of red. He ripped a right
hand into my jaw, making the noise of a butcher slamming beef on the wood block. I heard Tony yelling
frantically for me to get off the ropes, but I was blacking out on my feet, and feeling an aching echo all
through my head.

When the bell rang, Tony sat me down with a sense
of urgency and immediately pulled the elastic band of
my trunks. He poured water down my crotch and
grabbed the soaked sponge and sprayed water over my
face. My voice, strangled at first, came back to me and
I was gradually in control of my breaths again, but I
was still shaken. Tony gritted his teeth worriedly as he
pulled a cotton-tip swab out of my nose caked with
blood. He then crouched over me, taking my shoulders
in his hands, and he patted them, speaking intensely.
"Joey, you took his best. Go get him this round. Don't
let me down."

I got up from the stool waiting for the bell. I shook
my head to clear the grog. I was awakened to the realization that Tony was behind, watching me, and I was
inspired by his words. I charged at Sloan and he sidestepped to get out of my way, awfully fresh from having avoided most of my punches. My arms were feeling
heavier, filling up, congealing in the veins from all the
missed blows. Circling in the ring I caught sight of
Tony standing up on the lower rope in my corner and
motioning with both hands and shouting, "Go in on
him." I sprinted with a right hand that tore through
Sloan's guard and whipped his head around. He immediately tried to throttle my arms but I shoved him
away and sprung a left hook that caused him to bellow. He counterpunched with a right hand that stung.
Our tempers were flaring. Standing toe to toe, I buckled his knees with a combination. He stumbled backward and for the first time showed worry in his eyes.
He buried his jaw in his shoulders and raised his el-

bows, trying to hide and protect his jaw at the same time. I ripped punches at his exposed belly and he twisted and squirmed and his mouthpiece bulged white between his lips. When he dropped his arms, I caught him a roundhouse. The crowd was on its feet screaming. They could see Sloan staggering and in trouble. His eyes were glassy, his legs gluey. With twenty seconds to go, I threw a hard right to his jaw. He sagged and slipped along the ropes, losing his footing. The crowd was roaring and shaking the arena to its foundation. Another punch shot him off the ropes. His body went slack, he lurched backward and fell on his back. He moved his feet and his hands, but he was like a helplessly overturned turtle on its back, unable to right himself.

Everything was unreal to me when the referee raised my hand in victory. I was still feeling a mix of blood and adrenaline scorching and pumping madly in every pore of my body, breathing with a life of their own. It seemed while my body was on fire my brain was numb, as if drugged by the animal side of my nature. The haze was short-lived, because I was suddenly feeling a rush of exhilarated joy. I jumped up into Tony's happy arms, and he carried me around the ring as I waved to the cheering fans.

Another mood hit me in the dressing room. I started to come down from my euphoria and I could feel pains all over my face and body. One cheek was swollen and throbbing; my right eye was puffed, livid, and bloodshot. I had a split down the center of my lower lip. The insides of my ripped mouth were a faucet of blood. I watched, frightened, seeing blood in my urine. His kidney punches must have torn capillaries. The insides of my head felt like they were going to burst out. I was afraid that my brains might be bleeding inside the skull. I could not sit in one position in the car going home because of the pain pulsing in my head. I tried shifting my head from one position to another, but nothing would stop the aftershocks.

* * *

At three o'clock that morning my bruised and puffed eyes deep in sleep, I was faintly stirred by the lights flicked on and sounds of buzzing voices entering the bedroom and Dad calling my name in a hazy blur. Gradually his voice grew clearer and clearer and I was jarred to a drowsy state of awakening. Standing over me in his bathrobe and slippers, a nervous tightness on his lips, Dad clenched his fingers into my arm. "Get up, Joey. There are some policemen here for you." His head rotated in the direction of two beefy men in plainclothes standing in the doorway.

"At this time?" I groaned.

"Yes."

"What do they want?"

"They'll tell you. It's important."

"God!"

Rubbing the grainy flakes from my tired eyes I could see the two cops nodding. I sat myself up in bed and then a deep shiver of fright went through me. This was the real thing. I was not dreaming. There were really two policemen here to see me in the middle of the night. My mind flashed back to the rumble. I had to think that someone might have squealed on all of us. My gut was churning in knots as I got up from bed and went to the chair where my pants and shirt were folded over the backrest. My brothers blinked their eyes open and closed, asking Mom what was going on.

I took my clothes into the bathroom to change. Putting on my chino pants, I thought of climbing out of the skylight and escaping from the roof, but I decided against it because the glass door was sealed and it would cause too much noise breaking it. I laced my shoes up on the kitchen chair with the detectives standing nearby watching me.

"What are you taking me for?" I asked worriedly.

"Never mind."

"You can't bring me in without telling me nothing."

"Just get dressed," he barked.

"Can't you tell me why I gotta go with you?" I asked a little nervously.

"You'll find out soon enough. Hurry up."

On the verge of crying, her eyes filled with tears, Mom broke in. "He hasn't done anything. Why are you taking him?" She began to panic as they led me out the door. "He hasn't done anything." Her quavering voice broke. Dad came over and put his arm around her and stared at me with anger. He had to be wondering what new trouble I had brought the family.

Outside I walked from the apartment, feeling the detectives close behind me. Not knowing if they would shoot, I pushed down an impulse to bolt. Whatever it was they wanted, I was their prisoner, even though I had not yet been placed under arrest and no handcuffs had been locked around my wrists. The night air was hot and muggy and humming with pestering mosquitoes and from time to time pierced by the humanlike cries of alley cats. We stopped at the curb to get into an unmarked car, a fifties-model black Ford. The first to climb in on the driver's side was Detective Ryan, a tall broad-shouldered Irishman with a thick nose and beet-red cheeks. I got into the back with Detective Todd, the taller of the two, and rather good-looking with wavy black hair and clean-cut features and blue eyes, but tough in his ways with a hard and throaty voice.

Detective Ryan put the key in the ignition, and after the engine started, he released the brake and shoved the floor-mounted stick in gear. He pulled out of the space and left the apartment behind, riding through the dark streets, eerily silent and empty except for an occasional grocery truck lumbering on early-morning deliveries. Shafts of light from street lamps knifed in and out of the car windows and splashed in brightly whenever we stopped for a red light. The car moved slowly down Sixtieth Street, and we waited at a lonesome stop sign before moving up the ramp of the elevated Belt Parkway, a frozen burst of granite curving in midair around Brooklyn. I felt a deep coil of worry, wondering why they were taking me on the highway. This was not the way to the 64th Precinct station house. Detective Todd, who had been silent during the ride through the streets, straightened up and he turned my way, and asked rather casually, "You know Tony Bavimo?"

"Sure, I know him. He's a good friend of mine." My mood suddenly changed. I felt sure this ride had nothing to do with the rumble.

"Were you with him tonight?"

"Yeah, he was in my corner. I fought in the amateurs at Eastern Parkway."

"How long were you with him?"

"I left him at the pool hall after the bout. He was there during that time, playing Doodles Sangeorgio on the first table."

"You sure about that?"

"Yeah, I'm sure."

"Your father said you think a lot of this Bavimo. He said you look up to him."

"I respect him a lot. Everybody respects him. If you're in the Sixty-fourth Precinct you must know him."

"He's the leader of your gang, isn't he?"

"I don't hang out with the gang anymore. I spend my time in the gym training. I'm going into the Golden Gloves next year."

"Tony Bavimo was in the Golden Gloves, too. He did pretty well."

"Now he's a pro, undefeated. He's gonna be champ."

"Your father says you talk about becoming a pro boxer like him."

"Depends on how I do in the Golden Gloves."

"Your father says you copy this Bavimo a lot."

"I said I looked up to him." I didn't add that when I watched Tony climb into the ring at Madison Square Garden, it was like watching my god ascend his altar.

Heavy sixteen-wheel trailers went by us with bright beacons flaring on top of the cab and looking from a distance in the black darkness like low-hovering flying saucers. The driver wound up the engine and it purred as we sped on the highway, whisking by billboards with ads for Holiday Inn, American Airlines, and Chesterfields. I rolled down the window, inviting a rush of warm breezy air which prodded my brain to wondering and worrying about where they were taking me. Why the late hour? Why this rush? Why so secretive? Why the comments about Tony? What was going on? What kind of trouble was Tony in? Well, they wouldn't get anything out of me if they were trying to pin something on him. I tried to keep myself calm, but an uneasiness and fear were working around in my gut.

The two detectives sat quietly, not saying much to each other, glancing out at the sights along the road. We had traveled a good distance because the neighborhoods were thinning out; we were moving away from the populous parts of Brooklyn, and hitting the Levittown communities of Long Island. The lamps along the road changed from a luminous white to a gassy yellow when we got on the Sunrise Highway. Shortly, the headlights were illuminating wooded areas up ahead, which meant we were deeper into Long Island, and I was growing more worried.

Isolated service stations, islands of light in the darkness, flickered by at long intervals between my confused imaginings. The moon followed us over the treetops slicing in between the dense thickets. The steady hum of the engine grated on my leg-twisting nervousness. For long stretches there was nothing but black, empty road and uninhabited woods conspiring in a hushed silence which amplified the motor's guttural grind in my ears. Riding to the unknown can make a minute seem long, and we had been on the road for at least an hour and a half which seemed unbearably longer to me. Finally, the Ford slowed down as a fog of lights appeared off the road ahead. In vague blurred outline, I could make out dozens of people gathered around one spot in a ditch not far from the side of the highway. Pulling up, I could see twenty or so cars parked on both shoulders of the road. I wondered anxiously what was going on and I asked Detective Ryan, but he silently scoffed at my question. We stepped out of the car, and with one detective walking slightly in front of me and one behind, we moved toward the activity near the ditch. Everything looked too unnatural, all the cars, the blazing lights, the feverish movement. What was going on? I could feel cool sweat trickling down my armpits.

Since our car was at the end of the chain of parked cars, it was about a fifty-yard walk to the glowing lights and bulge of people. Out here in the woods the air seemed even hotter and muggier and smelled with strong scents of weeds, bark, and pollen. Beetles and crickets and other insects whined away in a steady, low din. We stepped over underbrush and growth, and I could feel leaves rustling and twigs cracking under my feet. Suddenly I was jolted by a blood-curdling scream coming from the clustered people, and I could hear the same voice break into uncontrollable weeping. The worries and fears I had before had never skirted near anything as ominously terrifying as that scream. My deepest fear up to now had been that Tony was in a jam and I was being brought into it. For the first time, as we moved closer to the faceless men moving briskly, I could pick up a strange stench in the air. I had known it before, but I had no name for it. The smell raised the back of my hair. I thought there might have been an accident; maybe Tony had been in an auto accident, but I saw no mangled cars, no broken glass or debris in the road, no ambulances, no fire engines, no police emergency trucks, not even a police car. There was not a uniformed cop to be seen. Somehow it was more eerie and frightening not having a uniformed cop around; at least you knew a regular cop was always ready to talk. He did not deal in psychological mind games, brainwashing, or third-degree tactics. All the men in civilian clothes shrouded the events in nerve-jagging mystery.

We walked along the side of the road and then moved down into the ditch. Bombarded with floodlights something was sticking up in the air, a tent, I thought at first, but as we stepped closer, I speculated that it might be a machine gun under a blanket. Among the large gathering of men I could see a number of my friends standing off on the sides looking dazed and stricken with sick grief. I could see Frankie Daggy deliriously sobbing, his face chalk-white. Richie was shaking his head in a catatonic trance. I could feel my heart race and my hands begin to tremble. They led me right up to the drab olive army blanket, and I could see it was speckled with mud and chilling smears of blood.

The detective in front of me yanked the blanket up, and for an instant the floodlights painted it a brilliant green. My eyes blinked in the blazing glare, but I did not turn away. Lying face down on the ground was a grotesquely unrecognizable dead body, totally nude, splatted with mud and blood, one hand stretched out stiffly clutching leaves. For a moment I shook in revulsion. Spasms gripped my gut. I could feel heat run up the back of my head. Still I did not turn away and kept my eyes on the body with a hypnotic compulsion. The floodlights trained downward poured a rush of the tiniest details into my head.

What was sticking up in the air like an ice skater's arc was the right leg, so high up it had to be broken at the joint, raised by rigor mortis and frozen stiff so that a passing motorist was able to spot the body in the roadside ditch. The skin color was a grayish white but the buttocks were a contrasting pale egg white. From the feet up to the shoulders the body was unblemished with blood, but around the nape of the neck and the ears and the lower head was a river of thickened, clotted dry cakes of blood. The head, bloated to a monstrous size, was pressed into the dirt showing only one side of the face, the side where the eye had been torn out, leaving a gaping hole so that I could see the slick gooey pink and white jelly inside the head. Unruly strands curled at the back of his hairline but most of the hair had been frizzed, singed, and burned away by gunfire. The jaw had a hideous tortured expression with the upper teeth protruding and hanging over the lower lip and parts of lip and teeth were blasted away. Under the blaze of floodlights the blood crystals studded in mud glittered like fool's gold.

"That's your friend, Tony Bavimo," Detective Ryan's voice boomed in my ear.

"Oh, my God, no! Tony!" I dropped my mouth and felt nausea and a powerful spasm to retch. "No, Tony!" I brought my hands up to my eyes and broke down and began sobbing uncontrollably. For a long time I went on crying, reduced to the same state of grief as my friends. I was in a trance during the ride back to the apartment, deep into my own head, oblivious to the world. I was in a deeply confused and emotionally overwhelmed state of mind. Only a few hours ago I had been with Tony, alive and laughing and strong, in the prime of his boxing career, a charismatic leader, an inspiring idol, a future champion. And now he was a bloody blob of wreckage.

It would be many years before I would lose the nightmare of that last vision of Tony Bavimo.

During the following months, there was a lot of wild talk about going after Tony's killers and even of my taking over the gang and having greater and grander days of gang glory, but I had no stomach for any of these ideas. Tony's death had disenchanted me with the streets, and so with no other available option, I joined the Marines.

CHAPTER TEN

The summer sun of the South stuffed the chow hall with sweltering heat. Scattered in shapes and sizes, the shaven-headed recruits moved through the chow line noisily jabbering to each other. Sitting at a long table with Marine recruits gobbling up mushy eggs and washing them down with briny coffee, I was silently staring into my plate at the blob of dry, lumpy powdered eggs. I had tried to swallow one forkful and my throat had heaved them back up. I decided there was no way I could eat them even though I knew the strictly enforced rule was you had to finish your food. I stuffed the eggs into my empty cereal box hoping to get by the mess sergeant when we bussed our trays.

At the rear of the chow hall, cans were filled with hot water and recruits lined up to put forks in one can and dishes in another and empty cereal boxes in a third can. The mess sergeant was a stocky southerner with a thickset neck, hook nose, fleshy cheeks, and clear blue eyes. It was an unmatching face with the air of a bully as he stood with his muscular arms crossed over his chest inspecting each recruit's tray. Glancing suspiciously at my turned-over cereal box, he stopped me and dumped the hidden eggs into the dish and smacked his lips in a sarcastic drawl. "You better finish your chow, private."

"Listen, I tried to. They make me sick."

"Oh, they make you sick." A glint of amusement came into his look.

"I didn't know they were powdered."

His voice snapped hard. "You're not talking to your mommy, private. You took them eggs. You damn better well finish them."

"I can't eat them," I pleaded.

His brows bunched together and the vein on the side of his forehead jutted out as he grabbed the front of my khaki shirt. He was used to recruits cowering like sheep. He pulled me forward and pushed his face up to mine, his jaws clenched and teeth bared. "You're gonna eat them, boy."

I could feel the blood rushing into my face. Instinctively, I was readying for a fight. "No, I'm not."

Seeing I refused to budge, he lunged at me and dug one of his thick hands into my throat and scooped up a gob of eggs with his other hand and tried to force it into my mouth. His movements were abrupt, catching me off balance and I tottered backward on my heels. When I regained my footing I ripped my arms up with both elbows to break his grip and I slammed a punch to his jaw which sent him crashing backward through a stack of used trays and knocking over a barrel of hot water, swashing the sudsy water all over the floor. The loud buzzing of recruits rippled across the chow hall like fans in a boxing hall. I dashed past the sprawled mess sergeant out into the street, without looking back to see if the D.I.'s were chasing me. I knew if they caught me it would be another month in the brig. I ran quickly and silently through rows of Quonset huts and shacks and through the bayonet course. Breathing in short, choppy nose sniffs, I sprinted up a dirt road along slopes pitched with tents in neat rows like tombstones. Rifle Range Baker was the last flat area before the everglades. No fences bordered the training area. The drill instructors said they weren't needed. The boondocks, as they called the swamps, were a densely endless maze of growth, quicksand, and bogs slithering with water moccasins and crocodiles. I had no idea how I was going to get off the island. I had no sensible thoughts in my head. I was a surge of powerful impulse on the move. I had cut the string back at the chow hall when I hit the sergeant. Emotion took over and it told me to run. They would have to find me first and drag me in chains to bring me back to that brig.

I waded across a silty creek with the water running up to my chest. I didn't know if it was Ribbon Creek where seven recruits drowned in a forced night march. The water raced and gurgled around my body and I could feel the current underneath drag and tug at my legs. Climbing up the bank into mangroves, I had to reach down and pull off the crawling vines snagging and tangled around my legs. Drenched and dripping, I continued to run deeper into the swamps, aware of and worried about quicksand, but running on nevertheless. The noon Carolina sun was savagely hot, beating down on my head. I could feel it sap my strength and weaken my stamina, making me dizzy and light-headed. Roving with no sense of direction, I was searching for a way off the island. There was no escape. Parris Island, the Marine Recruit Training Depot, is a forlorn island entwined by marshy water in the swamplands of South Carolina, bordered to the east and west by treacherous tidal rivers forming barriers two miles wide. The southern tip jutted into the Atlantic Ocean; along the northern horn sentries were posted at bridges, checking all persons coming on or off the island. The location for the most brutal military training in the world was not an accidental choice.

Breathing hard, I scampered over to a grove of reeds offering good concealment and threw myself down, trying to catch my thoughts. I had to be concerned about the M.P. patrols that must have been sent after me. I wondered if they were using hounds. Then I started to think about the future. I felt that I had blown everything this time. If they threw me out with a dishonorable discharge that would ruin my life. I had a faint inkling as I crouched sweating in the swamps that this act of flight was marking a habit of character for the rest of my life, that a response was riveting itself into my nerve centers, that in trouble I would always run.

It seemed wrong to me that because I signed a piece of paper, they owned my life and could lock me up in that bedlam brig again all because I wouldn't let some bully shove eggs down my throat. I couldn't believe this was really happening. It was like watching myself running in a nightmare. I couldn't see how close they were from me, but I could hear voices approaching. Breathing tightly, I brought my eyes down to my khaki uniform, noticing how splattered it was with mud from silty creek water. I was startlingly jostled from behind by a strapping black M.P. with his big .45-caliber pistol aimed at my belly. "I'll blow your guts out if you try anything."

Acting like an SS officer, a cocky corporal in full M.P. regalia, from white spats to white silk scarf, abusively cursed at me and then ordered me handcuffed behind my back and placed facedown on my belly in the back of a truck bed. During the ride to the brig, the corporal straddled my head, making me feel the hardness of his nightstick and a few times butting it against my skull. The brig was a fortlike mound of granite stones painted yellow with an armored, cumbrous door outside that opened to a corridor leading to a wall of bars slanting down to a large compound with two tiers of cells. The M.P.'s ushered me into a little office in the corridor and I was brought before the desk of the brig warden, who sat puffing on his pipe under a broad nose and jowly cheeks and protruding eyes glaring almost gleefully in their slits like an excited barn burner.

"I knew you would be back, Sorrentino," he said with smug satisfaction. "Fighting again."

"He shoved me around first." I stood rigidly at attention, my eyes on one plane.

"A malingering punk hitting a noncom." His eyes

creeped up to mine. "Nothing you can say will justify your actions. Respect for command comes above everything else. You didn't care to eat your eggs. Well, you may be ordered in combat to charge a machine gun."

"I don't see what good it does eating food that makes a man sick."

"Man! How dare you maggot refer to yourself as a man. You're not even a worm, less than a worm, a maggot, understand?"

"Yes, sir."

"We all have our roles to perform in this Corps whether we like them or not." He puffed on his pipe, with the light from the bulb showing the shining depths of his green eyes. "I despise playing jailer to a bunch of malingering scum, but I obey orders. The U.S. government spent twenty-five thousand dollars to train me for artillery. I hate this duty more than you hate powdered eggs. Another war better break out soon." He looked wistful. "How I miss combat duty. Standing over the cannons shaking the earth, blasting the gooks to pieces, smelling the sweet stench of death." He motioned for the two M.P.'s, who stepped forward jangling. "Take him up to the closet."

The two M.P.'s pushed me out of his office and nudged me with their nightsticks along the corridor to the cell compound and up a metal stairs and along a catwalk to "the closet," as solitary was known in the brig. Unlocking the heavy iron door, the light rushing in revealed a small square with walls of mortared blocks of stone thickly overlaid with rubber for soundproofing. The ceiling was a cake of concrete covered over with rubber padding. It contained no sink, no toilet, no bunk, no chair, not a single comfort except a metal pan for bodily functions and a rubber floor mat, the kind used in wrestling matches. They heaved me into the cell and slammed the solid door into its frame and turned the lock. The air was hot and sticky and smelled of rotting rubber. When the M.P.'s sealed the door, they had shut out all light and sound from the outside. With the darkness wrapped around my senses, I had to grope with my arms to know where the walls were from me. I sat sucking my gums for a moment, noticing how loud the sounds were, magnified in the hushed surroundings. The gruelling run through the swamps flayed by the sun had left me exhausted so I stretched out and quickly fell into a deep, undisturbed sleep. The next morning I awakened at the sound of the heavy door banging back against its hinges. A brig guard placed a breakfast tray down on the floor. With the door open I could hear the grating clatter of garbage cans being tossed at the cells in the lower compound as the brig inmates were being shocked awake.

When the door slammed closed again, I was back in dark, eerie silence. There was a Judas hole bored in the iron door, allowing air to come in, but a rubber mat had been pressed over it to block out the light and sounds. The first full day, I enjoyed the untaxing, unharassed quiet of being alone. I felt relieved not having to grind through the aching labor the other brig inmates were put through gruellingly through the day. Instead of straining all day in a duck walk scrubbing flooded floors, I could lounge back in a corner of the cell and listen to myself sing my favorite songs. The padded walls provided a resonant make-believe recording studio. Over and over I hummed the Fats Domino tune "Blueberry Hill" and after a while my imagination began to drift from the lyrics and I pictured, miragelike, an outdoor scene of hills overrun with blueberries and the hot sun melting the fruit into the earth, creating a blueberry land where I could lazily eat off the sweet of the hills.

The next day I began to feel the weight of the empty time and I tried to find ways to occupy myself. I took advantage of the freedom to work on exercises for all parts of the body. It gave a sense of satisfaction that even in the closet I was improving myself in some way. I had to endure the discomfort of feeling sweaty without access to a shower. With absolutely nothing to do for long stretches of the day, I found myself brushing my teeth by scraping with the tips of my fingernails. By the third day I was wishing I could be down in the compound scrubbing the floors, yearning for people around me and just mere sounds and shades of light.

Practicing a crude form of yoga, I sat on crossed legs in the lotus position, inhaling and exhaling, letting my mind soar in any direction. Staring off into space, I was flooded with memories, longings, and cravings for the warm softness of a bed, the spicy aroma of freshly baked calzone, the casually free feeling of a walk in the park, a triple scoop of ice cream. For the cold, refreshing taste of ice cream, I was willing to pay the price of a dishonorable discharge. A cool, foaming beer was another heady treat worth its suds in dreams. Most of all I pined and yearned to be with Dutchy; how I missed the pleasurable pang of the crush I felt being with her, the infatuation of holding her hand. I could almost hear her soft voice and feel her smooth black hair, and feel her dark brown eyes gazing at me warmly. I wanted to be with her more than anything else in life.

I sensed when it was night outside by the changed temperature in the cell. When the sun which baked the air during daylight left the island, it left a warmth that eventually evaporated and by late night was replaced by a damp chill. With no blankets I had a hard time getting to sleep. I tried wrapping my body in my arms and coiling up into a ball. I lay there shivering, and now and then a shudder would involuntarily throw my head up. I tried stretching out on my back with my arms parallel to my body and my hands palm down on the mat, but eventually my shoulder blades, jabbing the hard surface, became sore. The aching grew into a cramp around the spine. I sat up, rubbing my hands in the inflamed corners of my bleary, tired eyes, shivering from the cold. Finally all the hindrances to sleep were overwhelmed by the weight of fatigue and I dozed off in a crumbled heap. In the morning the cell heated up again slowly like an oven and I roasted in the hot, humid temperature, sweat pouring out of every pore in my skin.

The overpowering loneliness was turning me inward to find a source of activity for my senses. I was drilling into my own conscious interior with an intense laser of concentration. I felt myself trapped in a shadowy realm of pulsing fluids pressing and pushing on the walls of my skull. Horrible dreams and nightmares played in my sleep, and when I awakened, they continued to dance in the darkness. I was falling and tumbling down in a glowing, molten sea of blood. I saw the Marine Corps emblem break apart into teeming black widows astride black worlds. I leaped to my feet in the cell and began shrilly screaming and yelling for help. I banged against the door, begging like a child for someone to let me out. Delirious, I was agonized in fear over being left and forgotten about in what now felt like a coffin.

Finally, the nightmare ended. I was summoned on the eighth day before a military board composed of high-ranking Navy and Marine officers sitting erect and efficient in high-backed chairs at a long table. I thought, by the solemn authority present, that an important action was about to be taken. Their verdict was that I was to be expelled forthwith from the Marine Corps with a General Discharge. I felt a surge of jubilation. It was all over. I was finished with the Marines for the rest of my life or so I thought at the time.

The M.P.'s drove me back to my platoon where I was confronted by the chief drill instructor who addressed me with a cold and sterile brusqueness. "Get out of your Marine uniform. You will go home in this outfit that is suitable for your kind." He handed me a dress suit flamingo pink in color.

Changing into the pink outfit, I felt another mood coming over me. What did I care how they tried to chop me down. Let them toss all the degrading insults and slashes. What did I care about losing honor and dignity and all those other fancy words they talked about at the board hearing. They were only sounds coming out of the lips of strangers.

I was getting my wish, wasn't I? I was being sent home. What did I care if in the eyes of society I was being dishonored. If I had a son someday, I would explain it all to him. He would understand why I had to give up trying. He would accept my version of what had happened here in Parris Island.

The final round of humiliating ritual came on the morning of my departure. The drill instructors ordered me to march by myself up and down the company street in my pink suit so that my former platoon mates and others could see what had become of me. He then had me parade over the entire base so all recruits could see the penalty for being a rebel. I was painfully aware of how freakish I looked strutting in cadence in a flamingo-pink suit. My eyes raked the recruits standing along the walkways. I could see teeth and lips sneer. I could see mocking and hateful glowering from noncoms. I could hear snide curses. I tried to shut out their messages and fixed my features into a mask of aloof unconcern. For an hour I continued to march amid thousands of recruits, displayed as an oddity. I could feel their resentful malice toward me. I could almost feel myself being stoned. I ignored all the slurs and growling boos. Soon I would be leaving it all behind me.

Rolling into Grand Central Station, the train came to a lurching and jolting stop. I hopped off quickly, carrying my overnight bag over my shoulder and joined a swarm of civilians, which gave me a strange uneasiness after three months on a military island. Ashamed to face my family in a pink suit, I went to buy a uniform at an army-navy surplus store. The owner, eyeing my outfit, asked for a military ID and when I told him I didn't have any, he looked at me as if I was a contaminated grub and walked away. Eventually I found a place that didn't ask any questions but the only Marine uniform they had in stock was at least a size too small. I bought it anyway, and changed in a toilet stall at the Automat.

As I walked up my block, I thought about the glorious scenes in Marine movies when the young man's family has a big Welcome Home sign in the window and flags are draped over the roof and his proud mother and father rush out of the house and he scoops them both up in his arms. I recalled my Uncle Ernie coming back from World War II and Mom and my aunts racing out to him bursting in emotional tears, embracing him, weeping joyously at his safe homecoming.

Entering the front door, I went up to the apartment and let myself in. "Hey! Surprise! Anybody home?"

Mom was the first to see me and her face flashed her astonishment. "Joey? Well, what are you doing home?" She came over to throw her arms around me in a hug.

Dad, who was at the kitchen table slouched in his chair, looked up and for a moment there was a strained silence.

"Hi, Dad. I guess you're really surprised to see me, huh?"

He didn't move from his chair and his tone was neither friendly nor unfriendly but cautious. "Why aren't you at the Marine camp?"

"Well, I changed my mind. I mean, the Marines are nothing. Nothing like they make it. Where's Tony?"

"He should be home from work any minute." Mom's face lit up. "My, you look so, so nice in your uniform."

"Did they kick you out?" Dad's look became sullen.

"Nick!" Mom exclaimed.

"Did they?"

"It's a long story. I got a General Discharge. It really wasn't my fault, Dad."

"It's never your fault, is it?"

"You could at least give me a chance to explain before you go blaming me for something."

His voice rose. "Am I stopping you from explaining? I'm the one standing here asking you what happened!"

At that moment the door opened and Anthony came inside dressed in the uniform of a street cop. "Hey, Joe!" He moved quickly to shake my hand and pat me on the back.

"Hi, Tony."

"What are you doing here?"

"Wonderful surprise your brother brought home. He got himself kicked out of the Marine Corps."

"Joe?" Tony's face grew serious.

"You want to know the truth, I'm relieved."

"Sure, you're relieved," Dad said with an edge of scorn. "I mean it makes no difference to you you disgrace the family name. I mean why should Joe Sorrentino take orders from anybody else? Why should he be expected to put in a full day's work?"

"I'm not afraid of work! I don't know why you say things like that."

"Why? Maybe because you didn't keep a job longer than a month in your life. So you see me changing my job every two weeks?"

I lashed back. "So what's that to brag about? So you can hang onto a lousy job as a garbage collector."

"Hey, Joe." Anthony nudged me in a quiet tone.

I felt sorry I said it. "I didn't mean that the way it sounded, Dad."

"That's all I am, Joe," he said softly, emotion in his voice. "I hoped you'd be more. Maybe learn a skill like plumbing or carpentry. Or maybe even get a civil service job like your brother. But you fixed that now."

"I think it was God's will," Mom said. "He must have wanted Joe out of the Marines."

"Not half as bad as the Marines wanted him out." Dad shook his head.

"I mean God must have something else in mind for him."

"Yeah? Like what? With that bad discharge on his record he'll be lucky to get a job pouring concrete the rest of his life."

"Don't worry about me!"

"Don't worry, he says! How about you don't give me nothing to worry about for a change. For a big change."

Hurt by his words, I went into the bedroom and slammed the door shut. I could hear Dad's words to Anthony through the wall. His voice was husky with feeling. "I just don't understand. God gave me a son like you, Tony, that I've always been so proud of. And then turns around and gave me one like Joe who hurts me so much." A few minutes later Anthony came into the room and sat down next to me. He knew I was feeling very depressed.

"Hey, guess what? Theresa and I are gonna get married!"

"That's terrific," I said softly.

He seemed to be looking me over. "That's not the sharpest uniform I ever saw."

"I paid a hundred bucks for it at an army-navy surplus store on Forty-second Street. The one they gave me was pink." My voice trembled as I said it.

He put his arm around my shoulder. "Hey, it's gonna be okay, Joe."

"Well, at least I came back in time to dance at your wedding."

CHAPTER ELEVEN

The next day I went over to Dutchy's place. I felt uncertain about how she was going to receive me, and I was wondering what I was going to tell her, how I was going to break it to her. My mind was racing and I could feel my nerves acting like they were drowning in coffee. I knew I had to shut off my nerves. If I was a jittery wreck, it would only upset her more. I was wistfully hoping that the unpleasant part would pass quickly, like a little fish bone caught in the throat, and then everything would be smoothly back to where we were before. I tried to think of a way to put it in the best light, put it off on the Marines, and not on me. It was their fault. They were unreasonable, cruel, brutal sadists. I got kicked out because I wouldn't knuckle under to their brutal torture. I would tell her something along those lines. I had tried but they were too inhuman, a bunch of sadist savages. I had earnestly tried. It was not my fault.

My heart leaped with fear and a jab of passion at the sight of her coming out the door. She looked beautiful. She swerved down from the stoop, looking down at the ground. For a moment she didn't say anything, then she told me she knew. All the details had reached her. It was amazing how details traveled so fast from a remote island off South Carolina. I had developed a sensitivity to her moods but it was hard for me to judge how she was feeling. Her face was tight around the lips and eyes. It wasn't a happy look. Her smile was strained at the corners of her mouth. It wasn't her warm easy smile that warmed me inside. Her eyes, normally cheery and eager, were distant and cool. I could hear the enthusiasm go flat in my voice and a worried tone creep into my words. I could tell that I had slipped badly in her regard. As we walked and I put my arms around her waist, I felt a hint of her leaving me, not physically leaving me, but the person inside her lovely body had a restlessly dissatisfied feeling. We continued to walk silently, saying very little to each other. I wanted to respond to her inner mood, but I couldn't get out the right words. Finally, I tried to perk up the situation. "Hey, my brother and Theresa are getting married. He asked me to be in his bridal party. He wants both of us there. You'll like that, wearing a gown and me in a tuxedo."

The wedding reception was a festive "football" reception held at the Regina Pacis Hall, attended by hundreds of people, the Italian relatives and friends sitting at long tables on one side, the bride's Irish clan settled across the way. Waiters scurrying to the tables deposited piles of ham, corned beef, salami, and provolone sandwiches along with pitchers of beer, bottles of wine and soda, and for a memento, miniature plastic slippers laced with confetti. The hungry guests forked up gobs of steaming greasy peppers, sucked up mozzarella cutlets, ravished toasted lamb head, savoring the delicacy of the eyes, and stuffed themselves with rich pastry until they cramped from bellyache and burped from heartburn. Meanwhile, Grandma, seventy-five years old and wide all around, whirled gracefully on her Clydesdale legs, smiling with delight.

Everyone was having a merry time as the Irish and Italian relatives danced together mixing the jig and the tarantella. The beer and wine flowed and the music soared to the rafters. I was looking at all the activity from the stage, sitting with Dutchy as members of the bridal party at a long flower-bedecked table with

Anthony and his bride, the best man, the maid of honor, and other bridesmaids and ushers. My eyes were flitting around the reception hall, registering the happy expressions on faces, enjoying the sight of children eagerly ganging around the buttercream wedding cake, their little hands darting in and out to melt a mound of cream puffs. I watched a rosy mood slip through Anthony's smile as he basked in the well-wishing toasts of all the relatives. They were all proud of him. He was of them and he had become a policeman, a position of authority in the new country. He was now with the law, he had a voice of power in the system, he was someone these people of immigrant stock could come to if they were ever in need.

Putting my arm around Dutchy, I took a bottle of champagne and poured myself a glass, and sipped it slowly, watching Dad get up to waltz with the bride around the dance floor, wearing a big grin and waving to his Sanitation buddies. He was very proud that Anthony had won such a beautiful girl. He was also still glowing with pride over Anthony's position on the police force. With graceful, light steps he whirled in harmony with the balmy music of "The Merry Widow Waltz." At the end of the dance he escorted Theresa back to the stage and he returned to the table where he was sitting with Mom and the rest of the family. He leaned back in his chair, stretching his legs, and he reached under his breast-pocket handkerchief where he had tucked several Havana cigars, hand-rolled, strong, wrapped in clear cellophane with gold rings, each costing one dollar, which was a splurge on his salary. I pointed to him puffing on the expensive cigar, getting an appreciative nod from Dutchy. She knew that his normal smoke was the cheap, tart Dinobili, or "quinea stinker," but he felt that in a once in a lifetime event like a wedding, he was honoring his son by being extravagant in celebration. He shook off the flame with a little flick of his wrist and he tossed the match at an ashtray on the table in front of him.

He sucked in a deep drag, slowly savoring the taste of the expensive, aromatic smoke. Glancing at Mom, he affectionately threw his arm around her.

Just before they were going to leave on their honeymoon, Anthony and Theresa rose and moved to the dance floor for the traditional wedding ensemble. He held her closely, waltzing under the spotlight, ignoring all the staring eyes. I had taken Dutchy's hand and walked down to the dance floor where we watched on the fringe of the crowd. Dutchy was smiling. "Theresa's so beautiful."

"Not half as beautiful as you're going to be on your wedding day," I said.

"Joe, please don't talk like that." Her lips tightened uncomfortably. "I never said I'd marry you."

"I wasn't thinking right away. But you know how I feel about you."

"I don't see us having much of a future."

"Sure we do!" I grabbed her hand so she was facing me. The dancing continued behind us, holding the crowd's attention. "This job hoisting steel. That's until I get organized."

"When you came back from the Marines, you said the same thing. The next thing I knew you'd decided to become a boxer."

"Well, that made sense. I was a damn good boxer in the Golden Gloves and AAU. It was just that once I got close to it, I saw how guys were getting their brains scrambled and I didn't want that to happen to me."

"I understand that. I'm glad you quit, Joe. But the point is you quit everything, don't you."

"Look, tell me what you want me to do."

"I can't tell you that. All I know is . . . I used to think about what it would be like married to you. But I don't think like that anymore."

"Well, I'll get you started again." I put on a big grin.

"No, Joe."

"Hey, you know how much I care about you."

"I know."

"So let's think about getting married again."

"No, I don't want to. That's why I've . . ." She faltered. "I'm seeing someone else."

"You've been going with somebody else." I glared at her.

"I've been seeing Jimmy Antone."

"But you know he's a—"

"He's a very nice person, Joe. And he's got a trade and—"

"He's a butcher. He cuts meat in a lousy butcher shop."

"It's a good job. He's got a future."

"So you've been seeing this guy." I was feeling a storm of rage inside a deep, bleeding hurt. Suddenly moved by a furious impulse I gritted my teeth and whipped my hand across her face with a hard smack. Her head shot around tossing up her hair. I felt everything crashing down inside me. I knew everything was over between us forever, and I couldn't bear it. Tears were springing from her eyes but she fought them back. Suddenly the entire dance hall was silent and the crowd was staring at us in shock. Before I even sensed his presence, Dad was on top of me, burning a scowl into my eyes, and then turned to her. "Are you all right, Dutchy?"

"It's nothing, Mr. Sorrentino," she said in a soft voice. My sister Madeline came over and put an arm around her, and they moved toward the ladies room.

"Even at your brother's wedding," Dad growled.

I turned around and stormed out to the street, pacing back and forth under a streetlight, feeling a chaos inside my gut. I felt so terrible for what I had done. A voice called to me from behind. "Joe." I recognized the voice. It was Anthony. "Hey, cool off a little, huh?"

I shook my head. "Tony, why do I mess up everything. Why do things always go wrong? Why do I lose the girl I care about more than anything else in the world?"

"Come on. You still have a chance. You got a lot going for you, Joe."

"Sure, hoisting steel."

"What's wrong with that?"

"Mule work, shape-up work, no wonder she leaves me for a butcher."

"If you're not satisfied with that, do something else."

"What can I do? Get my brains scrambled in boxing? I'm not trained for anything else."

"Then get trained."

"How? I haven't been to high school."

"Go to high school."

"How am I gonna go to high school, I'm twenty years old."

"They have night classes."

"Sure, I'd be twenty-four when I got out. A twenty-four-year-old high school graduate."

"Is that some kind of magic number?"

"I'd be too old."

"You're crazy. You'd still be young and could land a decent job."

"I was a lousy student before. I failed almost everything. What makes you think I'd be different now?"

"Did you want to be a good student before?"

"Do you really think I could do something like that, Tony?"

"Yeah, I think you could and you'll meet somebody else, somebody else you can love."

Night school was five nights a week from the hours of seven to ten. During the day I went to my job as a steel hoister on a construction site. It was a priest, Father Russo, who had helped me get into the Teamsters Union so that I was eligible to be a steel hoister. We started at an early hour in the morning just as the sun was bursting over the city. All day I fastened up steel strips and hoisted them to the upper levels of the building. At closing time I changed into my street clothes and headed for the subway, grabbing a hot dog for dinner at Nedick's. On the BMT I cracked open my history textbook, studying the lesson for the evening. I found it hard to read alertly, being so drained from the sweaty hoisting all day. By six o'clock I was back in Brooklyn and getting off the train and walking three blocks to Erasmus where crowds of adult students made their way into the entrance.

Half the school was shut down due to the lesser number of night students. Ages ranged from twenty to seventy, with the majority of students immigrants attending school to learn the basic skills of the English language. Dialects in the air echoed the strains and tones of the Mideast, Western Europe, and the Caribbean. We all held full-time jobs during the day, and the drain of energy showed in heads bobbing, eyes drooping, and lapses into sleep during instruction. Classes in English were down to the basics, learning how to use a comma and how to use a semicolon and how to use a colon and when to capitalize a word. Because some immigrants in class were slow in catching on to grammatical rules, we often repeated the same simple lesson for hours. Reading assignments were short stories of modest vocabulary. Everyone seemed fatigued by the end of the night, including the teachers who were usually moonlighting for some extra money. The atmosphere in class was serious and mature with hardly any social exchange between students except during coffee breaks.

Back and forth on the subway from my house to the construction site, and on the bus back and forth from night school to my house was my daily routine. With this routine the weeks and months went slowly by. I went through this grind for two years and three summers before I was a candidate for graduation. I had no definite idea of what I was going to do with my diploma. While others talked about becoming a fireman or a cop I had no inkling. I was not sure that with a General Discharge from the Marines I was still eligible for civil service. As graduation neared, I found myself leaning more and more in the direction of becoming an insurance agent.

I never thought of attending college when I enrolled in Erasmus. The possibility of a college education was light-years away from my thinking. In my neighborhood, where everyone was a dropout, the view of a university was as distant as the stars. I had been on the job market long enough, however, to know that without a high school diploma you had to settle for the lousiest jobs, and I was no longer willing to resign myself to the bottom. I wanted to raise my qualifications to get a decent job, and to find another Dutchy.

The idea of college seeped slowly into my plans from a gradual coaching by several of my teachers. Mr. Troyan, an American history teacher, gave me the highest grades in his two courses, which was a terrific boost to my confidence. Mr. Arluck, my English teacher, said I had a good aptitude and he encouraged me to consider making application to college. My body felt it first, an excited surge of unexpected fervor, the slow hatching of a dream, and I started to feel that, if it was at all possible, going to college would be wonderful. I began hoping, dreaming, and wanting to go to college more than anything else.

Instinct, innate sense, told me that if I wanted to make a new life for myself, the best thing was to place myself in an entirely new mold, and so I knew I had to go to an out-of-state college. Going to a New York college would leave me too exposed to old influences and temptations. California loomed as my top choice because it seemed like a magnificent tropical paradise compared to the harsh canyons of the New York streets. *Look* magazine called it "the Golden Magnet;"

everything about California was touched by gold. Completing my high school work, I made application to the University of California.

The days went by slowly as I waited for my response from the university. My outlook fluctuated between grand optimism because of my high grades to deeply anxious doubts because I feared that an admissions officer would not place much stock in a night school. Two months went by with no word. I checked the mailbox every day and hounded my brothers and sisters to make sure they had not accidentally picked up and misplaced a letter for me. Another two months passed. Finally, the envelope came, bearing the crested gold seal of the University of California. I was jumping off the walls with excitement. The gold-embossed seal had a magical aura in my eyes. Never before had I received anything looking so solemn and significant with a seal of such magnificence. I held the envelope tightly in my hand, running into the bathroom with it so I could be alone. My hands trembled ripping open the envelope. The anticipation I felt at the prospect of a new life awaiting me had to eclipse the suspense for an Academy Award nominee. I was also filled with the fear of being turned down. The message leaped off the page in the opening sentence: "We are pleased to announce." I didn't have to read any further. The opening phrase did it. I was in. I jumped in jubilation. I felt waves of ecstasy. I had to squeeze my head into the back of my neck to calm the chills. Instantly, I felt drained of energy and adrenaline as if some mighty vacuum had sucked up all my vitality. The news was overwhelming.

And so it began. I worked arduously for four years at the university, achieved high grades and was elected student-body president. After graduation I reenlisted in the Marines to remove the blemish from my record, putting in a year of active duty and committing the rest of my time for reserve duty. I received an Honorable Discharge. I was then admitted to Harvard Law

School where after three years of hard effort I was selected to be commencement speaker—competing in an essay-and-oration contest to win the honor. Eighteen thousand people and representatives of some of the most distinguished American names were going to be at the commencement exercises. There were members of the Rockefeller, Roosevelt, and Kennedy clans; there were professors Kissinger, Galbraith, and Moynihan. All of them were there to hear me speak, Joe Sorrentino, the former four-time high school dropout.

It was like a transfusion of electricity to my confidence. I realized I had beaten some brilliant young men for this honor. I called Anthony to tell him the good news. I called my parents to tell them. My father had almost no comprehension of what I was telling him. The academic world was a remote artificial island to the working man, utterly devoid of real meaning or real value. It was thought that academics were out of touch; those who lived on islands in the South Pacific were no more remote than college university culture to the average working man in the inner cities of America.

I received a warm ovation and my speech was picked up by papers all around the country and even several magazines. Ready to start a new life, I moved out west.

CHAPTER TWELVE

Jaunting up the path to the UCLA law library, I was swinging my shoulders, not as exaggeratedly as my Brooklyn days, but with a macho swagger, feeling good about myself, happy about the way things were going. I threw my legs down with a dancing energy and took in deep breaths of the leaves and grass in the sunny air. My confidence was never higher. In heavy competition I had landed a prestige position in criminal prosecutions with the United States Justice Department. Instead of loading cabbage and doing other brute labor, I was going to be paid and given authority to use my intelligence. The heady, dizzying ego rush from delivering the commencement address at Harvard Law School had not yet subsided. I had received a tremendous outpouring of emotion from the eighteen thousand people who had attended. *Time* magazine had given full-page coverage to my speech, calling it "the year's most moving graduation address." My ego was feeling juiced and puffed.

My decision to join the Justice Department was motivated by the courtroom arena of action, and the element of a dynamic duel prosecuting big-time criminals. It had an exciting appeal, but also influencing me was the unsureness I still felt about myself. Technically, I had no record; all my offenses, fist fights, had been committed as a teen-ager, but I was still sensitive about my early mistakes. I was acting out of an insecure fear that I needed more legitimacy in my ledger. It was like someone getting out of dirty clothes who felt he had to put on a white tuxedo. I had to show the world that not only was I now a law-abiding citizen but that I had become a gung ho enforcer as well.

My academic record was a positive factor when I applied to the Justice Department, but it was former Supreme Court Justice Arthur Goldberg's backing that landed me the job. I was impressed that a man with so many weighty responsibilities and pressing issues clamoring for his attention could find the time to write letters and make calls in my behalf. No matter how drained and tired he was from the demands of his own job and family, he stretched himself to reach out to help others. He was quite a human being and an example I hoped that I could follow to the best of my ability.

I had lots of dreams and at that time I was of a frame of mind that believed anything was possible. I started to whistle a cheery tune to celebrate my good spirits when I spotted a lovely face rise from over the hill. Then, like a ship on the horizon, she came forward to where I could make out the streamlined shape of her figure. I stopped dead in my tracks and waited for her, not knowing what I was going to say but almost compelled by impulse to speak to her. Near, her facial features became clearer and the once distant good looks became to my eyes the ideal of a beautiful woman. Her blond hair fell gracefully to her shoulders, her eyes were as green and clear as a summer pond, her skin was white, and she smiled with even, white teeth. The overall impression of her features radiated the wholesomeness of a Scandinavian farm girl, which I later found out was her heritage. I waved my hands for her to stop, flashing a big smile. "Excuse me, miss, where is the college library?"

Her eyebrows raised slightly, but she turned and pointed and said in a friendly voice, "If you keep going on this path, you can't miss it. About a hundred yards up."

"Excuse me, do you know if they have the *Reader's Guide to Periodical Literature?*"

"I'm sure they do." She tilted her head, folding her arms around her books.

"I'm looking for *Time* magazine."

"I'm sure you'll find it there."

"Yeah, for this past June."

Her eyes rolled quizzically. "Go to the reference desk. The librarian will help you."

"You read *Time?*" I smiled, very much aware that she was lingering and revealing a spark of attraction for me.

"Well, I browse through it. Some sections I read completely like science, movie reviews, current news."

"Did you read June twenty-sixth's edition?"

"What was the cover?"

"I was in that edition," I said coolly.

"Really." She widened her lips in a big smile, amused by my subtle touch. "What did they write about you?"

"I'll tell you over lunch. It's almost noon. How about it? I know a place nearby that serves great guacamole. And to show you what an enlightened respecter of women's lib I am, I'll let you pay for it."

"Oh, you would, eh?"

"I'm teasing. It's on me. How about it?"

"As long as you're not in the crime section of *Time*."

"No, I'm on the education page. What's your name?"

"Sherrill Olsen."

The restaurant was up a flight of stairs and was in a house, the atmosphere of a Mexican ranch, flickering with wax-oozing candles, the round tables covered with red cloth and set up with bowls of corn chips and blazing-hot peppers. It was a family-run business with the mother doing the cooking, the outgoing father handling the money at the cash register, and the dark, smooth-skinned sons and daughters waiting on customers.

As we were being seated, a couple of single men sitting in a corner shot admiring gazes at Sherrill's appearance but even when she caught their eyes she seemed unaware of their attention. She clearly lacked a sense of herself as a highly attractive woman. Newly arrived in the big city from a rural town, she was refreshingly humble about herself. There was no detectable air of conceit in her personality. Her upbringing on a farm had kept her away from the male hordes and bombardments of flattery, with offers and propositions and pickup pesterings and whistles and comments which eventually glaze over many a beautiful city girl into a dead-skinned creature of consuming self-obsession. Sherrill was real.

"How did you find this place?" she asked, looking around, delighted by its coziness.

"A friend at the Justice Department told me about it."

"So you're going to be a prosecutor?"

"I'm being groomed for it. How about yourself? What are you studying?"

"I'm doing graduate work in biology. I don't know yet what I'll do when I finish. I work part-time for Professor Shoestran, maybe you've heard of him. He's internationally famous for his work in electron microscopy."

"No, I can't say I'm up on my electron mi— what?"

"Microscopy, the use of electrons to examine cell life. I may go into that field and teach it."

"Boy, this place is something." My eyes skipped around the wood beams on the ceiling and the saddles decorating the walls. "It's a vanishing phenomenon. You should put it on your endangered species list."

"What's endangered?"

"The home-cooking restaurant. McDonald's is the wave of the future. I was once driving through a remote wooded corner of Maine. . . ."

"I imagine that must be so beautiful."

". . . It was midnight, the moon was out, the trees

were a dense green cave, silver lakes around me, untouched nature, and then there it was, the neon yellow arch, McDonald's in the forest."

"Oh, it's profane."

"Homogenization, it's coming like a giant tidal wave, one big cow pasture society, all eating bland cud foods and plugged into the boob tube."

"Well, it has one redeeming feature. No more bigotry."

"What kind of farm did you grow up on?" I pulled my chest back to allow the waiter to put down a steaming plate of tamales.

"Truck corps, you know, tomatoes, carrots, turnips. We had the farm until I was sixteen, then Dad went into the packing shed, shipped Legrande nectarines."

"They are the most delicious fruit."

"You say that because you've never had water peaches off the tree."

"On the farm did you feed the chickens and hogs and that sort of thing?"

"I fed the chickens, but I picked out in the fields, that was the real work. In the summers when I was in high school Dad made me work in the cannery. Del Monte had a plant up near Reedley."

"Somehow I can't picture you in a cannery."

"Why not?" She laughed, having no perception of the incongruity of a beautiful girl slapping peaches into cans on an assembly line.

"How come your father made you work in a place like that? Steinbeck describes them as dark, sweaty places with a lot of Mexican aliens slaving."

"Dad believes hard work builds character. He didn't want to spoil us."

"Where is Reedley, your hometown?"

"It's between Dinuba and Sanger. The nearest major city is Fresno."

"Fresno is a major city?"

"It is compared to Reedley. They're all in the San

Joaquin Valley, a farming area. Dad wants to get out of farming. He says Madison Avenue is ruining the fruit industry. They want fruit for eye appeal now. Taste is out. Pretty fruit. Wax-looking fruit."

"Your father has the right sense of values."

"My father is a wonderful, sweet man. He has the heart of Santa Claus."

"I once dressed up like Santa Claus. I did it for an orphanage last year. Never again."

"Why?" She smiled curiously.

"Those kids stomped me. They were pissed at me for giving better presents to rich kids. They accused me, Santa Claus, of discriminating."

"Kids are so perceptive."

"The talk I gave to the older kids went better. I gave a talk to eight hundred black girls. I was the only white male in the place."

"Where was this?"

"This was nearby at the Job Corps center."

"Why would they call on you? How could you relate to eight hundred black girls?"

"I simply talked about my own experiences. I told them how I had been a delinquent and a dropout and failed at a lot of jobs and how I pulled myself up by going to night school."

"But they were girls. They couldn't understand your troubles as a youth in New York City."

"You'd be surprised. They loved the talk and went wild after. They mobbed me on the stage like I was Paul Newman."

"I'll bet that made you feel good."

"At first, but then I got nervous. These were brassy, hip girls from the ghetto. I thought they were gonna rip my clothes off right there."

Her head went back in a big laugh. "That's funny."

"You know, I asked these kids what they wanted more than anything else in life."

"What did they answer?"

"In one big chorus they yelled, 'I want to be seen.' I understand what it means because I want it too. It means you want to be recognized."

"I don't feel that need at all. I have never been interested in fame. I simply want to lead my own life, a private one, with time to go to the desert, and the ocean, and camping in the mountains, and hiking. Do you like the outdoors? I'm a member of the Sierra Club. Tomorrow morning I'm going to the desert with some members to catch rattlesnakes, sidewinders. If you're not doing anything, you're welcome to join us."

"To catch rattlesnakes?" I asked in disbelief.

"Sure, it's fun. We bring them back to the biology department where they're used for research."

"Catching rattlesnakes is one kind of fun that I will pass on in this lifetime in the interest of prolonging it. But I would like to explore some other paths in nature with you."

On Saturday morning I got into a faded pair of dungarees and laced up my old Marine combat boots and went to pick up Sherrill for a day of hiking and picnicking in Trancas Canyon. We drove up the winding curves of Pacific Coast Highway, looking up at the sun, brightly spinning a golden web in the sky, throwing down a broken spray of light on the tall trees of the rugged palisades, dimming behind a puff of clouds, but then breaking out in a glow that brightened the greenery on the hills and the blue sheet shimmering on the morning sea. Parking the car in a rock-strewn lot, we trudged up on foot through a clearing within view of the ocean to begin our hike into the densely wooded canyon. Sherrill eagerly marched up the trail, touched by an excitement that was strange to me, being a city boy. New Yorkers only got excited hiking into the blazing lights of Broadway. "Nature" was a word we once heard about back in the third grade when the teacher explained that acorns reproduced trees. In the big city the only stimulation to your senses was the electric energy bombarding you from neon signs. Trees you were aware of only insofar as you parked your car away from them to avoid bird droppings.

Sherrill led me into her world, taking me by the hand and guiding me up the terraced slopes overrun with thickets, trees, and broken by a glassy-clean country stream. Her emotions warmly rose watching the water stream ripplingly and refreshingly over the rocks and boulders and around tree stumps. Her hand squeezed mine as she gazed into the flow.

She kneeled in a field of wild flowers off the path, and gathered up a bunch, breathing in deeply, as though wanting to dream in their scent. Beyond the aesthetics, she studied the complex botany of the foliage. With her trained eye she divided the visual field into separate entities, cutting life forms into classes, species, and then parts and fractions, and further into bits and pieces, and finally into the invisible activity of the inner cell life. She picked up root samples and bird feathers and rocks of uniquely striking age or shape. While I tended to guzzle in the whole scape like a painting, she approached it with a balance and discipline.

We sat under a tree and had a basket of lunch she had prepared: fried chicken with cornflake crust, heavily spiced to make it delicious. The basket was loaded with bruised and spotted nectarines sent to her by her father and they were juicily ripe. We had the woods to ourselves. No other people ventured as high and far into the canyon. The air was calm, gentle, and picked up our voices which mingled with the brushing of leaves and the gurgling stream and cheerily chirping birds. I stretched out on the grass under a beautifully full hanging branch and put my head on her lap and was feeling content. The sun was floating down on my body and I let my whole being rejoice from toes to soul. In my exhilaration I was wondering what was happening to me. Our personalities were melding into each other as naturally as the rhythms around us.

Moving deeper into the woods, we came to a sandy slope scattered with rocks. Suddenly Sherrill let out an excited yelp. "There goes a gecko." She raced into the nest of rocks, visibly delighted.

"What is it?" I blurted, chasing after her.

"A lizard. The only lizard who can talk." She searched under the rocks. "I got it. I got it, Joe." She held up a slimy, horny-skinned reptile with a long tongue and transparent, watch-glasslike bulging eyes. "Isn't he cute?"

"Adorable," I said, looking at the prehistoric face. "Is he going to say something?"

"He can only make a noise in his throat. No other lizard makes sounds. I think I'll keep him for a pet."

"Hi, guy," I said, waving at it.

"He's got a double tail. It's a defense. A gecko will leave its tail in a predator's mouth, drop it, and run."

"How clever. He leaves the tail in the wolf's mouth and splits."

She stroked him on top of the head. "His scientific name is Gekkonidae of the reptilian order Lacertilia. His cousins are turtles and crocodiles. He's cold-blooded. Look at those eyes."

"He looks drunk. Can he do tricks?"

"He can eat roaches by the hundred. What do you think I should name him?"

"How about sending him into the ghetto and calling him Gecko Ghan."

We went to a movie together in Westwood later in the evening and after the film we walked down the boulevard holding hands and I felt robustly at peace with myself, totally content and that contentment made me feel bristlingly alive and happy. I did flying cartwheels and windmills on lampposts, acting like a boyish puppy and Sherrill laughed delightedly. I was feeling my spirit soaring. Hanging from a branch, I smiled down at her. "It's great to get this excited. It isn't often that I feel this way. When you feel this excited, you are really alive."

The days that followed were a spell of free-falling sublime moments for us. Before the year was over we were married.

After several years of working as an associate for other law firms, together with Sherrill's brother, Gary Olsen, as my partner, we proudly opened our own law firm in Century City, under the name of Olsen and Sorrentino. We had a general practice, doing small business work, domestic relations, some contracts, an occasional entertainment matter, personal injury, and criminal cases. It was in our second year of practice in 1972 that we took on the case of *NYPD* v. *Sorrentino*.

PART 3

THE GOLD SHIELD

CHAPTER THIRTEEN

Trotting down the subway stairs in a hurried, morning-rush-hour crowd, I had a tight grip on the briefcase under my arm containing the brief that I was on my way to hand-deliver to Deputy Commissioner Max Davidson at police headquarters. Seconds later the train, with sparks flying, came rumbling in and after a wave of jolts its multiton cars hissed to a halt. It had been a long time since I rode this subway at rush hour every day on my way to jobs in a sweater factory and cheese factory and shoe factory and other jobs in dreary factories around the city. With all the bodies pressed against each other, horny men jockeyed sneakily for cheap feels and embarrassed and nervous women twisted and turned to elude them. I caught one obese, ugly man with slits for eyes grinding and swooshing into an attractive young brunette, his breaths slobbering in a racing gurgle from his nose and his eyes rolling in lustful ecstasy while the girl grimaced in revulsion and fluttered near tears, unable to budge with him impaled between her thighs, not a loose inch of movement around her in the vacuum-packed mass.

As the train made its stops, the people got off the way they got on, in dense swarms, and the standees thinned out to where I could weave my way around the poles to take up a position by the front window of the first car. The train surged onward, clacking on the rails and regaining its mad rhythm, speeding under the city. A little window waist-high allowed me to see the engineer's hands at the controls in his phone-boothlike compartment. He was sitting in the tight quarters on a narrow bench with his entire body shrouded in darkness except for his hand under a glowing light on the throttle. When I was a boy, I often had daydreams of being a BMT train driver. I would picture myself at the controls, screwing the wrenchlike throttle on its column, and then turning up the electric power to launch into motion a hundred tons of steel monster. As the train got moving I'd give it more juice and more speed, to race down the glinting silver tracks, flashing blue sparks in the black underground hole, sucking up more juice with a little flick of my wrist, commanding the thundering train to move faster. Whipping the wheels into a whirring streak, twisting the throttle ferociously in my hand, raising the wheels off the tracks and breaking out of the bricks and mortar, I'd skyjack the train into the night sky, heading for the stars.

The building that housed New York City's police headquarters was a massive sixty-million-dollar structure with modern windows that strove to create a bright and cheerful tone. It did not strike me as bright or cheerful but rather as a bureaucratic monster like the Pentagon set with rigid cold lines. Everything was on this scale of ponderousness, heavy-handedness, a show of power. Virtually everyone who was in the upper police echelons was located in this building.

As I rode up in the elevator, noticing its lack of streamlined silence, I began wondering how seriously the deputy commissioner was going to take my mission. I glanced down at my briefcase holding the brief that I had worked so hard on for his inspection and knew legally was a good piece of work, but I began worrying about how much attention he was going to give it. I recalled a sign over the entrance of the CYO boxing gym which said, If you think you're going to lose, you've lost. Despite his authority and impressive title, I was not going to let this man intimidate me. He was still only a man. There is nothing threatening that is not curable by an act of will. I strode out of the elevator, throwing my shoulders back, sucking in and hardening my gut, clamping my jaw out firmly, and gearing up my adrenaline for a confrontation. From ten yards away in the corridor I could see stenciled on a glass-paned door, Max Davidson, Deputy Commissioner of Legal Matters. I knocked firmly, feeling the same assertive determination I used to feel waiting for the bell to ring in a boxing match. I felt that I was going up against a tough opponent, a man who had climbed high on a tough mind and good intellect. Max Davidson was one of seven deputy commissioners, all of whom were technically civilians, but in actuality outranked all uniformed members of the police force, including the four-star chief inspector. He had the power to suspend from duty, or to reinstate, or to grant a rehearing to any member of the uniformed force.

No one responded to my first knock, so I reexamined my appearance, brushing off a little dust and pressing my hands like an iron against the front of my three-piece dark suit, satisfied that I was impeccably neat and looked sharp, and then I rechecked my wristwatch, noting that I was on time exactly. Before I raised my hand to knock again, the secretary opened the door with a cordial smile and had me take a seat in the outer office while she went in to tell Davidson of my arrival. In less than a minute she was back out again, parting her lips slightly in a cordial smile. "Mr. Sorrentino, the deputy commissioner will see you now."

"Thank you." I rose and followed her into the inner office and she left me standing at Davidson's desk where he was holding the phone, intently absorbed, muttering, "Uh, uh-huh." He half smiled, looking up and gestured with his finger for me to take one of the chairs in front of his large desk.

My eyes first went to the mass of papers and documents littered on the desk and then to Davidson, whose body was long and lanky but oozing with intensity. He appeared to be of early middle age, with alert, darkly lacquered eyes. His black hair was dappled with gray around the temples and was smoothed back from his forehead and curled inward when it reached the nape of his lean neck. A slight trace of a New York accent rippled in his surprisingly flat and bland voice that contradicted the energy of his restless body. The lines of his brown suit flowed harmoniously with the shape of his form and were of a tone and style that were unobtrusive, presenting no risk of calling special focus on his presence.

As soon as he put down the phone, he rose to give me a handshake. "Mr. Sorrentino, I'm Max Davidson."

"Nice to meet you."

"I understand you wanted to have a little talk about your brother."

"A little more than that. I'm submitting a formal brief." I reached into my briefcase.

His lips twisted in mild surprise. "I see. To what request?"

"A new hearing."

"New evidence?"

"Legal error."

He paused, his eyes on mine, peering into them, not with hostility but curious searching, and then shifted into a shallow diplomatic mask matching the tone of his words. "Mr. Sorrentino, I can appreciate why it would be difficult for you to accept the fact of your brother's misconduct, family ties being what they are."

I spoke evenly. "In our case they're very close."

"I'm sure." His hands rustled into the stacks of papers on his disordered desk looking for something. "I'm sure you're close. But it would be a shame for you to lose your objectivity and waste a lot of time whipping a dead horse. This matter is closed for all intents and purposes."

"Which means you're not going to review the brief?"

"Which means I'll look at the brief but I have confidence in the original verdict."

"Look, my brother had a perfect record as a cop. I've known him a long time. I know he could never get involved in this kind of shabby thing." I could feel my nerve ends sparking toward anger but my tone stayed unexcited.

"Your brother had an excellent record. I'm aware of the high standings he achieved in his precincts. But when he was at the 92nd Precinct, his captain cited him for insubordination once."

I flustered a bit and swallowed. "I didn't know that. What are the facts?"

His hand brushed the air over his cluttered desk. "Mr. Sorrentino, I don't have the time to go into it."

"But that has no relevance to his conscience or integrity, insubordination."

"But you understand my position. You understand that we're satisfied with the verdict."

"I think so."

"And you realize the futility of trying to reopen it?"

"Not really. I want to follow it through just to hear an explanation of why the judge ruled that Tarras was a reliable witness when the official transcript shows he perjured himself eight times in that hearing alone."

"What do you mean?" He reacted slightly startled.

"Page three, line fourteen, he says he had no criminal-arrest record; page twenty-one, line five, under cross-exam he admits he's been arrested nine times." I fired them quickly at him from memory. "Says he 'misunderstood' the question! Page twelve, line twenty-four, he says he had been in the numbers racket for less than three months; page forty, line sixteen, he admits he started running numbers when he was nineteen years old! Nobody picked him up on that one including my brother's attorney." My adrenaline was racing. "There are eight instances of perjury, Mr.

Davidson, and the ruling on those makes up just one legal error, and there are fourteen legal errors pointed out in that brief! Does that give you some notion as to why I don't think it's quite as futile as you do?"

"Well, I'll have to read what you have written. We'll see." He seemed a bit shaken.

"I would appreciate it," I said. "Oh, I almost forgot. Can I have that brief back for a moment?"

He looked up at me, puzzled, handing back the document. "Is there something missing?"

"I want to see if the typist put on the carbon-copy notice." I leafed through the pages. "Temporary help sometimes isn't as reliable as our regular legal secretaries." Finding the covering letter I had put in addressed to the Solicitor General, I handed the brief back to Davidson, who immediately looked at the letter to see what I was talking about. He appeared somewhat disconcerted. "The Solicitor General of the United States! What interest would he have in this matter? Why are you sending a copy of the brief to him?"

"I thought he would be interested in seeing what the New York Police Department considers due process."

"Are you trying to put pressure on me?"

"This is my brother and I am going to do everything I can to see that he gets a fair shake. I trust the judgment of the Solicitor General a lot. He used to be the dean of the Harvard Law School and I think he will take the time to read this brief and see why I am so upset over what was supposed to have been a legal hearing for my brother. I appreciate your taking the time to go over this carefully and will look forward to your response."

And on that note, I shook his hand and left the office.

Later I asked Anthony about the incident of insubordination at the 92nd Precinct.

In the spring Anthony was assigned to Post 29 which covered Lee Avenue from Taylor to Rutledge. At three o'clock one afternoon he went over to elementary school P.S. 109 to direct traffic. He liked performing this duty of seeing that kids safely crossed the street. It affirmed his concept that a cop was more than just a tough enforcer with a gun and handcuffs in the ghetto. It made him feel a sense of being helpful to people in the community. He enjoyed these moments standing in the middle of the busy school intersection, raising his hand to stop cars and motioning for the kids to cross and exchanging friendly words with them. On this afternoon he noticed a little boy about five years old fearfully hesitant to cross.

"Go ahead, kid," he shouted, waving at the boy to cross.

"I be scared," the boy said and beckoned with his dark eyes. "I be scared."

"Okay, I'll take you across." He went over to him. He had to crouch down to speak into the boy's face. "Why are you afraid to cross? I told the cars to wait."

"I be scared the cars no listen. You be blowing your whistle and they don't gonna listen. That's why I be scared." He reached up and wrapped his little fingers around Anthony's thumb. "You be taking me across."

"Sure." He affectionately rubbed the boy's hair before starting into the intersection. He could feel the boy's fingers squeeze tighter as they walked by the halted line of cars. After he got the little boy to the other side of the street, he went back to his position. He continued blowing his whistle, waving his arms, stopping cars and letting kids cross, for another fifteen minutes until it appeared all the elementary pupils were out. As he was leaving the intersection, he spied a late-model Buick Riviera glide through a stop sign a few blocks down and head his way. His mind went back to a few minutes ago when there were so many children in the area. He sprinted out into the middle of the street in front of the oncoming car and flagged it down, signaling for the driver to pull over to the curb. He wasn't sure he was going to give the driver a ticket. He was more concerned about warning the man about the danger to kids. Quotas for tickets were low in the 92nd, roughly five movers and three parking tags a month per man. The cops at this precinct had their hands too full with real crime to be looking for cars to tag.

"What's this about, officer?" the driver said. He was a gray-haired, well-dressed man with a pudgy face with wide nostrils and short teeth highlighted by the flickering sun.

"You went through a stop sign back there on Jones Avenue." He lowered his shoulders to the window. "Can I see your license?"

"You must be mistaken, officer." He rolled down the half-opened window.

"I'm sorry, sir, but I saw you go through the stop sign. Can I please see your license?"

He looked at him speculatively. "Do you know the Businessmen Allied with Our Police group here in Williamsburg? I'm the one who started it. I'm Donald Colt." He expected recognition.

"Can I see the license?" Anthony was growing impatient.

"Donald Colt," he repeated. "Editor of the *Williamsburg Daily Press*." He shoved his card out from the window.

"I'm not interested in this card. The name means nothing to me."

"I'm in a hurry, officer. Can't we just forget this for now? I have a meeting." Colt's prominent eyes tightened.

"Sir, you see this school here. A lot of kids were crossing these streets a few minutes ago. You might have hurt one of them the way you were driving."

"I don't need a lecture from you."

"Will you please step out of the car, sir?"

"I know Captain Wilson," the man said. "I also know Inspector Wiles."

"Can we get this over with? Your license, please."

"Are you gonna write me a ticket?"

"Yes, sir."

"I'm an important man in this community." He leafed through a billfold thick with credit cards to find his license.

"It makes no difference to me who you are," Anthony said with an edge. "You violated the law."

"You'll find out who I am," Colt said snappishly.

Anthony said nothing, reviewing the date on the license to see if it had expired. He noted the address of the man was Huntington, on Long Island, an affluent community. Moving around to the back of the Buick, he set his foot down on the bumper and began writing up the ticket.

"You write up this ticket and you're in for trouble." Colt paced smolderingly in a back and forth rhythm.

"You broke the law," Anthony answered not looking up, continuing to write the citation.

"You smartass, you'll find out. I can get you bounced so fast your head will swim." Colt put his wallet back inside the pocket of his flannel suit. "A flake like you needs a lesson."

"If you keep quiet, I'll get this done quicker."

"Don't you talk to me in that tone." A nerve of ego had been touched.

While Anthony was continuing the citation, he felt the man's spraying breath behind his ear. The man was sputtering insults. The angry scene was attracting a crowd of onlookers. Turning around from the license plate, Anthony found his path blocked by the man, whose jaw was now gnarled and spewing curses with an unpleasant odor a few inches from his face. He pulled back his head and Colt shoved his blazing eyes and wagging tongue closer. He kept shouting insults like an enraged manager on top of a baseball umpire. "You dense rookie bastard, you're gonna be on unemployment."

"Will you mind stepping back, sir." Anthony was feeling his own temper fuming. "Aren't you blowing this thing up?"

"Don't you tell me what I am doing, you bitching flatfoot. Don't you ever talk down to me. Why aren't you out there looking for real criminals? What are you breaking my chops for with this nitpicking shit? This is harassment."

Anthony swiped by Colt moving back to the driver's side, his eyes glimpsing the large crowd that had gathered around them watching with avid curiosity. He knew the ghetto people were taking measure of how he was treating this big shot. He was sure they had heard all the threats and badgerings and were wondering if he would stand up. Completing the writing he handed his citation pad to Colt. "Please sign on the line."

"I didn't go through any stop sign and I'm not signing anything."

"This is merely a promise to appear. It is not an admission of guilt. If you refuse to sign, you'll have to post bail."

"You make me sign this and you're out of a job next week."

"Just sign and shut your mouth," Anthony said disgustedly. He wondered how much guff he was supposed to take from this creep.

"What's this?" Colt's face flushed red. "You told me you stopped me for a stop sign. It says here, 'stop sign,' 'no sticker,' 'failure to signal,' 'faulty signal light.' "

"Since you acted like such a gentleman, I gave you all you deserved." Anthony watched the incensed man sign the ticket with furious strokes. He then tore off the violator's copy and handed it to him.

A week later at the conclusion of his midnight tour, Anthony noted his name was on the bulletin board to see Captain Wilson. He felt a premonitory chill go through his body, but he had no clear anticipation of why the captain might want to see him. Observing department decorum, he held his cap on his chest as he knocked on the captain's glass-paned door.

"Patrolman Sorrentino reporting. You wanted to see me about something, sir."

"Come in and close the door." The captain spoke in a flat tone.

"Yes, sir." Anthony took up a position of erectness at the desk.

The captain shoved back from his desk and he looked up with his unswervingly stern mouth and matchingly dour eyes, which were the unyielding traits of his features, making him unpopular with the men, and an object of sardonic jokes in the locker room. His lips puckered with rebuke. "You gave a summons to Donald Colt last week?"

Everything fell into place. The incident on Lee Avenue, the tantrum, the threats. This meeting was because of that guy. He gulped nervously. "Yes, I did, sir."

Wilson eyed Anthony coldly. "You know who that man is?"

"Not really, sir."

"He's the founder of the Businessmen Allied with Our Police."

"I recall him mentioning it."

"And he's editor of the *Williamsburg Daily Press*."

"I don't mean to sound disrespectful, sir, but he deserved the ticket. He ran a stop sign near the elementary school."

The captain listened imperviously. "Did he tell you he was a good friend of mine?"

"He said he knew the bosses."

"How come you didn't acknowledge when he said he knew the bosses?"

Anthony weighed his answer carefully. "I would have given him a break if he had acted like a gentleman. He became crude and vulgar. I had nothing personal against him. His attitude showed no respect for the uniform. It's a joke for someone like that to claim he cares about policemen. He didn't show it with me. He lost all sense of decency, and became a hollering animal."

Wilson's lean head straightened and his eyebrows wrinkled, revealing surprise at this disclosure. His forehead dipped momentarily in pensive deliberation. He was having second thoughts about the matter. His friend had doubtlessly given him a one-sided version of the incident. His eyes came up sullenly. "I still want you to apologize."

"But, sir, there was a crowd of people watching. He was screaming insults in front of everyone, disgracing the uniform in front of all those people."

"You can take off an hour Monday." Wilson rubbed a fever sore under his chin. "The newspaper is on Thirty-four Selby Street. I insist that you apologize."

"Apologize!" Anthony repeated the word sharply, feeling stung. "Why should I apologize? I was doing my job."

Wilson's teeth mashed irately. "It's important that we maintain good relations with that newspaper and show courtesy to the business group supporting police." From the captain's viewpoint it made more sense to have the rookie bow submissively to the influential editor.

"I should have locked him up for disorderly conduct," Anthony said unflinchingly. "I'm not going to apologize."

"Take some time to think about it."

"Nothing will change my mind."

The top precinct officer pulled out a P.R. 1 form, a record that follows a cop through his department career, and in front of Anthony's stunned and speechless face, he wrote a notation that stated that Patrolman Sorrentino had become disobedient and uncooperative in the performance of his duties. He then looked up icily. "Okay, have it your way. Now get back out on post."

Badly shakened by what had just taken place, Anthony sat on the bench in front of his locker in inner turmoil. The blood was racing in his head in stunned confusion. He had just received a bad mark on his record because he refused to back down to a man who broke the law. His own boss was taking the side of the lawbreaker. It was not a serious offense, but still he was doing his job. He pondered the effect of the bad mark on his record. He gave thought to the threats made by Colt. He recalled Colt's mentioning Inspector Wiles. Maybe he was in for more trouble. His gloomy mood was noticed by Joe Leary when he entered the locker room.

"What happened, kid?"

"I just got chewed out by the captain."

"What caused it?"

"He wanted me to apologize to that Colt character."

"You should have done it."

"Apologize to that obnoxious creep! I want to wring his neck."

"You gotta learn two fundamentals on this job. The first law of survival is to bend. It's a fact of nature. Palm trees stay alive in a hurricane by giving. In marriage you gotta compromise, give and take, to keep it alive. When there's a war, both sides give at the peace treaty. You gotta learn to bend."

"What the hell principles do I have if I apologize to that hypocrite? You don't bend when you're one hundred percent right."

"You ever hear of Anastas Mikoyan?"

"No."

"He survived every purge in Russia. He was one of the greatest benders in history."

"Nothing's left inside if you bend outside all the way."

"Fundamental two of survival: The best way to pass your thirty years on this job is to do nothing. You still haven't learned with your eyes. You're still young. You're idealistic. You want to get ahead. Be a hero. If you go bust your ass on this job, nobody's gonna care, nobody gives a damn about you, the bosses are for themselves. The only ones who care are your wife and kids and they need you, depend on you. To the brass you're just a number. You go out there and try to be a hero and one of these days someone like Bigfoot gets his knife into you; you'll get a nice write-up in the paper, Colt himself will do an article, the law and order man, and your wife will get a letter of commendation, and you'll get an inspector's burial, but that's not going to put your kids through school, or pay the rent, or feed the family, or raise your kids right."

"I can't change the way I am."

"I did. So will you when you get it through your head that this police thing is not real."

CHAPTER FOURTEEN

The days went by slowly as I waited for a response from the police department. My expectation fluctuated between fair optimism, because of the strong arguments put forth in the brief, to deeply anxious doubts because of fear that politics would overshadow legal merits. Not hearing any word in two weeks, I was growing tensely irritated with waiting, and the knowledge that it could be long months before they got around to answering my request. There were no procedural pressures on the police department to answer my motion within a limited period of time. The silence was pulling my nerves taut. On some nights I tossed sleeplessly, wondering what was going down at police headquarters. I felt a sense of absolute powerlessness in the face of their dawdling. I couldn't do anything without risk of offending and doing damage by getting on the phone demanding haste.

Finally, Ernie came into the house one morning holding up an envelope bearing the embossed seal of the police commissioner. Light-years seemed to have passed between his handing me the envelope and my taking it in my grip. I held the envelope tightly moving to the couch in the living room.

"Is this what you been waiting for?" Ernie asked.

"This is it," I nodded solemnly as I began to peel the edge of the envelope.

"Would they let you know in the mail? Don't you think on something like this they would call you personally?"

"No, this must be it," I said in a low voice, trying to conceal my tension and apprehension. I knew the letter inside had to be the answer to my motion. I was impressed that it was from Commissioner Murphy's office directly and not from one of his deputy commissioners. I calculated instantly that the matter had been brought to his attention for his personal decision after being apprised of the legal issues. My fingers were slightly trembling as I ripped away the flap.

"Hey, the letter has come," Ernie shouted into the kitchen. "Joe has the letter from the police department about Anthony."

"What does it say?" Dad's muffled voice came from the distance.

"Give me a chance to open it," I said edgily.

Ernie moved closer and bowed his head over my shoulder and I could hear his breaths and I could feel the heat of his body and it made me nervous and uncomfortable. I shifted around in the chair for a bit more privacy in reading the letter. I don't know if it was superstition, but I wanted only my eyes to be the first to glimpse the content of the letter. Mom and Dad hovered on the edge of the room tensely waiting. Suspense hung in the air. No one said a word as I unfolded the fresh, crisp, thick-bonded official paper also bearing the embossed blue seal of the New York police commissioner.

The message leaped off the page. My eyes streaked over the preliminary explanatory language to the phrase "motion is granted." The meaning instantly hit me. I felt waves of elation wash over me and run up my arms. It was a profoundly satisfying feeling of accomplishment.

"Well, what did they say?" Dad asked.

"They said yes." I slapped the letter vigorously with my hand.

"They did?" Dad's eyes visibly brightened.

"All right!" Ernie exclaimed with fierce delight. "You did it!"

"Hey, easy now."

"Man, you got it." He swept up Mom in his arms and then moved to hug Dad.

Mom came over and planted a big kiss on my cheek. "Joey, we're so thankful. Oh, I'm so happy. What a wonderful thing you've done for your brother. You should call him right away."

Acting with quiet gratitude, Dad came over to me. "Joe, I'll have to admit what you've done is something."

"Hey, everybody! Hang on!" I said uneasily. "It's not all that much so far. It's just the first step."

Dad's smile faded and a confused expression came over his face. "But you got him a new trial!"

"That's right, but . . ."

"Which must mean they believe he's innocent."

"No, it doesn't mean that at all."

"Then why did they give him a new trial? They don't think he's guilty?" His face flushed deeply, growing frustrated.

"The new trial is because they agree there were legal errors in the first one. It has nothing to do with whether he's innocent or guilty."

"You know he's innocent," he shouted, his volatile temper flaring, the eyes flashing the way I remembered them looking down at me as a boy.

I whirled around at him with my teeth grinding in exasperation. "Of course I know it, dammit. He's innocent but we got a new trial on legal error."

"Well, why didn't you make them know he was innocent?" he rebuked.

"I don't believe this," I said, shaking my head.

"What good does it do to trick around with this legal rigamarole?"

"You're out of line, Nick," Mom intervened. "Why are you faulting him?"

"Just like old times." I frowned, and squeezed out a you-can't-win smile.

"He should have made them believe he was innocent."

"I will."

"Then what are you saying?"

"If just once in your life you could listen instead of yelling the first thing that comes to your head." My temper flared.

"I don't like your tone."

"You're spewing your spleen here out of ignorance. You don't know what you're talking about. Immediately you jump to conclusions. I'm the lawyer in this family. I understand these things better than you. Why don't you listen, and let me explain."

"A son shouldn't talk to his father that way. You don't talk down to me."

"I'm not talking down. I'm trying to make you listen."

"Give him a chance to explain," Ernie said.

"I don't want to get into an argument over good news. This letter is good news. It means the last trial is being thrown out and we're being given a chance to prove Anthony's innocence. We still have to prove it. I believe he's innocent but I'm going to have to persuade a judge. It's not enough to be innocent when someone accuses you. I don't want anyone here to have illusions about this news. I don't want you to build your hopes too high. But before we had no hope. Now we have a reason to be hopeful."

"You're satisfied, Joey?" Mom asked.

"Of course I am."

"Hey, like Joe says, it's just a first step, but it is a first step."

"It's wonderful." Mom smiled.

"You bet it is," Ernie said emphatically.

Dad shook his head, looked at me, started to say something, and then backed off. He went into his bedroom, closing the door behind him.

CHAPTER
FIFTEEN

The news of the reopening of the case by the police commissioner did not generate much coverage in the press but I was invited by News Center 4 in New York to appear for a five-minute interview slot with newscaster Pia Lindstrom. I felt a strange sensation entering Rockefeller Center dressed in a conservative three-piece suit, coming in the role of a Harvard lawyer, because the last time I was here, I worked in the basement as a mail boy. Memory cells were triggered off by the familiar surroundings and I could see myself pumping mail into the stamp-meter machine and it spewing it out like salmon jumping upstream. A rush of forgotten faces popped up in vivid clarity. I could refeel the emotions I used to feel licking the envelopes, listening to Martin Bloch's *Make-Believe Ballroom*. The big hit that year was the Platters' "Only You" and I used to gush with daydreams thinking about Dutchy. Physically, I was standing in the lobby of the RCA Building, but my mind was flooding with the scenes of the mail room below.

I was met in the lobby by a young member of the NBC news staff. She escorted me to the elevator, chatting amiably with me while giving me the first set of instructions on the interview. By way of curiosity she meandered through the news room before heading for the makeup room. Desks were scattered over an enormously large office that bristled with the staccato rhythms of tatting and tinging IBM typewriters, phones jangling, and teletype machines rattling off and stopping, and repeating the same sound in shorter or longer cadence. Everyone moved with an evangelic sense of urgency as if fighting a deadline.

In the makeup room the sounds were shut out by a pair of heavy doors. I slid onto an adjustable chair, one of three in the room, the leather-cushioned variety found in the better barber shops. The rather petite-looking makeup artist put a white paper towel around my neck. In front of us was a mirror blazingly alight with neon bulbs and a counter set out with the grandest collection of cosmetic tubes and casings that I had ever seen. With the tip of her finger she tried a shade of pancake makeup on my skin to get a reading of my complexion. The woman had been doing makeup for ten years and she kept a gallery of her famous subjects on the walls. She was slow and meticulous, a perfectionist, using a tiny brush to tip the corners of my eyebrows. She brushed my hair and even adjusted my tie.

Out on the studio set I sat opposite Pia Lindstrom in a comfortable chair with only a modular coffee table between us. Cables stretched across the room behind the cameras trained on us. Brilliant floodlights created a mini-sun of white light on our images. The daughter of actress Ingrid Bergman, Pia Lindstrom had a luxuriating lush and shining beauty to her features, the blue eyes pure and deep, the skin silkenly white and flawless, the hair soft and full and the blond yellow of new corn, the cheekbones high and fragile and the chin line the edge of a shadow. She was looking straight ahead at me, with the corners of her mouth creased in a smile, a smile of warmth and friendliness, a smile designed to make me feel relaxed and comfortable. I tried to compose my own lips in a smile, but they felt a resistance of self-consciousness and nerves. A skilled interviewer, speaking in a delicately soft voice, she was able to pull me away from my self-concern and get my mind working and my words flowing, and I was beginning to enjoy the interview, feeling a sense of my own uniqueness and potential. The five minutes raced by quickly. Because the trial was still pending, we did not get into much of a discussion on the legal issues. What she appeared to be more interested in was the human-interest angle of a former Brooklyn street kid returning in the role of Harvard lawyer.

When I stepped off the set, I was told that there was a phone call waiting for me at the reception desk. I had not the haziest notion who might be calling me at NBC. The news interview had been done live, so it may very well have been someone who had seen me on television calling out of the past. The receptionist said the person calling claimed to be an old friend. I picked up the phone, and recognized her immediately. It was the soft voice that I used to hear in my dreams. It was Dutchy. She said she wanted to see me.

For the meeting I told her to be at Rocco's Restaurant the next day at two o'clock. It was a small neighborhood place with a cube-glass front, specializing in Italian dishes on the weekend, but had very few eating customers during the normal days. The only person inside the place when I walked in was the stout, balding bartender, wiping glasses under a glowing Schlitz beer sign. The lighting was dark and my eyes blinked making the adjustment from the bright sunlight outside. There was no air-conditioning, only a small electric fan blowing a feeble breeze that did little to relieve the sticky, hot feeling in the air. The bartender chewed down on a cigarette and mumbled for me to take any seat I wanted in the place. I moved around tables decorated with red-checkered tablecloths, some splotched with unwashed-out sauce stains, and I took a spot by the jukebox. A waitress immediately came out of the back room and asked if I was going to have anything to eat. I told her I was meeting someone and only wanted a beer until she arrived. Sipping at the beer, I turned the chair so that I would be facing the door. I was nervous, excited, and in a thoughtfully nostalgic mood. I shifted my body around in different poses while expecting her to walk through the door at any moment. I became very self-conscious about my body language. I wanted to strike her eyes with the right pose after fifteen years of being apart. I loosened my fingers from a tight, rough grasp on the beer glass, my usual way of slugging down a beer, to a more gentlemanly Ivy League refinement. I wanted to project an air of dashing polish. I was glad I had decided to dress up to the hilt. I wanted to flaunt my success. Underneath, I guess I had a need to rub in how well I had done after being dumped by her years ago. I became annoyed with myself for selecting this hole-in-the-wall dive. I should have picked a classier place uptown. My reason for selecting this spot was the belief that one of those trendy lounges would make her feel out of place. I was too overdressed for this workingman's beer joint.

I fidgeted in my chair, worrying about how much friendliness to show her. It was a tricky emotional thing having a reunion with your teen-age sweetheart. I noticed from the clock that I had come fifteen minutes too early. I had too much time to worry over how I should act. My biggest worry was over how much affection I should show her. I decided that it would be better to kiss her, but then I wrestled internally over the question of whether the kiss should be on the lips or on the cheeks. We were both married, but I saw no guilt in a face to face peck on the lips as a token of my affection for what we once had together. Looking up at the clock, I noticed it was ten minutes past the hour, and I began to wonder if she really was going to show up.

She had often been late for things when we were dating. I had to feel somewhat confident, because it was her phone call that brought me to this place. It was a good distance from her apartment to get here. Neither of us wanted to be seen together, which began making me feel a pang of guilt. The meeting was going to be harmless, I told myself. There was nothing to be sneaky about. She had been my dream girl, the pure virgin, the Madonna on the pedestal, the girl I wanted for my bride. Her sweet face had been my inspiration to sweat and bleed to win the Golden Gloves.

I sipped a slow spot of beer, remembering quite clearly how in those days girls clung to their virginity with the tenacity of a bear trap and how the males, even though messing around with whores, clung to the ideal of marrying a virgin, regarding a nonvirgin as spoiled goods of cheap value. Hypocritically, the males never looked at themselves as secondhand goods, even though they had slept around, but rather bragged about their bed conquests as trophies of virile manhood.

Drinking more beer, I was mellowing out, losing an uneasy flux of nerves, and falling into a nice sentimental mood. In my head were pictures of Dutchy as I remembered her as a young girl. She was the curviest, softest, loveliest, most luscious dark-haired girl in the neighborhood. I could picture her in a bathing suit, wearing Wedgies with straps snaking around her ankles, somehow making her shapely legs sexier. There was no two-piece bathing suit ever made that could keep her round buttocks tightly in the suit. When she swayed her hips, men drooled. Her mother was responsible for the name Dutchy. She had thought that her child had been blessed with royally adorable features, and so she christened her Duchess, which later, growing up, became shortened to Dutchy. As I conjured up images of her, I realized why I was nervous about this whole idea of a reunion. The sight of her face or the sound of her voice might bring back a flood of all the warmth I once felt for her. I was worried about some kind of déjà vu suddenly breaking open a dam of locked-up old feelings. For years the name Dutchy lay dead and unmentioned in the distant, ancient layers of a rather heavily traveled memory.

I sat there, silently struggling against something inside myself. I was thinking about all we once had and wondering if I was trying to start up new emotional fires.

Plunking a coin in the jukebox, I pressed the button for one of the many Frank Sinatra songs among the selections. As the silver arm slid down the row, I caught my own face in the glass window over the record assembly. To my own eyes the insidiously slow, almost imperceptible changes in my looks, going from boy to man, were not strikingly noticeable. Yet I had to wonder how my appearance was going to strike someone after a separation of fifteen years. Why I was concerned about such trivia, I couldn't say. What difference would it make how I might have changed over the years? I guessed that she would have to be feeling much deeper insecurities. I was the one who had climbed out of Little Italy from the low status of "manuál" to go on to achieve all the right symbols of success. I was the Harvard lawyer with offices in Beverly Hills and a Mercedes 450 SL, and a wardrobe from Alondales, and a large, Mediterranean house in Brentwood, California. She was the little girl who had never left the neighborhood. She was the one who had to have insecure doubts about herself. I sat back in my chair and once again assumed a pose where I would appear the master in control.

The Sinatra song I played was "My Way," with which, given the zigzag improbable and unorthodox course of my own life, I could feel a bond of empathy. I imagined that every person wanted to identify with the piece, needing to believe in some kind of self-styled individuality. I laughed lightly at the ironies of events in the past. Nature had a way of balancing out the bad with the good. There were so many things that at one time seemed terrible and caused deep hurt which turned out to be the wings to a brighter future. All of my failures and disappointments in boyhood had aided my climbing destiny. If Dutchy had not dumped me for another guy, I would have remained in Brooklyn to marry her and would have continued to toil in the peanut warehouse and struggled with bills to raise a family. Drinking a beer at a place like Rocco's would have been my nightly treat. By losing her, I was cut loose from the neighborhood, to search for a new love. I raised the glass of beer so that the light was illuminating the liquid a clear gold color, and as I sipped some more, I thought how losing in other encounters had resulted in good things. My heartbreaking loss to Danny Russo in the Golden Gloves, which at one time seemed so painfully terrible, ultimately was a blessing because had I won the championship it would have propelled the momentum for a long and destructive career in pro boxing. In retrospect, the murder of my street idol Tony Bavimo became fate's act of salvation.

Time had freed me from the shallow and shabby measure of values I had acquired in the streets. At one time, in my young eyes Tony Bavimo held the heroic charisma and inspiring leadership attributes of a John F. Kennedy, but looking back on him, I saw a psychopath, sociopath, and fanatical hotheaded egomaniac moving fast toward megalomania. The fact that he could destroy other men with his fists made him my hero. How impressionable I had been as a boy. What I had once admired as the greatest way of life, the mean streets, I now looked down at as the lowliest form of existence. I wagged my head in disbelief, reflecting on the ironies, trying to make sense out of the elusive twists of fate, realizing that today's disaster may be the seeds of tomorrow's victory.

Tapping my fingers on the beer glass, I had to reconsider the presumption that I had come up a winner in life. At one time the feelings I had for Dutchy would have said no to anything in life. There was no price that would have made me give her up, and yet I had been forced to give her up which drove me up to a grander material life-style. Now I experienced a wonderful mature love with my wife, but I wondered if there was anything in life that generated the same magic as first love, or if there was anything so shattering and unhealing as when it broke apart.

I had to weigh the exaggeration of self-delusion in looking back. I had to understand that it could not have been as pure and perfect as I remembered it. Suddenly, I felt a spasm of anxiety over staying for the meeting. I had this great fear that I was going to destroy something beautiful that could only exist unopened and untampered with in a dark corner of memory. All of my thoughts about Dutchy, which still gave pleasure, were based on the image of the beautiful girl of fifteen years ago. I realized that the woman who would be coming through the door in a few minutes would have to be a frightening disillusionment. From what I knew, Dutchy had been living a hard life, married to a butcher, giving birth to three children, cramped with her family in a small Brooklyn flat, spending her days cooking over a hot stove, washing clothes for five people, mopping floors, scrubbing walls, and mending and ironing clothes. The toil of housecleaning and the births and the pressures of raising children and heavy pasta meals must have taken their toll on her appearance. I formed this horrid picture of her with a thin moustache over her lips. From the weathering of a hard life she could have deteriorated beyond recognition. I was setting myself up for a jolt. I was not going to be meeting with my teen-age sweetheart. The woman coming through that door was going to be the middle-aged butcher's wife.

* * *

Nearly a half hour late she stepped inside the dark tavern, and I was excitedly stirred by the sight of her. I was beholding the womanly version of the beautiful girl. Her blue-black hair was up in a fresh set, gold earrings glinted from her ears, and she was wearing a high-necked blouse with a frilly early American collar and a pale yellow silk scarf whipped down over the shoulder of a stylish white suit molded to an astonishingly preserved figure. Every sensuous curve was set in the same flow of fifteen years ago. Her chin and cheeks and angelic features were the same, but there were differences I noticed as she strode toward me with a new walk and new smile. Up close, she revealed a few more inches around her hips and bust line. Her soft feminine voice was a slight register deeper. The liquid crystal, the innocent sparkle of girlhood in her brown eyes had been pushed out by the hardening jell of time's tensions and cares. The skin was still creamy-smooth but nicked with a hint of line here and there around her eyes and pulled tighter near the mouth. Spontaneously, I rose to pull her face to mine and gently touched her lips in an affectionately warm kiss. She sat down and crossed her legs under her dress and clasped her hands together, poised and gracious, and leaned back to survey me with a glowing smile of pride. Vicariously, my appearance on television in an interview with Pia Lindstrom had reached back to sprinkle a little luster of glamour on her. Her friends had called her to tell her her old boyfriend was on the news.

Immediately, I helped her off with her suit jacket, putting on my warmest smile and sincerely complimenting her on how wonderful she looked. I ordered a bottle of Chianti wine and reached over the table to tenderly squeeze her hand, trying to make us both feel at ease. I could sense strangely strong emotions passing back and forth between us. Although she was a woman, changed from our days together, enough of the former girl still showed in her face. The dimples around her smile were still the same. A part of who she had been was very visible and I responded to it with a wish to be especially tender and warm to her. Even though she had dropped me in a bad way, I cared now only to think about what she had given me, all those days of soaring emotions and nights of dreamy dazzle. Her name would always be special in my memories. I was flattered that she had gone to the trouble of setting her hair and putting on an elegant outfit and attempting to look her best. Underneath there was more emotion than I allowed to show in my voice, and my breathing was a bit quicker than when I had been sitting alone.

"You look wonderful," I said to her again.

"You look great, too, Joe. You've lost weight, trimmed down. You were a lot huskier in those days."

"Yeah, being husky was a big thing to me. The more you looked like a bull, the more you felt like a man. When people said I looked like a bull, it choked me up inside, I felt so flattered." I broke out into laughter at my own teen follies, and she laughed with me.

When the waitress came over with the bottle of wine, I poured a glass for each of us, and then picked up my glass for a toast, clinking it against hers. "Here's to our youth." After taking a sip, I slowly brought my glass down and looked at her seriously.

"Why did you call?" I asked.

There was a silence. Out on the street the siren of a police car screamed, and the silence fell again. She sat with her chair pushed back from the table, her voluptuous legs crossed, her hands clasped on her lap, her eyes looking straight into mine with a smile in them. "When I heard you were in the city, I wanted to see you. I thought about you a lot over the years. When I heard you finished night school and went to college in California, I couldn't believe it. No one would have believed you were going to do those things. You were such a crazy kid, a wild man in the streets in Brooklyn. Going to Harvard of all places to law school. Everyone figured you were heading for Sing Sing, hanging out with the pool hall crowd. You did such a change, it was a miracle. God must have had a hand in it. I wondered what you had become like with all this education."

"I don't know if inwardly I have changed that much."

"You've grown so much, Joe. Look at what you have accomplished. Becoming a lawyer, to hear you talk on TV, I couldn't believe it. When you were with me, all you talked about was fights. All you cared about was punching hard. This bull thing you talk about, wanting to be another bull like Jake LaMotta, and a bull like Tony Bavimo, no talking, only brute strength and smashing."

I drained the wine. "You know I was almost twenty when I started night high school. I didn't know any words."

"But you are so educated now." She brushed her hair back self-consciously. "I've done some things but nothing compared to you. I have so much respect for how you pulled yourself up."

"I was almost a mute when I started night school. You're right, all I knew about was punching hard. You didn't have to know words. You could shadow box to make your points. Bam! Bam! Bam!" I laughed. "That was my vocabulary in those days. Plus I knew a lot of curses and slang and the obscene Italian gestures with the hand. These street kids today are lazy and unimaginative. They use one finger to flip the bone. We used the fingers of the both hands in a ballet of obscene gestures, like sign language."

"You don't have to remind me how little you talked. That's why I've been saying how amazed I was to see you interviewed on the news. You couldn't talk to me, and there you were talking smoothly in front of the cameras to Ingrid Bergman's daughter in front of millions of people."

"What a trip. I went from a 'bam bam' dummy to a verbal florist. I had a dry rock for a head until the teachers fertilized it with learning. Now I can be floridly pompous with my vocabulary."

"I wish I had your way with words." She wrapped a finger around her wineglass. "You make me so self-conscious about my own lack of education. I regret more than anything else leaving school. The kids came fast. By twenty-four I had three children. I had no time for myself. Kids can take it all out of you. It's something, isn't it, to have three beautiful kids to show for your life?"

"You should never be embarrassed about what you've done raising a family. It's not something to be embarrassed about. Personally, I don't care what a person does; it's what the person is as a human being that's important. I've met a lot of famous people, so-called successful people, celebrities, who are nothing but shallow assholes. It's not what I think anyway that's important. How do you feel about your life? If you feel proud then it's good. Love and enjoy your kids. All the glitter and glamour you see on the tube is like the Wizard of Oz, a lot of facade. You'd go through it like a Chinese meal."

"But I see there's a lot more to life than what's here in Brooklyn. You're with such class people now, I can't believe it. You were on TV with Pia Lindstrom. You talked to her so relaxed and smooth. You always talked inside your head when we were on a date."

"What did I know to talk about in those days? If I was upset, I could say I was mad. Now I can spend a week spewing analytical theories aimed at fathoming the roots of my vexation. That's an educated man. The man who can say something in a million words instead of one."

"Do you really feel that way about education?"

"You mean viewing it as a tower of empty words?"

"Yes."

"No, I don't. It is much more a lens that looks at everything with questions, that examines beliefs, that turns on itself, freeing the mind and shaping potential. Education remade me."

"I was never attracted to you because you could beat somebody up. I admired that you were not afraid and stood out in the crowd, but the hitting upset me. All that moved me away from you. I never would have believed education could change you so."

I felt a need to change the subject, her talk was reaching a sensitive thread. "You know I see Richie from time to time in California."

"Oh, how is he doing?"

"He's still struggling in the movie business. He had a great role in the movie *Play It as It Lays*, but it was too artsy for the public. No action, and too many boy-girl scenes."

"He was another one interested in fighting."

"We once went to the Olympic Auditorium together to see the bouts. And we looked around at the crowd in the arena, loud, boisterous, crude, throwing beer bottles, yelling dirty stuff at girls, screaming for blood during the matches, and I remember at one point we both looked at each other, both of us having been fighters, and he nodded to me, 'To think, we wanted to play this audience.'"

"I hope he gets a break, but that's such a gamble wanting to be an actor, but I give him credit for leaving the streets."

"The streets might help him in movies, but I'm not sure the same is true for me."

"Why do you say that?"

"The streets are a weakness, by creating a blind rage of stubborn pride, a chip-on-the-shoulder oversensitiveness, an anger that bulls forward without admitting error or outrageous misjudgment in its objective. It twists your vision."

"That's quite a speech."

"I like to get carried away with words. I like to hear myself say them. Words got me out of the streets and into a top suite in Century City."

"But the streets gave you drive and made you hungry to succeed. You learned a lot about people from the streets. Didn't some kind of wisdom come out of all you went through?"

"The whole crux of wisdom is having insight into the nonrepetition of human error. I have made a lot of mistakes and I have not forgotten them. I guess that gives me a little wisdom."

"You have changed so much, yet I know people who have not changed a bit all their lives. Joey Lot is the same. It's still the fifties for him. He's in his thirties but still drives around on a motorcycle with tight polo shirts. Still chases young girls."

"Whatever happened to Ralph Shades?"

"You knew he was going to have a bad end. I wonder how many people he killed. You heard that he killed Tony Bavimo."

I felt a surge of anger, but it abated quickly. "Yeah, I heard. He was bragging about it in Sing Sing. Word traveled by grapevine all the way to California."

"They found Shades buried in the floor of a fish market."

"The way he lived that was a fitting burial. He would have never done it to Tony's face."

"You still think about Tony?"

"Every now and then. I don't know why but no matter what I do now, nothing matches those days. Every day was so big. Everything was so exciting. I have met some of the biggest movie stars and biggest political leaders and rock stars and most famous people in the country, but it was nothing like the thrill as a boy meeting Tony Bavimo."

"You were very young. I was so young. We were impressionable. Our eyes hadn't seen much. The neighborhood was the whole world. Tony was a god. It was like riding the roller coaster. The first time is the biggest thrill."

"You are a very intelligent lady, Dutchy."

"You know, I knew you cared about me, but I only appreciated how much after I became a woman. You never expressed yourself. That was part of it. I was also vainly self-centered in those days."

"I guess I loved you the most after I slapped you and your tooth flew out of your mouth and you fought back the tears and stared at me defiantly. You wouldn't give me the satisfaction of crying. It sounds so brutal. Why that should make me love you more, I don't know. How screwed up I was."

"Those things were important to you then. Toughness was like a religion. You fought in the streets, in the ring, you even joined the Marines."

"Everything to show how tough I was, and I wasn't really. I forced myself to be tough."

"You liked me more because I showed spirit. Tooth and all, I wasn't going to give in to you. I cried when you left."

"You always seemed to have a better grasp of my character than most."

"It's a more basic understanding. My life hasn't been cluttered with a million ideas."

"Word games."

"Knowledge."

"I wonder what it would have been like if we had stayed together."

"We'll never know."

There really wasn't much more to talk about. We no longer had anything in common, no plans to see each other again, no places to go anymore. We got up and walked to the front door. Once again my eyes adjusted from dark to light in the sun. Somehow the dark setting inside Rocco's had been appropriate for our backward journey in memories. I whistled to a cab from the curb and gently helped her get into the backseat. Before closing the door, she sat facing me. My face was flushed and I was feeling a warm affection for her and a sadness, too. We looked into each other's eyes and I leaned inside and gently kissed her on the lips, and closed the door and watched the cab speed off in traffic. As I waited until the cab was out of sight, a strange mood came over me. I had the emotion of having just left a cemetery. It was as if we had just placed a wreath on the grave of our youth.

CHAPTER SIXTEEN

With the trial a week away, I still had time to go visit the sites of old memories, and one morning I decided to go see the Fourteenth Street Gym. As I left the house for the subway, I stepped out to a beautiful sunny day with the air full of vibrant and invigorating smells and feelings that awaken in spring and grow stronger and warmer every day.

I looked up at the sun and stretched out my arms in the fashion of a prophet praying to the sky. I could easily understand the ancient Egyptians enshrining the sun into a god. The warm weather had a rejuvenating effect on my body. I imagined that I was once again a street kid strutting down the avenue.

I walked by produce displays loaded with firm and ripe peaches, plums, and tomatoes freshly picked and lustrously juicy. The street noises and kids' shouts rose above the voices of store owners and shoppers. I watched a woman suck the juices out of a handful of grapes and then spit the seeds into her purse and I laughed at the sight.

I looked up at the blue sky stretching to the end of the harbor where Lady Liberty was visible in white serenity and at the towering skyscrapers of Manhattan knifing into clear skies with silent eloquence. The royal, pure lines of the Empire State Building streaked up proudly over the shoulders of all the high-rise structures of the city, and I recalled how I used to spend hours staring at it, and feeling a simmering anger. That building represented a challenge. It was a symbol of imperial magnificence that belonged to the elite society across the bridge. Anchored near those chic and elegant shops like Tiffany's and Saks on Fifth Avenue, it was an arrogant monument of the rich. I would wonder about that world across the bridge, and my dream was to reach it.

Familiar sounds of bodies in furious motion greeted me as I climbed up the rickety stairs of the Fourteenth Street Gym. At the doorway of the barnlike room, my eyes swept in numerous boxers in satin trunks or sweat suits, bristling over the floor in various phases of training. Over in a corner a middleweight was rhythmically peppering a speed bag—whappity, whappity, whap—and not far from him a burly heavyweight was crashing his fists into the heavy bag, jangling the chains and crunching the stuffing. Out on the floor other fighters jumped rope with swishing speed. I paid an ex-pug with lumpy ears and he let me enter. I stepped into a wave of familiar old smells, the bitter dry bite of leather, the oversweet aroma of oil of wintergreen, the musky stench of stale socks, dirty jockstraps, and hairy sweat. I stopped after a few steps to watch a pair of wheezing welterweights slugging it out grudgefully in sparring, spilling drops of blood in the ring. I thought with relief how glad I was to be only a spectator, that those days of smashing exchanges were forever over for me.

I recognized Keen Jones, a veteran black heavyweight, as he crouched by flashing his irregular snaggled teeth and nodded a greeting to the young black near my old locker. A powerful man thewed like an oak with thick arms and massive thighs, his body movements told everything about the punishment of a long ring career. It could be seen in the way he plodded ponderously and slowly rotated his scar-puffed face and insensibly blinked his eyelids and slightly twitched his lips before speaking. He uttered his words in a gravelly voice with a stammer. His black eyes were dull, filmed over with a glassy haze. He was a crowd pleaser who waded in flat-footed to slug wildly. Keen had been knocked out six times in his career; the last two times he hit the canvas hard, plummeted like a shot, and was sprawled on his back and went into convulsions with his tongue spastically twitching and was nearly semicomatose. They had to get a doctor in the ring to revive him and he was carried out on a stretcher. To protect him from risk of severe concussion and possibly death, the New York Athletic Commission had slapped a year suspension on his fighting. The commission's ruling did not apply to sparring sessions in the gym, so to earn fifty bucks, he headed out for three rounds of hard punching exchanges with a heavyweight contender.

Going into the locker room, I passed the open shower stall, looking down at melted soap oozing down the drain. The names of contenders and ranking fighters could be seen on the silver-painted full-size lockers. The half-size lockers were left unpainted and held the names of the new and the fading, and some of them were bashed in from frustrated fists. I glanced around at the walls and I could see the names scratched out with keys in the paint or written in pencil or ball-point and more names on the poles and even in the toilet stalls. Thousands of boxers had come through this gym over the years, hoping their names would be immortalized in boxing's hall of fame. Except for a handful the final memorial was usually the wall or toilet stall. The chance of winning a boxing championship was more a Cinderella dream than movie stardom. In all of professional boxing there were only eight titles and only one, the heavyweight championship, gave household-name fame. I moved to my old locker, where my name was buried under several name stickers. A young black wearing street clothes came down the row to the locker next to my old one and he clicked off the combination, listening to a low whizz, and he removed his training gear of bag gloves, jump robe, head protector, and hand tape and set them out neatly on the bench. He got into a sweat suit that was raggedly scissored at the shoulders to streamline his punching. Watching him wind his tape around his hands stirred a stream of memories for me.

As a boy, during those days I followed Tony Bavimo to arenas around New York, I saw an awesome glamour in the muscular physiques of boxers and adulating crowds and blazing ring-lights and TV cameras and flashbulbs shining on the winner, and I could think of nothing in the world that could more fulfill my dreams than to become a champion. But over the years I found myself moving and fading out of that mentality. My attraction to the ring had been part of the cult of macho manhood I had learned growing up in New York City. I had listened hundreds of times over from older boys and men about fighting legends.

Over the years my eyes had imperceptibly, very slowly, creepingly but progressively, opened up more and more in a sobering way to violence in the streets and ring. As a boy the storied images of fists flying had the harmless and enchanting sparks of a toy tank, but the first time I stepped into a ring and another boy smashed his fist into my face, drawing a stream of nose blood and painful tears, I began to learn the very different reality behind youthful fantasy. I began to learn about the reality behind the cosmetic luster of the sports pages. The day to day action of the ring, the hundreds of rounds of sparring, the tournament matches, the thousands of shocks of pain from the hard-balled fists crashing into my ribs, kidney, and face eroded the glamour of boxing and reduced it to a raw collision of meat. What was seeping into consciousness, penetrating the layers of propaganda, was the emerging realization that earning a living by pounding another human being was not glamorous but rather a dull brutal drama. The supposed heroics of rumbling I had come to realize even earlier were an insane illusion. Whenever I thought of a rumble I saw a meat rack of severed jawbones, ripped flesh, lips hanging like flank steak, gored skulls, bloody mucus pouring from mouths, hysterical screams, twitching bodies, wailing ambulances, police sirens, and forever haunting me, Tony's bullet-mutilated head. With these thoughts I left the gym to continue my walk.

Out on the street I paused for a moment, gazing at the manhole cover that was once home plate in boyhood stickball games. All kinds of sensations and memories were clicking off as I took in the neighborhood. It had been ten years since I had been to the area. Looking around, everything seemed weary and worn, but underneath was a rugged and enduring strength, a solid hardiness and a hibernating vitality and color that soared during feasts and church parades when people danced in the streets. It was a teeming Italian neighborhood of working-class people, first generation and immigrants clustered with their families. Some of the blocks were in better shape than others. Typical of the streetscape was the fading, aging apartment building with fire escapes, but there were nicer blocks where skilled tradesmen lived in brick houses and drearier blocks where poor families were crowded into dilapidated wooden buildings that were peeling paint, losing shingles, and decaying inside the walls.

I walked along Fort Hamilton Parkway, the main thoroughfare where gas stations alternated with tall apartment buildings and small stores occupying the sidewalks. Unrecognized, I watched an older, grayer, more wrinkled Dom Basoni, the fish peddler, wrap a slithery squid in newspaper sheets for a woman, the same way he used to wrap Mom's cod on Fridays. At Aiello's Italian Dairy I could taste the salt-milky sweetness of the cream-oozing mozzarella balls displayed in a glass case. I stopped in front of a store with a large painted sign, Red Hook Civic Club, and inside through the venetian blinds I could see men playing cards at tables. Out of view was the back room where bets were being placed on horses. I weaved my head, trying to spot an old friend in the smoke-filled gathering. Scores of men were standing, scanning the racing pages of the *Daily News*.

I could pick out Capo Losino moving through the men, giving orders to his soldiers. He was a bulky man with a pouched belly, thick and wavy black hair grizzled with gray, bushy eyebrows, tough creased skin, and a wide nose gutted with burst veins. His scissory exhalations were due to a congenital lung problem, but ten years in Sing Sing must have also taken their toll on his wind. His manner was gruff and hard, his lips showing no trace of kindness, his eyes flickering alertly and distrustfully. He glanced suspiciously out at me, wondering why I was staring in the place. The capo had to be nervous because the FBI's organized-crime unit was always snooping around these days. In his treacherous business he also had to be on guard for a possible contract out on his head. Quite a number of men had been shot down in the streets of the old neighborhood. If it was really a big shot they were after like Frankie Yale or Charlie Sige, they came prepared with machine guns to blow him apart so there was no chance for a vendetta. They hit Charlie Sige in broad daylight, coming right in Mike's Candy Store, where he was sipping an ice cream soda. They quickly unslung their machine guns, and holding them at hip level, they opened fire. The mafioso's whole body violently jerked, shuddered, and slammed forward as the bullets ripped smoking through him and splashed out blood, bone chips, chunks of hairy scalp, and skin, leaving the soda fountain a gruesomely splattered mess. Rounds of deadly bullets ricocheted wildly and hit buildings outside, chipping off puffs of stone and brick. People shouted and screamed, dropping to the sidewalk, and some rounds came terrifyingly close to striking a child. Frankie Yale was buried in a silver coffin under the unloadings of five open limousines carrying thirty-seven thousand dollars worth of flowers. I remembered how horrified Dad had been over the killing and often talked of moving the family to Flatbush, a nice Jewish neighborhood where a father didn't have to worry about his sons growing up around gangsters.

I felt a surge of excitement nearing my old apartment building. The building which showed the wear of years was fading and peeling and painted a whitewall white. It had three levels of windows and the frames were cracked and creaky and I could hear them creaking in my mind. Out front to one side of the door were trash cans brimming with garbage and a few feet away, stuck in a patch of dirt, was a plaster of paris Madonna, the Holy Lady with a solid flowing cape of blue and carved-out slits for eyes, frozenly set in sadness. I went up to my apartment door on the second floor. I didn't knock to go inside, but could picture it all. I knew what used to be inside by heart and I could go from room to room in my mind picturing exactly how it looked. In addition to the three small rooms, there was a big enclosure that could have been deemed a closet, but we always called it the half room, and it held two long cribs with ladderlike sides that were decorated with teddy bears. Three of the children slept in these cribs. A few paces away was Mom and Dad's bedroom, furnished with sturdy, old-fashioned oak pieces except for their bed which was falling apart and never fixed, the mattress slanting down at the foot from broken supports, so that my parents always slept on the angle of a hill. I could see the big, flesh-toned plaster body of Christ on the cross hanging from the wall at the head of the bed, and again I thought of how I emotionally related to that icon, talking to it like it was a supernatural miniature with a part of the ear and heart of the heavenly God. The scene shifted to the bathroom, tiles flaking off into the claw-foot bathtub, the toilet not refilling unless the moldy ball in the tank was lifted by hand, the bathtub bobbing with balled-up diapers, streaking with a greenish wake. There was my bedroom where I slept with my brothers Anthony and Ernie in the open Castro sofa-bed, jagged springs snaking up from the raggedy mattress, the venetian blinds drooping lopsidedly, the round wall mirror missing some glass and the carpet a fading straw color with only a corona of its original brown. In the doorway was a rubber doll danglingly lynched to a necktie as my adolescent punching bag. At night the floors squeaked with mice. The walls were covered with holy calendars imprinted with Christ's face, some years old but never taken down because Mom could never throw her Savior in the garbage, and the same was true for palm crosses from Palm Sunday corroding to a tobacco brown. Cluttered all over were miniature glass slippers, plastic cupids, sequined angels, porcelain valentines, and other romantic knickknacks tracing Dad's weekend gigs as a horn man. The radio squawked and had to be slapped, the odd pagoda-shaped dish cabinet was missing a glass pane, smashed out by Dad in a fit, the old iron radiator hissed and clanked and had to be hit with a hammer, the sockets shorted, spitting out blue sparks, and from time to time on stormy days the power lines went down, blacking out the entire neighborhood. I recalled how on those blackout nights Dad made the whole family huddle around the kitchen table, our faces glowing by the light of little white kosher candles, while Mom and Dad told us stories. We felt closer then as a family than any time I could ever remember.

Standing in front of the door, I noticed that the hall was filled with a smell of pasta sauce, but the strongest and most familiar smell was the imbedded musty odor that belonged to the walls themselves and was part of my every trip up and down the stairs. Past epochs never vanish completely and blood still drips from the most ancient emotional wounds and it can be healing to return in adulthood to look back at bad things through a wiser pair of eyes. Deep down there was a feeling of loss. I felt that pieces of myself had died and were pressed down and petrified under layers of accumulated memories. Staring at my apartment door I had a desperate yearning to turn back the clock and return to boyhood, to once again look at life through the eyes of unlimited wonders. Whatever the bad times, it was an age of innocent faith. There wasn't an ounce of disillusionment in my boyhood bones.

I moved down the block feeling the wind pick up energy and drive howling and fluttering across the street, sweeping up clouds of ashes out of trash cans and lashing shutters and gates and pummeling a blanket hanging out on a wash line. On Seventy-fourth Street I had to pass the buttermilk-colored brick building of P.S. 259 and I slowed as I passed the classroom windows. I remembered how Dad, who used to beat the hell out of me for playing hookey, didn't care much about my dropping out as long as I was going to get a job where I would be bringing home money to help with the bills. He had been unmoved when Miss Lawsen, my eighth-grade teacher, wrote home that I had a good chance of getting into Brooklyn Tech, one of the finest technical high schools in the country, supposedly open only to students with high potential. None of that mattered to Dad, a third-grade dropout himself, who was struggling in those days to feed nine mouths on a garbage collector's salary. Under heavy pressure, he didn't know where to turn except to his oldest sons for support in the job market. Dad's outlook on schools was an attitude he learned from his own father who told him: "You don't need to know books to work. Books are for the rich man's leisure. The workingman must develop his hands."

I went on to visit the relocated Pop's Pool Hall. Out front were a few husky, aggressive-looking figures, dark-haired and shuffling back and forth restlessly.

The generations had changed, the hair styles were longer, the faces were unfamiliar, but the atmosphere still bore a resemblance to my own day. Pop's was a loud and boisterous hangout, with players cracking off exploding break shots, and pinball machines clanged with bells and onlookers horsed around, wisecracked, and rooted raucously with cheers and hoots for the pool shooters. I spotted one person, Philly Lane, whom I had last seen when he was a boy younger than me. His toughly bearded face glanced my way and suddenly there was recognition and his eyes shifted from a neutral hardness to a cold, flinty hostility, and before I could say anything to him, he hurried outside to get away. At one time he looked up to me, but now he was making it clear he didn't want to have anything to do with me. His brusque flight was intended to let me know I was an unwelcome outsider if not an enemy now.

Gagging clouds of cigarette smoke made me cough, the smoke hanging thickly and stagnantly in the air. An open door revealed a cracked toilet with cigarette butts littering the sloshy floor around it. The pool shooters were all a new generation and unknown to me, but in the back at the poker tables I saw men my age and some older with heavily salted gray hair, and among them were faces I knew and could vividly recall sitting back here playing poker twenty years ago. Nothing had changed for these men. For twenty years they had remained as fixtures in this pool hall, turning grayer watching their cards. Except for a few curious glances no one paid any attention to me.

Glancing outside, I noticed a boy staring in from the space of the partially opened door. I knew what was going on in his head. When I was his age, I felt that I was missing something being barred from the pool hall. It held an adventurous and colorful lure to innocent eyes. It had a seductive mystery with its black-painted windows and smoky clouds steaming up the air and its menagerie of exotic characters. In a way, it tugged on a teen's imagination the way a circus enchanted a child with its wild and strange creatures and costumes. The atmosphere and pulse of the pool hall was excitingly alive, always jumping with action and motion and roaring with juke rhythms and cryptic crap games and smooth dapper con men and hustlers wearing dark glasses and tough tattooed gang members moving restlessly like animals in a cage.

The boy was enchanted, while I was feeling slight nudges of an undefined pain. I didn't know if it was the pathetically empty impression of the pool hall that was once my magic kingdom that bothered me or the fact that none of these young pool players acknowledged my existence. About to turn and leave, I heard someone shout to me by a name I hadn't heard since I was a boy.

"Hey, Sarry." One of the poker players started toward me. "Joe Sarry. I wasn't sure it was you." He broke into a warm, enthusiastic smile. "It's me, Frankie Dagostino."

"Frankie." I went to shake his hand.

"Joe Sarry." He threw his arms around me with a lot of emotion, as if he was reliving a moment in his youth. He stood back examining me. "Still keep in good shape? Still run ten miles a day?"

"I still run, Frankie, but not ten miles."

"You still work out on the bag?" He smiled. "Boy, you could hit."

"No, I don't work out. My values have changed."

"Values?" He looked at me clearly puzzled.

As we were standing there talking I noticed over his shoulder an old fight poster from Madison Square Garden, the cardboard yellowish and flaking in shreds but with the date, 1955, still readable and one of the bouts still noticeably circled in crayon, the six-rounder between middleweight slugger, Artie Chuback, the crowd pleaser from Hoboken, and Tony Bavimo, the pride of Fort Hamilton. The memory of Tony was still alive in the neighborhood. Though he had been dead for more than twenty years, he was still revered as a legend. Suddenly I felt a cold chill come over me and I felt myself reliving every moment of that entire night. I could feel my skin the way it felt when they pulled the blanket from his corpse. I could see the face. I said a quick good-bye to Frank and turned to leave. "Only the dead know Brooklyn," Thomas Wolfe wrote.

I had seen enough of my past. It was time to return to the present, to the work I had come home to do.

CHAPTER
SEVENTEEN

All during the ride to police headquarters, I wondered how I was going to react seeing this character Tarras face to face. At the entrance to the parking lot, a uniformed police officer looked into the car, and when I identified myself, he handed me a temporary official permit which I jammed into the windshield, to leave there for the duration of the trial. I thanked him and drove on to find a space.

Nearing the steps of the massive building, I was reminded of what was at stake in this trial. My brother's future was riding in my hands. It was a heavy responsibility. I couldn't dwell on that kind of thinking, knowing it would interfere with my performance. I had to concentrate all my energy on the tasks of trial. You always felt a pressure defending someone in a criminal trial, the tense fear always nagging at you that you might blow it, that you might not do something right or that you would fail to hammer away enough on a critical point. Yet in virtually every case, once it ended, your involvement faded; win or lose the names and faces soon left your life. In this case, if I lost, the failure would not dissolve in the fading past. I would be seeing my brother for the rest of my life.

My nature was basically emotional and I knew it was going to be hard to restrain the emotion in my voice in this trial, but I had to discipline myself. A trial lawyer has to think on his feet and keep himself under control and not have his mind ruled by blurring unruly emotion. I also knew that judges tended to be scornfully intolerant and egotistically offended when an attorney got forcefully passionate in pressing his arguments. Melodramatics were viewed as both insolent and insulting.

I walked a few steps ahead of Anthony into a small courtroom which lacked a jury box and had only a half-dozen rows of benches for witnesses and spectators. In other respects it was set up with the usual judicial arrangement of a long counsel table facing the bench across a well and a witness chair to the left of the judge, who in this case was a deputy commissioner for trials in the New York Police Department. We were the first ones in the courtroom. Glancing at the wall clock, I unbuckled my briefcase and spread my notes and pads on the counsel table. It was a strange feeling having my brother sitting next to me as the defendant. The pressure from the emotional undercurrents could be felt in my knees as I flipped through my notes. While it had been encouraging winning a new trial, it had been done on purely technical grounds, a total of fourteen prejudicial errors in the first hearing, but they had little to do with the facts of the case. All of the incriminating statements and evidence established against Anthony were still to be discredited, and I honestly didn't know if I could succeed. I knew in his last-ditch desperation Anthony was relying on me to put in the extra fight his first attorney seemed to lack. Yet I was feeling and thinking that the first attorney, the former police captain, had done a decent job. His problem was that he was up against a stacked deck and I had to be afraid that same stacked deck was going to rule the outcome again. I glanced around curiously, and saw the other parties coming in the courtroom. My eyes immediately went on Tarras without anyone needing to point him out to me. I knew a street character when I saw one. A dark-skinned man, he was wearing a shiny pressed tan suit with a new white shirt, tight and stiff around his neck, and his tie was neatly knotted and straight on center, the combination striking me as unnatural for him. The overly innocent look in his eyes matched the clean crisp neatness of his clothes as he sat with his hands properly clasped in his lap. "Jesus," I thought to myself. "Why didn't they buy a halo for him, too."

He avoided my gaze, keeping his head attentively on the American flag up front, his eyes holding reverence for the stars and stripes. The exaggerated tone of his respectable looks and moves betrayed a devious mind to me. His childlike, innocent bearing did not blend with his facial features; the skin was coarse and dark, the lips slack and colorless, the eyes glassy-dark, the black hair neatly combed back from his forehead but shining wetly from Vitalis. Overhearing him speak to the men flanking him, I noticed that he had a nasal, unresonant voice with a sinking rhythm, which was definitely a Bronx street pattern. The realization of the harm he had done to my brother surged up in me again.

Next to him was Tom Colby, the police department's prosecutor, a man in his early forties with a touch of haughtiness and smugly patronizing flair in his manner. I could see his lips whispering in Tarras's ear. On the far end was a nameless man with a cold expressionless pair of eyes from Internal Affairs. Not only were we taking on Tarras and Colby. The real opponent I felt was the Division of Internal Affairs.

When the judge came out of his chambers, the bailiff, a chesty police sergeant, sprung to attention and announced, "In the case of New York Police Department versus Sorrentino, Deputy Commissioner Ralph J. Crippen presiding."

I studied the man in whose hands the outcome rested. He was a sizable man with wide spacing between his ruddy cheeks and thick-browed eyes and high, square shoulders that stretched his judicial robe and heavy hands bristling hair up from the wrists. He swung his swivel chair to the prosecutor and swung it back at me, registering our appearances, and nodded a silent symbolic bow to us as members of the same legal fraternity. I wondered how fair he was going to be, since he was a high-ranking official within the police department. Socrates once wrote that a judge had four duties: to hear courteously, to answer wisely, to consider soberly, and to decide impartially. I could care less about his courtesies, but it mattered a great deal to me how he handled the other three duties. If he chose to ignore them, we were engaged in a political ritual, not a proceeding to determine justice. In medieval days superstition governed the fate of a trial, which seemed terrible but not nearly as deplorable as a predetermined political charade.

"The clerk," the judge announced, "will now read the charges."

In a loud clear voice the clerk, a slight man with soft gray eyes, began reading the specifics of the charges. When he was finished he sat back down at his desk near the bench. The acts of misconduct cited were several alleged incidents of bribery. Out of the corner of my eye I could see the Internal Affairs man hawkishly tracking all the proceedings.

The judge then looked down at me. "Attorney for the defense, I understand you have a motion to present."

I rose to my feet. "I have, Your Honor."

"You may proceed."

I cleared my throat, swallowing down my nervousness. "Your Honor, at this time I would like to move for a dismissal of the charges. I would like to repeat the arguments contained in my brief for a new trial. It is well established in this matter that the only testimony against the accused is uncorroborated. There is no physical evidence at all, no photos, no wiretaps, no fingerprints, no life-style changes, no other witnesses. And the story told by the sole accusing witness bears on its face strong indications of improbability riddled as it is with inconsistencies, contradicted as it is by physical evidence, and unreliable as it is by virtue of the disreputable character of the prosecution's only witness."

"Objection, Your Honor." Colby heaved himself up. "It is up to Mr. Tarras's community to characterize his moral worth, not the defense attorney."

"Overruled."

"Your Honor, the cases I have cited clearly show that a court should look with serious doubt upon the testimony of an informer who stands to gain by falsely accusing a police officer. The total omission of any corroborative proof is the omission of a vital safeguard against the likelihood of gross injustice. To allow an informer to be the only basis for convicting a policeman sets up a dangerous precedent. It puts every policeman at the mercy of lawbreakers. It makes every policeman an easy mark for his criminal enemies in the streets."

I paused for a moment to look over at Colby, copiously writing notes in his yellow pad, breaking a pencil point, but quickly supplied with another by the Internal Affairs agent at his side. I paced within the confines of the counsel table, citing cases to support my points. I bowed my head to let the ideas roll down to my tongue. I clapped my hands together lightly and rubbed them watching my brother's eyes fill with surprise wonder at his kid brother orating in court instead of pleading with the judge for a chance. It took a bit of adjusting for him. I registered his impressed look but immediately plunged back into my argument. "In this case we are not talking about a man with a mediocre, lackluster service record but a policeman with an exceptional, unblemished record."

Suddenly I was interrupted by Colby up on his feet objecting, and I broke off my argument and turned my eyes away from the judge and looked at him. "Your Honor," he snapped, "I object to counsel's referral to the defendant as a policeman. He is no longer with the department. His position is not one of suspension but expulsion."

I shot a resentful stare at his blue eyes. "Excuse me, Your Honor, technically the prosecutor may be correct. However I hope that after my motion that situation will be rectified."

The judge dipped his head from the bench. "Is there anything further you wish to add?" He spoke in a softly polite voice, leaving me with the impression that he wanted to be cautious against any charges of unfairness and was ready to give me as much time as I needed.

"Yes, Your Honor. I was saying that when a man has one of the best records in the department, he should not be vulnerable to a criminal he has arrested. This court should not permit a case to be based on the word of a convicted felon alone against Detective Sorrentino."

"I object." Colby leaped up. "He cannot use the description 'detective.' He keeps doing this."

"Well, I'm sorry if counsel is so upset over my slip of semantics."

"I want him to stop doing it."

"This is a petty minor issue."

"I consider it important. He has no right to call him Detective Sorrentino."

"The exact purpose of this hearing is to determine whether that title should be removed from him."

"He is no longer a detective. He has been expelled, and that is the fact."

"Your Honor, if this hearing replaces the previous one, then—"

The judge slammed his gavel down. "All right, gentlemen! I don't think the court's opinion is going to be swayed by the defendant's title or lack of one. But since it offends the prosecution, I'll ask the defense to use the title 'Mister,' and I promise not to hold it against his client."

"Yes, sir," I said, feeling rather foolish and a touch rattled.

"Now, I believe you had just submitted a motion to dismiss."

"Yes, Your Honor, if I may speak to the motion."

"Go ahead."

"In sum, what I was telling the court was that no one ever accused Mr. Sorrentino of any wrongdoing during his distinguished career with the police department until this man of shady character and with a shaky story came forward who stands to gain by falsely making this charge. For this reason and the other grounds outlined in the brief, we ask dismissal."

Anthony leaned over to whisper as I retook my seat. "Wow! Do you think we'll get it?"

"Not if Colby's sharp," I whispered back. "He should argue that no charge against a policeman should ever escape full trial."

"You care to respond to the motion, Mr. Colby?" the judge asked.

"I certainly do, Your Honor." He rose to his feet. "The whole thrust of the Serpico investigations is to let the public know that this department is going to dig out corruption, and that no one is privileged. If any policeman is accused of wrongdoing, the public deserves that charges be brought to trial."

His mouth moved deliberately and he stood straight with his shoulders erect, slowly and firmly making his points, occasionally bobbing his head rhythmically for emphasis or looking my way with a sarcastic flip of an eyebrow. He was a tall man of limber form, no doubt an agile tennis player, with blue eyes as clear as stained glass that shifted from the frisky friendly gaze of a fraternity boy when looking at the judge to flashes of cold ice when confronting the defense. His hair was ashen, combed straight and short. The nose was sharp, narrow-bridged, and short, curving down over his tight lips, adding a measure of determination to his face.

He continued his argument. "I don't think any

charges against a cop should be swept under the rug. No wrongdoings should be dealt with in the dark. That's the trouble with this city. Police have come to feel beyond the reach of the laws themselves. If there are any faults in the testimony of the accuser, it is up to this court to weigh and make judgment."

I whispered again to Anthony. "I don't think the motion is going to make it."

"And if it may, Your Honor." His tone became sarcastically biting. "The defense refers to the danger of accepting the word of an informer who stands to gain by falsely accusing a police officer. Strangely, his brief suggests no explanation as to how our witness had anything to gain. If John Tarras had something to gain by speaking out, it's the duty of the defense to bring it before the court." He looked challengingly at me. All I could do was stare back in silence.

"Thank you, Mr. Colby." The judge slid his hands together with a quick move, suggesting his mind had been made up a long time ago. Half rising in the bench, his brow furrowed as his eyes peered my way, pulling in his chin to emphasize the weight of his words. "I shall judge on the merits of the evidence the issue of guilt or innocence. This matter will proceed to trial. The motion is denied. Do you have an opening statement, Mr. Colby."

"A brief one, Your Honor." He put one hand on the end of the table, acting smoothly steady. "We will show here that Anthony Sorrentino while in the performance of a public trust did wrongfully and unlawfully accept a bribe and did commit further unlawful acts of conspiracy to commit bribery. For this we ask a verdict of guilty."

Colby then turned to call John Tarras to the stand. Sworn in by the bailiff, the short dark man sat with his knees angled outward, his hands on his thighs, and his eyes directed unswervingly at the prosecutor.

"Mr. Tarras, on May 1, 1967, did the then police

officer Anthony Sorrentino come to your house with a warrant?"

"Yes."

"Do you remember what time that was?"

"I remember it was one-thirty, because I had to make a call that afternoon and was keeping an eye on the clock."

"When you were brought back to the police station under arrest, did something unusual happen?"

"One of the cops asked me to go with him." His mouth twisted around the word "cops." He took me into the bathroom and he asked if I wanted to copy the plays."

"Did he mention a price?"

"He said he wanted whatever I had in my pockets. He knew I carried a lot of cash because of my business."

Anthony's body next to me was tensing and tightening, making his chair squeak. His hands clenched and unclenched. Though he had heard the story before, he could not keep from reacting angrily. I was writing quickly in my note pad, trying to catch all the testimony.

"What time did this take place?"

"The trip to the bathroom?"

"Yes."

"Three o'clock in the afternoon, I'd say. It didn't take long. I gave him two hundred dollars. All I had in my wallet."

"You indicated he said he would allow you to copy the numbers. Did you do it there in the bathroom?"

"No, he set up a meeting place with me the next morning after court."

"The former policeman who took you in the bathroom of the 43rd Precinct, and to whom you handed over your money, is that man in court today?"

"Yes, he is," he said in an even voice, and then rotated his head toward Anthony. "He's the one in the blue suit over there."

Anthony's face turned red and his knees bumped together as he looked piercingly at his accuser and steadied himself with considerable effort. I felt a disturbed jab in my own gut sensing an unshakable rivet was being bolted into our side. It all sounded so clear and simple, so convincing, so unmistakable, an account of what happened between two men standing inches apart in a sneaky place.

We broke for lunch at noon. Anthony and I walked a few blocks to a sandwich shop, taking a table near a beak-nosed redhead cashier. I picked up a newspaper left on the table and opened it to banner headlines about a teacher being assaulted. Below was a picture of an attractive young blond teacher who had been savagely raped in Central Park. I breezed through the story, thinking about how the public needed a cop like Anthony out there and what a waste of the taxpayers' money it was to be going through this trial. "He was rehearsed letter-perfect." I looked over at my brother. "The whole testimony has been drilled. He's been coached to know all the little details to give his story credibility. Notice how five years after the arrest he has all the times down perfect."

"But he's contradicted things he said at the first trial."

"We'll take care of that on cross-exam."

After lunch we returned to the hall outside the court and waited for the trial to reconvene. I watched the Internal Affairs man leaning against the wall staring out a nearby window, saying nothing until Colby came up to him and he perked up and his mouth jumped into a spirited murmur. It made me feel I was being ganged by a team of two minds in concert with all the resources of Internal Affairs. Shortly, the doors were opened by the bailiff and we returned to our places at the counsel table. Tarras took the stand again.

"On the following morning"—Colby's pale lips twirled up at the corners—"did you get into a car with Sorrentino?"

"Objection." I leaped up. "The prosecutor is leading the witness."

"Strike the question. What happened, Mr. Tarras, on the morning of May second?"

"After court I went out to the parking lot where I got into Sorrentino's car, a black Ford, 1961 or '62 model. We pulled away fast. I remember Sorrentino wanted to get out of there."

"Out of where?"

"Out of the court parking lot. I guess there were a lot of judges around there."

"And did he take you to Mosk's Fruit Market on Terminal Street?"

"Objection." I jumped up. "He's leading the witness again."

"I'm just trying to save the court time."

"Follow the law," I bristled at him.

"Don't advise me on the law."

"Gentlemen!" The judge beckoned us to the bench. "I don't want any more of these outbursts."

Colby resumed questioning. "After you left the parking lot, where did you go?"

"We drove to a parking spot down the block from Mosk's Fruit Market on Terminal Street. I could see the guys working with the hand trucks, bringing in the crates of lettuce and potatoes. They were wearing those high rubber boots like when you go in a freezer."

"Where were you sitting in the car?"

"I was up front next to Sorrentino."

"Can you recall the time of day you stopped on Terminal Street?"

"Yeah, it was eleven o'clock. I know because I looked at the clock leaving court. It might have been ten minutes after or something like that."

I pursed my lips in annoyed distaste knowing his

marvelous memory must have been the result of frequent rehearsals.

"Backing up a moment. When you were in court that morning, what took place?"

"I was arraigned on the charges of the arrest."

"And then you went to the fruit market."

"We weren't exactly out front of the market. We parked down the block a ways. No one was around. Those are warehouses there. No one lives there."

"What happened in the car?"

"Sorrentino had a manila envelope with him. I think he called it the evidence voucher. Inside were all the gambling slips he had taken from my place. He handed me this voucher and let me start copying the slips. He even gave me a pen, a ball-point, the cheap kind, a Bic, the yellow one."

I saw a furious redness suffuse Anthony's face and he pressed a hand frustratedly against the table.

"Do you recall how long it took for you to copy the slips?"

"Four hours. There were a helluva lot of plays. Around ten thousand. My hand cramped from all the writing."

"What happened after you copied the slips?"

"Sorrentino asked me if I wanted to go on the pad."

"For the record would you explain what he meant by pad?"

"He was going to protect my operation, let me take action from the streets and not arrest me. He was after a monthly payoff." Tarras smacked his lips and sucked his upper gums, removing a bit of lunch. "He asked for more money on the spot. Called it goodwill or good-faith money. I gave him another four hundred bucks, cleaning out my wallet, and he stuffed it in his pocket."

"And did you have any further meetings with him?"

"Yeah, I met him again to work out details. How much it was gonna be." His eyes flicked to a memory screen. "We met at ten o'clock the next morning, May third, in front of the Amsterdam Avenue subway station. I got in the car and we drove to the upper Bronx, away from the neighborhood. Sorrentino wanted twenty-five hundred dollars. He said he'd put me out of business if I didn't come up with it. This was for the month, twenty-five hundred dollars, payable on the first of the month like rent."

"You talked with him about a drop in Jersey, another time, didn't you?"

"Objection, Your Honor." I swiftly rose. "Mr. Colby is assuming facts not in evidence, and is once again leading the witness."

"I'll rephrase it in a general way. Mr. Tarras, did you have a subsequent meeting with the defendant?"

"Yeah, on May eighth. We met at the Burger's Nest, a coffee shop on One Hundred Thirty-fourth Street. I got into his car and we went across the tunnel to Jersey and came back, talking in the car. The drop place was gonna be an abandoned tenement building on Grand Avenue."

Colby proceeded to go over the same line of questioning with a little variation, repeating over and over again the same incriminating facts, and he then got Tarras to say that he was bringing these accusations against Sorrentino in an effort to be cooperative with law enforcement and that he had nothing to gain by these accusations. The prosecutor stressed this spirit of cooperation. Tarras remained on the stand for the rest of the day for direct examination. Finally Colby's body sagged out of its intensity as the judge interrupted him to say that court was adjourned until the next morning. Colby swung his arm back over his chair, dropping his pencil, wearily relaxed.

Later that night, for perhaps the twelfth time, I began going over the transcript of the first trial. I had papers, notes, and photocopy sheets spread out on a coffee table and on the bed. I was writing down some ideas when Ernie came into the room. He was ready for bed. Looking at the materials all over the bed, he looked at me with a faint, puzzled smile. "What is all this stuff?"

"Mainly records from the first trial."

"All this?" He examined a stack of papers the size of laundry slips.

"Those are copies of the numbers plays, the ones Tony cought Tarras with."

On one of the sheets in Ernie's hand was a list of handwritten names, each followed by a four-digit number. "Names and numbers. You'd never guess a list like this could cause so much trouble."

"Right."

"What are you doing with these?"

"I just look them over."

"What for?"

"I don't know, really. Probably no good reason. It's just that when I go in there, I want to know as much as possible about the case. And all this stuff is part of the case."

"Well, I'll tell you the truth, Joe, it makes me glad I decided to become a recording artist."

"Right now, if I could sing, I'd join your band."

CHAPTER EIGHTEEN

Vivid splashes of morning sunlight filling the room woke me before the alarm clock on the dresser. Opening the window, I drew in a deep breath of fresh air, knowing I had a difficult day ahead of me. For a few moments I remained motionless with my eyes closed, drawing in breezes rippling across the curtains. Stretching my legs to the floor, I sat on the edge of the bed and rubbed my eyes with my hands, regretting the long hours of grinding with the transcripts and notes and missing vital sleep. I could have used another cup of coffee to spark and charge my body, but the idea of another drop of that black poison made me wince. I could be puritanical about touching harmful foods, but in times of stress or when confined for long times in a tight space, the munchies overwhelmed me, and I devoured mounds of cookies and ham sandwiches and downed pots of coffee. The transcript and notes and scraps of paper were scattered all over the floor and bed and unwashed coffee cups and saucers bearing gritty dark stains and junk-food wrappers were left in a chaos everywhere. Mom would react with a critical remark to herself but would not say anything to me until the right moment, when serious things were out of the way. I knew she felt no burden of crisis justified not taking the time to leave a room neat.

Mom and Dad said they wanted to come along to court. My sister Madeline acted as a baby-sitter so that

Theresa could also join us. I wasn't pleased with their insistence on being spectators. I knew it was going to place an added pressure having them watching me conduct the defense. We arrived at court at nine o'clock and the early sun was shining through the window on one side but still blacked by shadows on the other. We drove into the parking lot and parked in an open space next to where Colby was exiting his car, dressed in a conservative Brooks Brothers-looking suit with a button-down shirt and slim striped tie. I spotted the silently quiet presence of the Internal Affairs agent moving at his side, the two of them smiling about something. I felt an odd intuition, judging from their overly pleased looks, that we were in for a surprise. Shortly after nine-thirty the bailiff announced that court was in session. I relaxed a little while the judge made his way through the space up to the bench. He looked down at some materials in front of him and breathed deeply through his wide mouth with an air of putting aside preliminaries and getting down to business. Once again John Tarras was sworn in as a witness.

"Yesterday, Mr. Tarras"—Colby leaned forward—"you indicated you rode to Jersey with Sorrentino working out details of the pad. Is there anything that stands out in your memory about the ride?"

"Yeah, when he paid the attendant at the Lincoln Tunnel, he kept his face sideways when he took out his wallet. He held it that way, getting his change like he didn't want anyone being able to identify him. That really stuck out."

He continued to testify on details of the alleged four meetings with Anthony. He spoke very quickly at times and at one point there was a flaw in something he stated, and I mulled over it to myself but in the rush of words I couldn't pin it down and let it go by in the record. He was cutting Anthony up into saturated pieces of guilt, portraying him as a crook with precise facts and convincing details. I was feeling an accumulated burden of damaging proof burying us where we sat. I was trying to read the judge's state of mind, guessing at this stage he was sure Anthony was a guilty man. When Colby finished his direct examination, the judge turned toward me. "Will there be cross-examination of the witness?"

I heaved myself up. "Your Honor, we have no questions at this time, but we reserve the right to cross-examine later." Slipping back into my chair, I found Anthony staring with astonishment.

"What the hell is going on?" he whispered with a sense of urgency.

Dad leaned over the railing, putting his head between us. "Aren't you gonna take that crumb apart?"

"I hope so, but I'm not ready yet," I said flatly.

Court adjourned and we drove back to Brooklyn with everyone in the car confused and baffled on why I had not immediately lighted into Tarras on cross-examination to discredit him. I did not go into my reasons with them, but I was certainly not going to pass up my chance to go after Tarras with effectively sharp questions to tear his story to pieces. Shortly after we were back at the house, Mom told me that Sherrill was on the phone.

"Hey, how are you doing?" I said, feeling a lift in hearing her voice.

"The question is how are you doing? But even that is not the main question."

"Oh? So tell me what the main question is."

"Well, you see, Dr. Blanton told me today it will take him a week or so to read those two new papers, and so—"

"The answer is yes," I said excitedly.

"I haven't asked the question yet."

"The question is, Do I want you to come to New York for a few days."

"Wrong, the question is, Will you let me come to New York for a few days."

"Stop nit-picking. The answer's the same."

"I thought I'd take a night flight and get there Saturday morning."

"Great! I won't be in court so I can meet you." I sighed a deep breath. "God, I've missed you."

"I know the feeling. Your mother said things were going well."

"She said that?" I raised my brows skeptically.

"Aren't they?"

"Tarras was a damned good witness. He really chopped us bad. And I'm not sure how we can get to him. The prosecutor keeps asking, 'What was his motive?' and all I can do is change the subject or stay mute."

"Are you really worried?"

"Well, I'm hoping we'll come out okay, that is if Colby doesn't throw any big surprises at us."

The next morning, with a studied casualness, Colby rose from his chair and turned toward the back of the courtroom and looked ahead once again, pausing dramatically. "Your Honor, the prosecution calls Mrs. Mildred Tarras."

The name hit us like a lightning bolt. For a moment we were both speechless, disbelieving what our eyes were telling us was happening. Anthony bridled. "Did you know about this?"

"How could I know about it?" I whispered back to him as I rose to my feet. "Your Honor, I object. This witness invoked marital privilege in the first hearing and did not testify."

"There is no barrier to Mrs. Tarras waiving that privilege in this new proceeding."

"Your Honor, I received no notice of this development until this moment." I felt Anthony's hand lightly jostling the side of my suit coat. I glanced down at him.

"Let her testify. We have nothing to hide."

"No, she can't pull this stuff."

"Your Honor, the purpose of this proceeding is truth." Colby raised his voice.

"And fairness," I snapped back, eyeing him hotly.

"She can testify," Colby shouted.

"I object." I wasn't sure of my grounds or the strength of my argument, but it was a lawyer's instinct to object when faced with a damaging flanking movement against him.

The judge stepped down from the bench inviting the two lawyers into chambers. The room behind the clerk's desk led to chambers which were not surprisingly unelaborate but rather plain and functional with shelves of lawbooks and a worn leather chair and a desk that looked shuttled out of classroom, the only object of indulgence a little white portable TV set.

"Sit down, counselors." He wheeled around in the chair. "Mr. Sorrentino, I understand your personal involvement in this matter. I know you are defending your brother. I appreciate your intensity, but you must keep within the bounds of court decorum and restraint."

"Yes, Your Honor."

"Now let's get to the issue of Mrs. Tarras taking the stand."

I took my time preparing my argument, pretending not to hear while my mind raced ahead to absorb all the strategic meaning of this question. Even if I could prevail on my objection, which I strongly doubted, and I knew it would upset my brother, I wasn't sure of the wisdom of keeping Mrs. Tarras off the stand since it would leave the record open to faultfinding by the press even if we won. The last thing I wanted was some reporter screaming that the reason Sorrentino was put back on the force was not because of his innocence but because his attorney injected a technicality to bar a key witness from testifying. Technical objections were also not lost on a judge or jury in reaching a verdict. I decided to withdraw it.

* * *

Six years older than her husband at thirty-nine, Mrs. Tarras was a woman of attractive features, her hair black with highlights, her dark-skinned face pink-toned on the cheeks from cosmetics, her hazel eyes shaded by long, natural lashes, a nice but mildly nervous smile on her face glancing up at the judge. She was dressed in a subdued brown knit suit with the sleeves of her blouse over delicately boned hands and the hem of her skirt down to the ankles of her slim legs. She raised her right hand, facing the clerk for the oath.

"Do you solemnly swear that the testimony you are about to give in this matter is the truth, the whole truth, and nothing but the truth?"

"I do."

"Be seated please. Please give your full name and address."

"I am Mildred Tarras, and I live at Fourteen Thirty-seven Daymin." She leaned back comfortably against the chair clasping her hands.

Colby took over. "Are you the wife of John Tarras who has testified in this hearing?"

"Yes sir, I am."

"To clarify a point, would you tell this court why you did not testify at the previous hearing."

"John didn't want me to get involved. He said these things are not pleasant, they could get nasty."

"So your husband was trying to protect you from what could have been a harsh experience."

"And someone had to take care of the store. If both of us were in court every day, no one would be at the store."

"You and your husband run a grocery store?"

"Yes. John does it full-time now; he no longer has anything to do with gambling or policy things."

"Objection!" I called out. "Not responsive, no question pending. I will ask that her answer be stricken after the word 'Yes.'"

"Sustained. It will be deleted," the judge barked.

"Mrs. Tarras, to your knowledge does your husband have any connection with the policy game at this time?"

"None. He's only in the store now."

"What do you sell in the store?"

"Irrelevant and immaterial," I snapped. "I will stipulate it is a grocery store, and that it sells what its name suggests."

"Mrs. Tarras, in addition to the time you put in at the grocery store, do you also do the housework around the apartment?"

"Yes."

"You do the cleaning?"

"Yes."

"And the cooking?"

"Yes, and I love to bake." Her face brightened with a smile.

"What types of things do you make?"

"Objection. I don't see the relevancy of this line of questioning."

"Your Honor, it's simply for background. I'm trying to show the type of person Mrs. Tarras is by her activities."

"Overruled. She can answer the question."

"I love to bake breads. I make all my own breads. John's favorite is corn bread."

Colby was piling on points with this line of questioning, making her appear as a guileless, humble housewife. Her demeanor was thoroughly composed. Colby shifted on his feet. "Mrs. Tarras, I'd like you to think back to the day of May first, 1967. Do you remember that day?"

"Yes, sir, very vividly. I can never forget it."

"Why is that?"

"Because it was my birthday and . . ." She paused. "My husband was arrested."

"Do you remember what time he was arrested?"

"I was watching a game show on TV, and it came on at one. I'd say about one-twenty."

"Is the officer who appeared with a warrant here in the courtroom?"

"Yes, sir. That's him." She pointed at Anthony.

"What happened when he arrived?"

"He came in and said we were under arrest."

"Both of you?"

"That's what he said at first. Then John begged him and said I didn't have anything to do with his operation, and knew nothing about it."

"Was that true, Mrs. Tarras?"

"Yes, sir." She came across with a gentle sincere voice. "I mean, I suspected John was involved in something but I never knew what."

"How is it that you didn't know?"

"John insisted that I shouldn't know anything about it. He had six phone lines coming into the apartment, but he told me never to answer five of them. They were for his business. He wouldn't go into it with me."

"I see. So did Sorrentino arrest you?"

"No. He finally took John's word that I knew nothing about it."

I could hear my own breaths blowing through my lips nervously. I turned to Anthony. "Is that true, what she said?"

"Yes."

Colby noted our heads together almost with a jeering note in his eyes. He turned back to his witness. "After Sorrentino took your husband away, what did you do?"

"First I made calls to my brothers to see about raising bail for John. Then I went over to the station house myself."

"Did the police let you see your husband?"

"They were very nice, especially Sorrentino."

Colby braced his hands on his hips. "What did he do that was so nice?"

"John had told him it was my birthday, so he had bought a little cupcake and stuck a candle in it. We all laughed about it, but I thought it was a nice gesture. Cops usually don't go out of their way like that."

"So Sorrentino was very friendly to you?"

"Very. When we were alone, I commented on that to John. And John said he had reason to be nice, that he'd taken everything in John's wallet, and he showed me the empty wallet."

"Objection, hearsay," I shouted.

"It should come in," he lashed back. "There's an opportunity for confrontation and cross-examination, both parties are in court. Mrs. Tarras was a percipient witness to the empty wallet. It was a spontaneous declaration. It certainly has circumstantial value at least."

"Overruled. The rules of evidence will be liberally construed in this forum to admit all relevant facts."

Colby bared his teeth triumphantly. "Will you repeat your husband's exact words?"

"He said Sorrentino had reason to be nice, that he'd taken everything in John's wallet."

Anthony's eyes went up at her and his lips tightened and he simply shook his head. I had my left fist pumping into my grimacing face and my right hand writing down her testimony. I could feel the weight of the evidence building against us. Her every word was a killing indictment.

"Was there any other occasion when you saw Sorrentino?"

"Yes, sir, the next morning." She nodded. "It was after John's arraignment. We were out in the parking lot and he came up to us and asked if John was ready."

"Then what happened?"

"I saw John get into this car, a black one, and they pulled out. I didn't see John until late that afternoon. He was very upset. He said Sorrentino wanted money every month, or he'd make a lot of trouble for us."

Anthony's eyes were blinking attentively but his body was tensing and I could feel the anger gripping inside of him. He finally dipped his head slightly front of my shoulder, and whispered tensely. "Is she convincing anybody with this garbage?"

I swallowed grimly. "About as convincing as a nun in church."

All afternoon Colby continued to hammer away and ram every accusing word with corroboration. Speaking slowly and clearly and apparently evoking a sympathetic look from the judge, she was a marvelous witness, beautifully rehearsed, I thought, because I knew she was lying. I still had an unbreakable faith in Anthony's innocence, but I could see the tide running against us so heavily it seemed it could not be overcome.

When court adjourned, I was almost afraid to look at the faces of the family. I stole a glance at Anthony and found him momentarily silent and grim, but he bounced out of it when Theresa came over to us. Tensions and doubts had to be plaguing him. Mrs. Tarras had confirmed virtually every point her husband had made on the stand. The momentum was devastatingly moving with the prosecution. Coming off as the sheltered housewife, she had been brutally damaging. I put my notes back in my briefcase and fumbled with the clasp, having a hard time getting it to stay closed. I told myself that I should have been alerted to this development by the elusive wiles of Colby. I should have known that he was going to pull something like this on us. I should have been prepared for it. Homework for a trial lawyer is being prepared for every damaging turn a trial might take, and being ready to deal with it. At least I would have a night to think over how to handle her. There was an inconsistency there. She didn't testify before and I thought her explanation on why not was weak, but somehow in balancing the two things, the inconsistency versus the impact of her testimony, it was clear what she was saying was going to have greater weight. Throughout this case she had been looming like a dark-horse threat, the prosecution's secret weapon to tilt the scales, making it a two-on-one game.

I was thinking to myself as we walked out to the parking lot. I kept my vision straight ahead but out of the corner of my eye I could pick up Colby talking to the Internal Affairs agent by his car. Their voices dropped to a whisper when they saw us approach. I knew we had been badly stung by them, and the only question was what I was going to do about it. I opened the back door to let Mom and Dad in Anthony's car and I was surprised by the expression on Dad's face which showed none of the worries and concerns I was feeling. The impact of Mrs. Tarras's testimony had not registered with him. While Anthony went around to the driver's side, I let Theresa in on my side and then got in myself. Anthony's head bobbed, agitated, as we pulled out of the lot. "That woman is some actress! What an actress! She was lying through the teeth."

"I know that," I said. "But she was one helluva witness."

"What are you going to do?" Dad said quietly.

"I'm not sure."

"I don't understand why she did so much damage." Theresa glanced at me. "She only repeated the lies that Tarras himself has been telling all along."

"Right!" Mom injected.

"No, it's different now. Everything's changed."

"A woman lies, and everything's changed." Dad's voice rose annoyedly.

"That's right! Because up to now my whole case was based on putting Tony's word up against Tarras's. Now there are two people against one."

"It's simple." Dad pressed forward against the front backrest. "You gotta make 'em understand that she's lying."

"Oh, I don't know why I didn't think of that," I replied a touch sarcastically.

"You're supposed to be a lawyer." He wore a steely glare.

"I'm a good lawyer."

"That's what you tell me," Dad snapped.

"Okay, Dad," Anthony intervened. "Let's not argue again."

"Well, what's a good lawyer if he lets her get away with lies?"

"I haven't let her get away with anything yet. I'm going to cross-examine her tomorrow."

"And you say you don't know what you're gonna do!"

"I might do better if I got a little support from you, Dad."

"Now I'm the one to blame."

"Yeah," I hollered. "It just might make a difference to get some support from you for once in my life."

"You think I never supported you, Joe?" His temper flared back. "You think I never got out of bed to come down to the police station because you'd been fighting? You don't think that's support?"

"Whenever I did something wrong."

"That's the way it was!"

"That's not the way it was! Not always, Dad! Criticism, mistrust, discouragement, that's what I got! Exactly the same as today!"

"And what I got was disappointment! Tell me about that, Mr. Big Shot Lawyer!"

Everyone had been galvanized by the exchange, not interfering, until Mom spoke up. "I want you both to stop now. Please."

When we pulled up to the house, I got out quickly and went up to my room. I was suddenly overcome with weariness, feeling the heat along with the drain of all the bad events of the day. I was deeply upset. I had to face the possibility that we could lose. I had to ready myself for it. I tried to take a nap but I lay there thinking about the next day. I lay there for a long time staring blankly at the ceiling, seemingly unthinking, if viewed, but my head was racing and speeding like a rewind button or a fast-forward track on a tape player. Restless, I popped up and grabbed my court notes out of my briefcase and burned my concentration into them again. In my intensity I was barely aware but not oblivious to the moon gradually peeking in the window and bringing a silver light that seemed to cool the scorching hot air. From time to time I would push the stack of notes away from me, and reluctantly, as if defying a guilt compulsion, get up to listen to a few minutes of the news. It was sometimes hard to know if I was doing more harm than good by incessantly grinding away without taking time out for a breather to clear my mind. I looked out the window at the glimmers of fireflies appearing in almost a Big Dipper line of flickers. I turned my eyes up to the night heavens not too educated to hope God was reading my mind's plea for a change in the way things were breaking on my trip here. The facts were so clear, preponderant, and overwhelming as to leave no doubt in the judge's mind. The greatest legal minds can do nothing against facts. I had to find some weakness in the facts, some toehold or crack to burrow into and gain a defense footing.

Ernie walked into the room rather casually and plopped down on the bed. "So how are things with you, Joe?"

I snickered at the absurdity of the question. "Ernie, leave me the hell alone, will you? I got a lot of things on my head."

"Mom told me what happened today."

"Yeah, Colby dropped a bombshell on us."

"I mean about Dad."

"I can't deal with him. I got a fire in my hands and he throws kerosene on it."

"I came here to tell you something."

"Make it fast. I gotta get this cross-examination ready."

"I want to tell you something about Dad."

"Look, I have been jumpy about this trial. That's all that was in the car with us. It's no big deal."

"Bull!" he said strongly. "It's a big deal to both of you."

"You said you wanted to tell me something about him. He's all right, isn't he?"

"He could lift a bridge if you gave him a place to stand."

"Then what is it?"

"One night about a year ago I was talking to Mom. She's always felt she could talk with me, you know."

"Okay?" I said. "And?"

"Well, I said it really didn't make sense to me. That Dad should be proud of you, the way you turned your life around. And she said I didn't understand about Dad and his clarinet."

"His clarinet!"

"He was good, Joe. I remember him playing when I was little. He was still dynamite."

"Sure he was good."

"Well, there were these two other guys he was playing in the band with who decided to go out to Hollywood and really try for the big time. One of them had some bookings, and he thought they could get work. So Dad decided to go with them."

"So why didn't he?"

"You."

"And what the hell does that mean?"

"Mom was gonna take Tony and live with her folks while Dad was gone. Then she found out she was pregnant. There just wasn't room there for two kids."

"So Dad didn't go."

"I mean, whatever else he is, you know his sense of responsibility, Joe. He figured he had no choice. He had to stay here and take care of his family, which meant working on a garbage truck."

"I thought it was the Depression. I always thought it was the Depression that killed his dreams and made him run for security."

"I'm sure it was the main factor."

"But what are you saying, he also blames me? He became upset with me for being born at the wrong time?"

"Joe, you're smarter than me. The Depression ruined thousands of hopes and dreams, but it doesn't live with you as a reminder. You were part of that whole chain of events. I know it sounds crazy but you're a reminder to him every day. He gave up most of the joy in his life. That's gotta make a guy angry inside, don't it? And doesn't that have to come out some way?"

"Against me?"

"It was probably a vicious circle. The way he was that had to make you depend on your friends in the streets and look up to this guy Tony Bavimo. And the more you disappointed him, the worse everything got."

I paused for a long minute. "Why didn't Mom tell me those things?"

"How could she? She told me not to tell you, but she should know me better than that."

"I've kept thinking all these years, I could prove myself to him, show him I'm worth something."

"He knows that! He loves you, Joe, I'm sure of that. God, he moved the family away from Little Italy to try to save you. He dragged you out of a pool hall because he cared. It's just that he's built this damned wall."

"You know, when I was about eight years old," I thought back quietly, "he and I went to a public swimming pool and it was just him and me. We had a great fun time. After we showered and were ready to leave, he combed my hair for me, kneeling down and doing it with such care, wetting it and slicing a part straight down my hair like his own. And all of a sudden he gave me a hug and he kissed my cheek. He said, 'It's been a wonderful day, Joey.'" I paused. "It was the last time he ever called me Joey. I know it's the last time he showed me any affection."

CHAPTER
NINETEEN

A good lawyer once said that the object of cross-examination was to let the witness bring his hands up around his own throat and let him poke and press and tighten his fingers until he strangled himself by his own words. I was up early the next morning before court preparing the questions that I hoped would lead to the self-strangulation of Mr. and Mrs. Tarras. I had been over the testimony countless times, but I went through the trial notes one more time, hoping that I would not miss any critical points in the interlocking links of evidence. If there was a time to reverse the momentum in the trial, this opportunity to cross-examine the couple was going to be it. I had a plan of questioning mapped out and I was going to stick to it undeviatingly so that I remained in control. The chief aim of my strategy was to chop away all credibility in the people accusing my brother. While I put the final touches on my line of questions I realized that it was going to be difficult to trip up witnesses so obviously well rehearsed and composed on the stand.

Because I had a stop to make at the law library I grabbed a cab instead of driving with my brother and the others to court. Though we had started out at different times all of us arrived at court at the same time and I waited on the steps out front to go in the building with them. It was a balmy, breezy, sunny day.

"Good morning," I greeted as they came up to me.
"Did you get what you needed at the library?" Theresa asked.

"I don't really know what it is I need," I shrugged.

Dad faced me and a beat passed with neither of us speaking, but while I sensed no warmth, I didn't sense any hostility. His face softened. "You feeling okay?"

"Fine. Why?"

"It's gonna be a tough day, isn't it?"

"Probably is."

"Yeah, probably so." He nodded. "You question them today, don't you?"

"We begin cross-exam today, right."

"Well, I hope you cook them in chili sauce."

As we entered the courtroom, I glanced to my left at the group of people around the prosecutor, their faces smoothly framed in contented smiles. I unsnapped my briefcase and spread out the sheaf of notes I had made, staying up into the early morning. I watched Mildred Tarras, wearing another modest, conservative outfit, again demurely stroll up to her husband, confidently waiting to be called to the witness stand. Colby had his back against his chair, loosely relaxed, sensing he had piled up an unbeatable lead. He folded his hands under his chin, waiting for trial to get under way. Absorbed in my preparation, I hardly noticed Mrs. Tarras take out a small note pad and a ball-point and write something which she handed to her husband who read it and looked our way smiling. He then looked back at her big smile, the two of them sharing a private joke. Their cute, sardonic action grated on my nerves, but something was breaking through to my awareness precipitated by Mrs. Tarras writing out the note and it was hitting me with astonishing force and clarity. With my eyes sharpened in concentration, weighing the idea that had come into my head, I was startled when the bailiff shouted, "All rise."

All parties in the courtroom rose and waited for the judge to take the bench before being seated again. His robe billowed as he swung in his chair to look down at me. "Mr. Sorrentino, do you wish to proceed with cross-examination of the previous witness?"

I heaved myself up. "I do, Your Honor, but first, I would like to request a ten minute recess."

"For what purpose?" The judge appeared startled, as did Colby, leaping to his feet, and everyone else in court.

I stammered, "To, ah, confer with my client."

"Why didn't you confer with your client before we started?"

"It's something that's just come up, Your Honor. I think it's important."

The judge pondered for a long moment. "Very well. We'll stand in recess for ten minutes." He got up and went back into chambers.

I scampered out hastily to the corridor with Anthony following me, looking bewildered. We went into a small conference room provided for attorneys. I sat down at a table and scooped my hands into my briefcase, pulling out stacks of paper. My brother sat silently baffled, watching me dig eagerly and scavenge among the papers.

"What is it you need to talk to me about?" he asked.

"I don't need to talk to you. Just relax for ten minutes."

"You told the judge . . ."

"I couldn't very well tell him I needed ten minutes to dig around in my briefcase." I went through the papers not explaining what I had specifically in mind to Anthony but murmuring little grunts of satisfaction to myself as I set aside sheet after sheet that had been the object of my search.

"What are you trying to do, Joe?" Anthony asked.

"I'm trying to find a way to undo some of the damage she did."

Back in court, I put aside the papers I collected, keeping them in view for a special purpose in my cross-examination of Mildred Tarras. She was sworn in, and I began my questioning.

"Mrs. Tarras, you testified that it was your birthday on May first, 1967."

"Yes, I turned thirty-four on that day. I noticed my first gray hair in the mirror."

"Isn't it true that when Sorrentino picked up a little cupcake for you, a Hostess Twinkie I believe, out of courtesy he also stuck a candle in it for you, and even sang a line of 'Happy Birthday'?"

"I object." Colby bolted to his feet. "This line of questioning is not only irrelevant and immaterial, it is a frivolous waste of court time."

The judge dropped his head, pointing a reproving finger at me. "Where does this lead?"

"Your Honor, I think this has some bearing and it will only take a minute."

"Hurry it up, counsel."

"And didn't he buy sandwiches for dinner for you and your husband, to be nice?"

"I object," Colby shouted irately. "I don't see what Sorrentino's singing and sandwiches have to do with any material issue in this trial."

"Let her answer." I shot a glare at him. "We heard her version of cooking corn bread." I turned to her. "Isn't it true he got dinner for you and the birthday cupcake?"

"I think so."

"He showed you some decency?"

"Your Honor," Colby said with disdain, "will counsel please get on with the issues instead of this cupcake nonsense."

"Yes, he did, but John said—"

"Please only answer my question. He showed you some decency?"

"Yes."

"Mrs. Tarras, isn't it true that before the first trial on this issue, you were questioned by Captain Timmons and told him you knew nothing of the allegations being made by your husband against Anthony Sorrentino?"

"I don't understand the question."

"Could you rephrase the question, counsel?" The

judge flicked his brows at me. "It is rather cumbrous."

"Mrs. Tarras, did you have a meeting with Captain Timmons at police headquarters on October seventeenth of last year?"

"Yes, I recall sitting with him for a short time."

"And isn't it true that at that meeting you told him you had no knowledge of what your husband was accusing Sorrentino of?"

"I was afraid to get involved."

"Afraid of the truth?"

"No."

"Answer the question, please. You told Timmons you didn't know anything?"

"I did because I didn't want to testify."

"The truth is you really didn't know anything?"

"The question has been asked and answered," Colby steamed. "He's bickering with the witness. This is argumentative."

"The point is well taken." The judge rubbed a finger on his cheek. "You must refrain from bickering with the witness, engaging the witness in clashes and conflict. Restrict yourself to asking a question."

"Mrs. Tarras, how much time did you spend at the police station on May first, 1967?"

She looked over nervously at her husband and Colby before answering. "I can't give a definite amount of time, only an approximate amount of time. An hour, I'd say."

"Mrs. Tarras, you have testified that you have never had any active involvement in your husband's syndicate business, isn't that right?"

"Yes, he kept me away from it."

"To protect you, right?" I said sarcastically.

"Yes."

"The six phone lines in the apartment, you never answered five of them, is that correct?"

"Yes. The ones that had to do with John's business I never answered."

"You ever get curious about those phones ringing all the time?"

"Of course."

"And when John wasn't at home and the phone rang, you ignored them, right?"

"I only answered the phone our friends called us on."

"And the others you let ring until the callers hung up, is that correct?"

"Yes."

"Your Honor, may I approach the witness?"

"For what purpose?"

"I would like to ask her for a sample of her handwriting."

"Objection!" Colby heaved himself up. "Irrelevant."

"Your Honor, I can show relevance in a just a few minutes, maybe. Besides, I'm sure that Mrs. Tarras doesn't mind. After all, she has nothing to hide. She's only a hard-baking American housewife. All she has been trying to do has been to help us get at the truth. Isn't that right, Mrs. Tarras?"

She eyed me warily but maintained her calm poise. "That's what I'm after, yes."

"Then I presume you have no objection to, say, copying a couple of sentences on a legal pad?"

As if calling my bluff, she answered swiftly, "I have no objection at all."

The judge leaned over the bench in my direction. "I don't want you to spend much time on this, Mr. Sorrentino."

"I'll try not to, Your Honor." I went back to my briefcase removing a legal pad and felt-tip pen and handed both of them to her.

"What would you like me to write?"

"Whatever you feel. How about the first couple of lines of 'The Star-Spangled Banner'?" I smiled. "I'm sure we all know it, even if we can't hit the high notes."

Everyone watched us curiously, wondering what the purpose was behind this writing exercise. After she finished writing a few lines, she handed me back the pad. I looked down at it searchingly. "Thank you. You have very attractive handwriting." Without saying anything to the judge, I moved back to my briefcase on the counsel table. I trained my eyes on Mrs. Tarras's eyes, moving around slightly uneasily as she watched me pull a stack of slips out. I compared the sample of her handwriting with the writing on the sheets of paper. I gave a little nod of satisfaction, believing the two were the same. I moved back to confront her on the stand at an arm's length. "Mrs. Tarras, I have here an evidence exhibit with writing on it. Would you please take a look at it?" I handed her one of the slips in the stack. She appeared momentarily stunned, seeing what was on the slip. She shifted a bit in the chair, uncomfortably looking it over.

"Mrs. Tarras, can you tell the court what is on the slip?"

"Some names and numbers."

"Is it your writing?"

"I don't think so."

"Oh, it's not." My mouth dropped in mock bewilderment. "Are you sure?"

"It may be my writing."

"Oh, so you've changed your answer from a definite it's not yours to a possible it may be yours. Will you look closer?"

"Yes, this is my handwriting on the slip."

"But you couldn't recognize it a moment ago when I showed it to you."

"I was nervous."

"What is there to be nervous about some names on a piece of paper."

"I know what this is." She recovered her calm. "These are something I copied for John."

"I thought you never got involved with the syndicate business." My eyes stared. "I thought he kept it away from you to protect you."

"I can explain."

"I don't think anybody would interfere with your right to explain. In fact, I suspect most of us are intensely interested in your explanation. How it happens that an entire page of numbers records were written in your handwriting when you've assured us that you didn't even know what your husband did for a living."

"There's no mystery. It was obviously a unique situation."

"How do you mean?"

"Well, I seem to recall that he was in a hurry, and he asked me to copy some names and numbers on a page for him. But I had no idea what it meant."

"You mean it just happened once?"

"To the best of my memory."

"A unique situation?"

"That's what I've said." Her voice was a bit strained.

"I see." I went back to the counsel table and grabbed my briefcase and resumed my close face-to-face confrontation with her. "I wonder if it was also a unique situation when you copied this page." I took a page out of the case and smacked it down on the armrest of the witness stand. "And this one." I smacked another one down. "And this one." I put an emphatic cadence in my voice. "And this one." I pulled out another. "And this one." I watched her face grow redder and redder with each page. I piled twenty pages of syndicate transactions in front of her, all bearing her handwriting. "Isn't it true, Mrs. Tarras, you were a partner in the syndicate business?"

"That's a lie," she blurted, swishing her black hair back and forth agitatedly.

"And isn't it true, the reason you didn't go along with the false story in the first trial was because you didn't think he'd get away with it?"

"That's not true." She shot a trapped glance at Colby.

"What's true, Mrs. Tarras, that you are a humble housewife with no knowledge of your husband's syndicate activities?"

As the hours wore on, she grew more snappish and contradictory, and it became clear that she had been falsifying and perjuring herself under oath. I walked back to Anthony signaling with a hand gesture that I thought we had chopped down her sweet innocent act. It was a good exchange for us. I was beginning to feel a sense of hope. I could also see in my brother's face that he was feeling good about the way things were turning. I watched her take her seat in the courtroom with an unmasked scowl on her face, smoldering. Her husband seemed filled with bitter disappointment and worry over what had taken place on cross-examination. The Internal Affairs agent gazed around with darkened eyes, hiding whatever emotions were going on inside him, but it was obvious he was not pleased. Colby was furious.

My family was in buoyant spirits as we walked down the corridor for the elevator. My brother Ernie was wearing a happy grin. He wagged his head, laughing. "Did you believe that look on her face when you showed her the slips? I loved it."

"You really shelled her, Joe," Anthony chimed in.

"Hey, you guys, this is premature."

"We know you haven't won it yet."

"All I did was shake her credibility."

Dad, who seemed lifted by events, put in, "And that's not important?"

"Sure, it's important, but it's not what's gonna determine the decision."

"What will, Joe?"

"Same as it's been all along. Tarras's motive. All Colby has to do is keep asking the question: 'Why would Tarras have come forward and volunteered all this information if he were lying?' As long as we can't answer that question, we're in real trouble."

Anthony stopped. "Well, maybe we should just go up to the South Bronx and start walking."

"I wish I had an idea that made more sense."

CHAPTER TWENTY

The sun rising painted the sky with a streak of scorching red that gradually blossomed into a glowing yellow color as I watched from the observation tower at JFK airport, waiting for United's red-eye Flight 424 from Los Angeles. I was getting rather excited knowing that I would soon be seeing Sherrill after being apart for three months. I moved down to Gate 16 when United's TV monitor for incoming flights blipped the plane's landing. The first-class passengers were the first to disembark and they were met and welcomed good-naturedly by fellow business associates. When the coach section started coming off the emotions grew exuberant. The passengers were waving and smiling and rushing to hug and kiss long-unseen relatives. These reunions at the gate seemed like such a wonderful moment for these people and I was touched by it. I loved being with the crowd gathering to meet relatives and loved ones at the gate of a plane. I felt my heart leap with happiness at the sight of Sherrill hurrying toward me in a black dress that accented her sunlit blond hair and the beautiful sparkle on her face. I rushed to her and swept her in my arms, and we held each other tightly without saying a word.

We picked her luggage off the conveyor belt and walked out to the parking lot. She had her arms wrapped tightly around my arm holding her suitcase. I had held back from telling her my plans for the day because I knew it would make her uneasy. "Sherrill, I'm gonna have to go with Tony to The Bronx today."

"The Bronx?" She reacted with surprise.

"Look, I'll take you to my folks' house. You can have a nice day getting acquainted."

"Right." She nodded blankly.

"And then tonight, we'll go out somewhere for dinner, just the two of us." I could sense her upset. "Hey, it's okay, isn't it?"

"Sure. I'm disappointed and a little scared, I guess."

"They'll love you."

"Promise?"

"I have to do it, Sherrill. We're in real trouble in this hearing. I don't think Tony or my folks honestly realize if we don't come up with a motive then we're going to lose. It's that simple."

She nodded, showing in her expression that she understood my problem. She then made me stop to kiss her in the parking lot.

I dropped her off, picked up Anthony, and then I pulled into the Sunoco gas station around the corner to have the car checked out. I didn't want to get stuck in the South Bronx with a lame car. We pulled out into light traffic until we reached a bottleneck at the Brooklyn Bridge. Heavy trucks inched in front of us, belching smoke, crawling across the bridge in bumper-to-bumper congestion. I leaned over the wheel, craning my neck for a view of Manhattan's skyline and caught chopped-up swaths of it behind the crisscross cables rimming the bridge. Nearing the other side of the East River, I got a better picture with less obstruction. The tenements on the Lower East Side seemed unchanged from the days I passed them riding the train to my various factory jobs. The only noticeable new sight was an increased flock of Jesus Saves signs painted in black and yellow lettering beckoning to souls from the rooftops.

Once we arrived in the South Bronx, there was no mistaking it. Marked off by short square blocks, the six-story tenements, standing shoulder to shoulder, were all darkly discolored, shabby, disintegrating into a shambles of rubble, splintered bricks, and teeming fragments of jagged glass. Openly, on sidewalks and stoops, young Puerto Rican and black teens passed around beer and wine, guzzling or sucking drags from marijuana cigarettes, going into abandoned buildings for the harder stuff, the youngest appearing to be no more than twelve.

It was a volatile breeding ground for crime and violence. No one dared to walk the South Bronx streets at night without a razor or gun to fend off the mugger, murderer, or rapist who might pounce. Virtually every store had steel gates barring the windows, and storekeepers kept guns below the cash register. One store owner alone reported being robbed or burglarized a hundred times. The aggressive savagery was becoming the equivalent of Hobbesian civil war, with each man a predator against his neighbor, a social condition where life is nasty, brutish, and cheap. One addict assassin confessed after his arrest that his going rate to have another person killed was thirty dollars, the price of a morning fix. In another drug-related killing, an old man was found crucified with bullets in the pattern of a cross.

Few cars were visible on the streets, which was not surprising since most drivers were willing to go far out of the way to avoid passing through the South Bronx with its known bands of muggers. I had a certain feeling of uneasiness being in such a hostile and lawless slum where you could be killed casually for the few dollars in your wallet. But I had been here before and didn't feel an excessive degree of self-conscious worry. I had the physical confidence that I could handle myself and with Anthony along I felt an added assurance because of his physical abilities, and even more so from the likely appearance we gave of being cops. No one was going to take us for a pair of well-heeled tourists or a couple of local workingmen coming home from the factory.

The sun, moving higher over the buildings, radiated

a stronger heat. I took in breaths of the hot air, picking up the garbage smells. I braked hard, spying a space between two battered compact cars, and backed up a bit before cutting into the curb. The space proved tighter than I imagined and I had difficulty getting in, my tires badly scraping against the curb, but I finally nudged the car in front enough to make room. Across the street a little woman kept watching us with dark, suspicious eyes that moved back and forth between us.

About five minutes' walk from the car there was a building on the west side of the street, an old brownstone, five stories high, better kept up than most of the buildings on the block, with a freshly painted black fence out front and a fairly clean stoop that faced a fire pump. I felt a strange sensation of spying as I looked up at the apartment Tarras used as headquarters for his syndicate activities. He owned his own house in New Jersey, which is where he returned after business every day. The grocery market the couple owned was a half block away from the building. It was a fairly good-sized store, framed in dairy-white panels inscribed with the name Tarras on the awning and dangling with stalks of little green bananas in the windows.

Anthony led the way inside. He hopped up the creaky stairs, going onto a landing that was filled with the smell of chicken frying and the sweet odor of bananas browning and the strong spice of achiote, that pinkish red spice heavily used in Puerto Rican cooking. We could hear the blaring of acid rock laced with Spanish-speaking programs and conga drums and clashing with the bland, serious conversations of TV soap operas.

We knocked on the door of an apartment marked 5C. The door was opened by an odd-looking man with dark hair of Indian blackness and a blunt nose and fatty bulk and facial skin with hints of puffy damage from too much drinking. He held a cigarette at his hip while he moved back to let us inside. He knew Anthony and took his handshake without much enthusiasm and made his eyes sullen to discourage us as if our visit could not lead to anything good for him.

"I wanna talk to you for a few minutes, Victor."

"I don't know nothing, Tony." He plopped into a cheap, wooden casting-director's chair with his bulk spreading over the edges.

"Don't be negative right away." Anthony sat on the side of the bed in the small flat. "I haven't asked you anything yet."

"On my dead mother, I swear I don't have any information for you."

"This is my brother Joe." He pointed a finger at me. "He's a lawyer in California."

"A long way you come." His eyes squinted through a puff of his cigarette smoke.

"I came for a reason. I'm working to help my brother."

"I hope you don't expect me to help. I can't help anybody. I got my own problems."

"Listen, we just want to find out a few things. You're always home." Anthony got up and moved to the window, glancing down at the street. "You know what goes on on this block. You know when something happens in this building."

"I mind my own business. I don't stick my nose in what goes on with other people. That's their affair. The less you know around here the better."

"But you can't help but know some things," I said.

"I don't wanna know about nothing."

"What kind of trouble was John Tarras having last year? You see him get busted or know about him getting busted on something heavy?"

"Even if I did know, a man doesn't talk. A man doesn't pull that stuff on his neighbor."

"A man doesn't pull weak shit either," I snapped. "This neighbor of yours is a real creep. He's not a man. He pulled some slimy stuff on my brother. You got a wife and kids?"

"No," he said, surprised by my unlawyerlike tone.

"You got a brother."

"I got a sister."

"How would you like it if someone who had troubles tried to put those troubles off on your sister, messed up her life to get out of a bust. That's not being a man. That's what your neighbor pulled."

"I can understand how you feel. Something like that, it's not right. I can dig where you are coming from." He shrugged. "But I don't keep tabs on who the cops are busting. I ain't running a bail bond service. Shit, you see the police and it could be because some chick wasted her man, or some junkie just went plain OD."

"Well, that wasn't too encouraging," I whispered on the landing.

"We're just starting. Most of the time you come up with nothing. A detective doesn't expect to learn anything from almost all the door-to-doors."

On the same level we knocked on a door marked 5B. The black man who came to the door had a frizzy mop of hair that brought to mind a Ziegfield girl. He was wearing a white T-shirt splotched with ink smudges and drops of beer from the bottle of Rheingold beer in his hand. He touched his hand nervously to his lip and arched his eyebrows up when he saw us in his doorway.

"Can we come in?" Anthony asked.

"I'm clean." His response was automatic and took for granted we were a pair of cops.

"This is not official business." Anthony swung inside a sloppy, dish-cluttered kitchen.

"Listen, nobody from the police pays me a social call. You didn't come here to sell me ties."

"We're here to check out something in this building. It's a private matter."

His eyes flickered over at me. "What's that suppose to mean?"

"It means don't get uptight. We're not here to give you a hard time or make trouble for you. We're looking for a little information."

He wiped sweat dribbling down his cheek. "Boy, it's a mother hot day. If I give you information it means trouble for me."

"Maybe you know something about John Tarras. We heard he was in big heat last year."

"Well, you would know better than me, you're the cops."

"We know it but we want to confirm it."

"What you're asking from me is not too cool. It can only bring me trouble to mouth off about Tarras. You wanna make a stoolie out of me. I never been a stoolie and today's not gonna change me."

"Do you know if Tarras was busted on something big last year?"

He wiped his face again. "This damn heat. It's like an oven in this pad." He buried a finger into his nose weighing our question. "No, I don't know about any big arrest."

"You seem worried. You got nothing to worry about. We're not asking you to be a witness. You don't have to sign any statement or come down to the precinct."

"I have nothing to talk to you guys about."

Shortly, we left his apartment and moved to the next apartment on the level but no one was at home so we clambered down to the next level to repeat our door-to-door questioning but we again ran into tight-lipped, suspicious people. No one in the entire building was willing or able to tell us anything.

After lunch we went back to the streets, questioning all kinds of characters, still coming up with nothing. The light was fading rapidly as the sun began to set, coloring the eastern sky a shade of bluish gray while staining the west a glowing rose pink. Up at a stoplight Anthony spotted a man crossing the street he recognized as someone who once worked for Tarras. His name was Hank Diggs and he was a mainline junkie. Excitedly, Anthony plunged into the street, dodging traffic to catch up with him. He felt that since Diggs had worked for Tarras, he would likely know everything that went on. Moving with quick long strides he intercepted Diggs before he stepped into his car. I hurried to come abreast of them. Up close, Diggs was a sallow-skinned man in his mid-thirties, stoop-shouldered and wiry, sporting a drooping stump moustache. He faced us with his head tucked and his hands jammed into his pants pocket, staring at us with a gleam of hostility in his dark eyes. His fast-moving tongue appeared to be as robust as his teeth were tobacco-stained and decaying.

"You remember me, Diggs, I'm Tony Sorrentino." Anthony's tone was low-key friendly.

"I remember ya," he snapped with sullen lips.

"Listen, I need some information?"

"What sort of information?" He spoke tonelessly.

"I understand John Tarras was in some heavy trouble with the law last year. I'd like to know more."

"I'll bet you would." He creased a humorless smile.

"You don't have to come to the station."

"That's nice to know." Diggs pulled a cigarette out of his shirt pocket and lit it.

Anthony flushed slightly. "Can we talk a little? Let's step into the coffee shop." He put his hand on Diggs's arm.

Diggs pulled his arm free. "I got no time for you. I ain't going nowhere with you."

"Come on, Diggs. I'm not gonna—"

"Don't hand me orders. I ain't gonna nothing with you."

"Okay, but . . ."

He grinned nastily. "I know you're not a cop no more. They cut you off with a long knife. Everybody knows that. You're just an ex-pig."

My temper was smoldering, watching Anthony almost grow stiff in his frustration and humiliation. I jumped in front of him with angry energetic force. I jabbed a finger at Diggs. "Okay, he's not a cop, but I am, creep. I'm one of his old partners, and I'm helping him out."

His eyes flashed fear. "That don't mean you have any right to do anything. I'm clean."

"You better improve your manners. You're gonna be in big trouble."

"Like I said, you got no right—"

"I got a right to nail your butt on the wall."

"What for?" He angrily stamped out his cigarette.

"We'll start with littering!"

"Come on, get off it."

I grabbed his arm, and he pulled it free. "And resisting arrest! That ought to keep you on ice for a few months, shouldn't it?"

He looked at Anthony worriedly. "This guy's crazy. You know that. He ain't got no probable cause for shit."

"I got probable cause for resisting arrest. You don't put your hand on a policeman. I'm gonna write up the arrest. You're gonna do a little jail time."

"What is this?"

"What's a matter, Diggs?"

"Man, you can't be serious."

"Test me. What's the matter, you don't like the idea of being off the stuff? That would improve your health."

He started to panic. "Hey, I don't need any trips like that."

"Then maybe you better talk to us."

"What're you looking for?"

"What kind of trouble was Tarras in last year?"

"I heard something heavy did come down on him. I don't know what." He flinched his eyes under my stare. "But if you give me a little time, maybe I can find out."

I looked over at Anthony who gave me a little nod signaling trust him. I took out a piece of paper and wrote my folks' number on it. "Okay, I'm going to be at this number. If I haven't heard from you in twenty-four hours I'm going to come looking for you."

"I'll call you just as soon as I know anything."

"Take off."

We watched him scurry down the block, occasionally looking back at us with a pout. I shrugged my shoulder turning to Anthony. "Maybe we'll get lucky."

"Maybe." He sounded skeptical.

"You don't think Diggs is worth a penny for a lead."

"I guess it's really hitting me."

"What?"

"If Tarras made a deal with Internal Affairs, there aren't going to be any records. It's the way it works. When they make a deal for testimony against a crooked cop, they wipe everything clean."

"As I said. Maybe we'll get lucky. I don't know what else to hope for, Tony."

Anthony nodded and then grinned. "You handled him real well. They teach you that at Harvard?"

When we got back to the house, I immediately sensed something had gone wrong with Sherrill and my parents. I found them sitting in the living room in stiff, tense discomfort. I smiled at my wife. "Hi! You all have a good visit?"

"Yes. It's been very nice."

"Good." I was trying to figure out what had happened.

"She's a very smart young woman," Dad said, in a voice that was genuine. He seemed to be impressed, but Mom remained tight-lipped.

"I told you, she's a biological scientist, or a budding one."

"You did something smart for yourself for a change, marrying her."

Sherrill did not know how to respond. "That's very nice of you."

Finally making a firm, subtle show, Mom got up and headed for the kitchen. "I'll get supper started."

"Uh, Mom, Sherrill and I will be eating out."

Mom gave a little whatever-you-say gesture and disappeared. Dad looked over at Sherrill. "Don't worry about her." He then left the room. Anthony and I looked at each other. "What's going on here?"

"I guess I blew it." Sherrill shook her head.

"How?" Anthony asked.

"Everything was going very nicely. Your mother was just as sweet as she could be."

"Until?"

"Until she asked me about some of the things I'm active in. I started telling her. It just never occurred to me."

"You didn't mention." I brought my hand up to my head.

"First thing I said. 'I'm cochairman of the Abortion-on-Demand Committee at the University.' I don't recall anything moving in the room for the next hour. Oh, Joe, I'm sorry."

"You've got a right to your opinions."

"Mom never stayed angry for more than three hours in a stretch her whole life," Anthony reassured. "Don't worry."

At that moment the phone rang in the next room. I went over and picked it up. "Hello?"

"Are you the cop I talked to this afternoon?" The voice belonged to Diggs.

"Yeah, I'm the one you want. What is it?"

Anthony came over alertly and whispered, "Diggs?"

I nodded, and then got back to Diggs. "Say that again. Yeah, I know what it means. Anything else? Good." I hung up.

"Well?" Anthony waited.

"We got lucky."

I was not saying much as I thought about the importance of this call. From the beginning of the case, gnawing at my mind subconsciously was the big worry over the need to come up with a motive. Without a concrete showing of motive, I had to fear we were going to lose. Even though I might be able to show the Tarras story was full of illogical flaws, contradictions, and inconsistencies, I knew from prior experience that all of those flaws could be explained away by confusion in the mind of the witness. Only when you can show a motive do all the discrepancies take on the clear focus of a sinister scheme. Almost axiomatic in law is the principle that to prove misconduct, one must prove a malicious state of mind. I realized that in the summation, Colby would hammer away at this deficiency in the defense, reminding the judge that in all the hours of questioning I had not come up with one shred of evidence to show motive.

I was further aware that the streets were almost mystically imbedded in a brutally enforced code of silence, and that anyone who gave information on a neighbor, who violated the taboo of silence, was condemned to the status of squealer, a social ranking degraded in the streets below child molester, and that severe punishment could be meted out. Where the betrayed man has ties to the syndicate, as did Tarras, it could mean having the squealer's genitals chopped off and stuffed into his dead mouth. Yet I also knew that behind street codes was a lot of empty swagger. I knew there was not much honor or character or guts in the street mentality. I could recall gang rumbles where virtually everyone but a handful out of hundreds had the nerve to be aggressive against fear. Make no mistake about it, the streets have a lot of tough cookies, vicious, ferocious, fearless, and even disciplined men, but they constitute the small minority, the elite of organized crime. Behind closed doors and guarantees of secrecy and some money passing hands, endless betrayals were going down every day against the so-called code of silence. Sometimes money wasn't even needed to get information against a neighbor. Not even a saint can be assured he has no enemies itching for a chance to smash him. Tarras was far from saintly, and I was betting that he had a lot of neighbors in the South Bronx who were not especially fond of him. After I hung up with Diggs, I knew I had found one.

CHAPTER TWENTY-ONE

Awakened, I had my face buried in the pillow so that only one eye caught a clear glimpse of the sun gleaming in through the window on Sherrill's blond hair. I jogged my head a bit for a full view of the bright blue sky filling up the spaces between buildings. I could feel the onset of a beautiful summer day. I slipped out of the sheets slowly, not to awaken Sherrill, who was still catching up on sleep lost from flying the midnight coach. In my Jockey shorts I did a falling tree dive for the floor, putting the brakes on with stiffened arms, and I began pumping myself up and down in push-ups, counting to myself. My body felt fresh and strong and I was feeling a good day was ahead of me in court. Whenever the sun was bright, I started the day feeling a better sense of possibilities. I didn't believe in astrology or the stars or planets affecting my luck, but I knew for sure when the sun was shining, it picked up my spirit. After showering and dressing, I went downstairs to the kitchen and fried myself an egg with a strip of crisp, crackling bacon. I gathered up my notes that I had worked on the previous night, stuffed them into my briefcase, and left for court a jump earlier than the rest of my family. I was feeling good about the information we had learned from our search in the South Bronx. What Diggs had told us was the missing link in understanding how this whole thing got started. After long perplexity I was finally piecing together what had happened.

On my way to court I made one stop at the federal courthouse to pick up a certified document and then I drove over to St. Francis Church. I had not been in church in a long time but on this morning of the final round of trial, I found myself going back to my spiritual roots and feeling a humble need to appeal to a higher force for guidance in my task. The rows of darkened pews were empty and the air was heavy with incense as the sunlight glowed red and gold on the stained-glass windows. I made my way up the aisle, glancing up at the empty organ and choir section hushed silent, but in memory I could hear the rich chords and moving voices. Up ahead were thousands of votive candles flickering in red glasses cluttered around interior grottoes. All light from candles and sun slicing in from the stained glass angled in toward the altar converging with floodlights, drawing my eyes to a floodlit sculpture of a tragic Jesus on the cross. I kneeled in the dark church in prayer.

When I arrived in court, I felt ready. I had regained some of the confidence and vigor with which I had begun the trial. I collected my thoughts, spreading some notes in front of me on the table and looked around behind me, seeing that all my family was in court including Sherrill. I was fairly well satisfied that I was prepared to expose the fraud of Tarras's story if the judge would listen with an open ear. I chatted quickly with Anthony on some details while we waited for the judge to take the bench. The moment court was announced in session, I heaved up to my feet. "Your Honor, at this time I would like to have the prosecution's witness John Tarras retake the stand for cross-examination." I glanced across to the cluster of three men, Colby, the Internal Affairs agent, and Tarras, feeling a flutter in my gut, knowing that this was going to be the last and critical confrontation, and I felt the same upheaval of adrenaline that used to come to me before a street fight. Tarras sat down and slightly raised himself to push further back in the chair and tapped his fingertips on his lap, looking confident.

"Mr. Tarras, when you were arrested in 1967 by Anthony Sorrentino and went to court, how many runners did you have working for you?"

He considered, then answered slowly. "I don't remember the amount of them."

"Well, approximately, as best as you can recall."

"About thirty."

"Now, bearing in mind the collectors you had, you were doing a gross business of about ten thousand a week, isn't that right?"

His voice took on an uneasy tone. "Somewhere in that neighborhood."

"Do you recall the judge saying to you, 'Is it your desire to have me appoint an attorney for you?' And you saying to him, 'Yes,' do you recall that?"

He looked annoyed. "Yes."

"Mr. Tarras, do you also recall what you said when you were asked your occupation?"

"I think I said I operated a grocery store."

"That's right, that's what you said." I leaned back. "And didn't you tell the judge that you only earned a hundred dollars a week and came under the category of indigent in need of a public defender?"

"That's right."

"Isn't it true you were taking in about a half-million dollars a year in your syndicate business?"

"Somewhere around there."

"Do you know the term for untruthful answers given under oath, Mr. Tarras?"

"Sure, I know."

"What is the term, Mr. Tarras?"

"Perjury."

"Right, and since you failed to tell the truth under oath, would you agree that you are an admitted perjurer?"

"You can call me whatever you want to!"

"Not quite. I have too much respect for this court."

Colby leaped to his feet. "Defense counsel is being antagonistic."

I tucked in my lower lip. "Mr. Tarras, I have subpoenaed your income tax record for the state of New York and also for the United States government and have them with me here for the years 1966, '67, '68, '69, and '70."

"Objection, irrelevant." Colby came to the rescue of his witness, protesting to the judge that I was going into immaterial and prejudicial matter.

"Your Honor, this bears on truthfulness."

"Overruled. He can go into this area."

"Mr. Tarras, I notice on these income tax returns that you only put down the grocery business. I see no inclusion of the half million from your syndicate business. You pocketed what should have gone to the government."

"Yeah, so does everyone else." He flashed a malicious smirk.

"So you are an admitted cheat?"

"You use whatever words you want." He licked his mouth.

"I'm using them. You're a cheat." I glared at him.

Colby snarled. "Counsel is being antagonistic again. He is out of order. He's harassing the witness. His speech is inflammatory."

"No, my speech is straightforward," I retorted hotly. "I'm not going to let him bluff his way with doubletalk."

"Get on with the questioning." The judge peered down at me, showing no great sympathy for Tarras.

Anthony, who had been following the line of questioning, said softly to me, "Ask him about May fourth."

I nodded to him, and turned back to the witness. "Mr. Tarras, I notice that in your original affidavit making charges against Sorrentino, you said that the last meeting you had with him was on May fourth, but you later changed that to May eighth."

"Yeah, I straightened it out."

"Is it possible that someone refreshed your memory?"

"I don't know what you mean."

"Oh, for example, that it couldn't have been May fourth because Anthony Sorrentino was in court on May fourth testifying in another case. Did anyone tell you this so you could get your story straight?"

His feet scuffed under the chair. "No, I just checked my mind."

"Oh, you checked your mind," I said in a higher sarcastic register. "Your mind told you you had the wrong date?"

Colby sprang up. "The question has been asked and answered."

"I'll withdraw it." I swung my arms behind my back. "Mr. Tarras, could you tell us how long you and the Internal Affairs agent spent talking about this case?"

"There were a number of meetings."

"And did you basically go over the same questions and answers that have come up here?"

"Generally speaking."

"So you were coached?" Slowly at first and then more rapidly I began to hit the points that he was a man whose testimony was blatantly full of lies and that his story had constantly been under the direction of Internal Affairs agents.

After a brief recess he was back on the stand glaring at me with belligerence in his eyes. I calmly got up. "Sir, you testified that it was Anthony Sorrentino who took you into the precinct bathroom in 1967, isn't that correct?"

"That's right." He wiped his forehead of sweat.

"But in your original affidavit you stated it was his partner, Detective Ward, who dealt with you in the bathroom."

"No, I said it was Sorrentino."

"Sir, I have the affidavit signed by you. You wrote here that it was Ward." I brought forward the affidavit.

"I must have gotten the names mixed up." His voice dropped.

"You knew who Ward was and you knew who Sorrentino was, they could not be confused in your mind, could they?"

"I made a mistake when I wrote down Ward. I mean at this time it would be hard to pinpoint an individual."

"Only one man went with you into the bathroom, isn't that your testimony?"

"Yeah, it was only one with me in there."

"Well, which was it?"

"Sorrentino."

"Well, why did you write down Ward when you first brought these charges?"

"Objection," Colby boomed. "Counsel is throwing flak."

"Your Honor, I believe this is very important."

"Overruled."

"You were in the bathroom for fifteen minutes, wasn't that what you said?"

"Yeah, about that time."

"And you were standing arm's distance?"

"Yeah."

"And in fifteen minutes standing at arm's distance you didn't get a good look?"

"I got a close look."

"Well, if you had so much sureness and clearness, how is it that you said Ward in your affidavit and Sorrentino at trial?"

"I'm clearing up the mistake now." He squirmed making the chair squeak.

"Oh, you checked your mind again?"

"Yeah, I checked my mind."

"Was your mind blank when you wrote down Ward?"

"I told you I made a mistake."

I continued to cross-examine him on the many contradictions in his testimony. He kept looking up at the clock, seemingly eager for the lunch break. At noon I met my family out on the steps. "You all go on. I'm not gonna eat. I want to go over my summation."

"You okay?" Sherrill squeezed my hand.

"Yeah, I'm fine." I gave her a little nozzle kiss.

"I'll join you there."

She joined Anthony, Theresa, and the others heading down the block. Dad lingered on the steps. "Could anyone believe what he was saying? He was lying through his teeth with that check-his-mind routine."

"I hope not."

"You know?"

"What, Dad?"

"I want to say you've been doing a good job in the court."

"It's still not over, Dad."

"But you've been doing a good job." He looked about to say something else, but it didn't come out and he avoided my eyes turning to join the others.

When Tarras took the stand again, he was no longer calm and composed and seemed rather rattled. In contrast, my brother's face was growing brighter and more optimistic. I was not allowing myself to presume anything, so that I would not relax my effort. I went back to cross-examination. "Now let me make sure I have this right, Mr. Tarras. When the so-called Serpico scandal broke, that's when you were called before the grand jury."

"That's correct."

"And you gave them the names of some officers who had accepted bribe money from you?"

"Yes."

"But you did not give them the name of Anthony Sorrentino?"

"I didn't want to involve him. I needed him."

"You needed him?"

"That's right. To provide the protection I was paying for."

"That certainly would explain it."

"It certainly would."

"Except for one fact."

"What's that?"

"The fact that Anthony Sorrentino was transferred out of the South Bronx two months before you were called before the grand jury. I'd like to hear just how he managed this wonderful protection when he wasn't even in that precinct anymore?"

Tarras was becoming visibly unglued and unstrung. He mumbled a little. "Well I—I, ah, maybe I got dates mixed up or something."

"Isn't it true that you didn't name him because he'd never been bought! Because he never took any bribe from you?"

"No!" he shouted.

"Isn't it true that you named him later because you had to name someone and you'd already turned in the cops you actually had paid off?"

"I paid him, too."

"You had to name someone to protect yourself."

"Protect myself from what?" His face regained a confident glare. "If I was trying to protect myself, I'd just like you to tell me from what."

I looked at Anthony. This was the moment. I walked back to the table and picked up a document, and moved to the bench. "Maybe from this." I looked up at the judge. "Your Honor, we submit as defense exhibit C a certified copy of an indictment filed in federal court in Newark, New Jersey, on October eleventh of last year—four days before Mr. Tarras suddenly remembered the terrible things my client had done to him."

"What is the indictment, Mr. Sorrentino?" the judge asked.

"A charge of violating the Travels Act. The charge was dropped because of 'insufficient evidence,' Your Honor. One week later."

"Objection, Your Honor!" Colby boomed. "The witness's past criminal record is irrelevant."

"Do you really expect me to take that objection seriously, Mr. Colby?" The judge spoke with an edge.

Colby sat down uneasily as I put a copy of the document in front of him and handed one to the judge. I then faced the witness. "Well, Mr. Tarras, wouldn't you say that might answer the question of what you were trying to protect yourself from?"

Nervous for a moment, he blurted defiantly, "The record says the charge was dropped for lack of evidence. And you can't prove otherwise."

When Tarras stepped down he stared over at me, and I thought I saw a look of hatred on his face; then he looked away and took his seat next to Colby at the counsel table. There being no further witnesses for the prosecution, Colby rested his case and the judge then invited me to summon witnesses for the defense. Sergeant Ted Roarke was a squat, stocky man in his early fifties who had been the desk sergeant at the 43rd Precinct on the day of the arrest. I introduced into evidence his ringbook showing entries for Sorrentino on May 2 at 11:53 and 12:25, which showed that Tarras was lying when he testified that Sorrentino had been with him uninterruptedly during those hours. Lieutenant Michael Mirow was the next witness I called to the stand, a police veteran of thirty years with an upstate accent. A tall, slightly balding man with gray sideburns and rangy shoulders, Mirow in a freshly pressed uniform bearing the brass lieutenant bars strode forward and eased himself into the witness stand. His brown eyes met the judge's unblinking as his lower lip pushed into his teeth firmly.

"Lieutenant Mirow, what is your duty assignment?"

"I am with the Bronx Borough command working out of the 43rd Precinct."

"On May first, 1967 were you supervising the execution of a warrant for the search and arrest of John Tarras?"

"Yes, I was."

"Do you recall the time you entered the apartment?"

"We went in at two-fifteen or two-thirty."

"How do you recall that?"

"We had been staging outside, getting ready to make our move, and I was aware of the time."

Colby, who had jumped to his feet during Mirow's comment on surveillance, did not say anything until he had finished and then put in, "I will ask the court to strike that testimony on the grounds it constitutes hearsay, and no foundation has been laid."

The judge eventually overruled the objection when I established that Mirow had checked his watch. I next moved to the events at the station house. "Now when Tarras was brought back to the station house, were you present during the booking?"

"I assisted in the booking."

"At any time during the booking did you see Sorrentino take the prisoner to the precinct bathroom?"

"No, I did not."

"And you were with him until the business of the day had been completed?"

"Yes, I was."

My next witness was Inspector James Timmons. A tall, masculine man, he was in a blue uniform, spanking new, with the black shoes freshly shined. His hair was brown but slivered with gray, his blue eyes alert and moving around under dark brows. Settling into the chair, he sat erect, looking like a leader, and a man who would make a good witness. In police circles he had a widely respected reputation for integrity. He was born in Queens, one of eight children, the son of a Flushing fireman who drove a hook-and-ladder with

Engine Company 32 in the fire-fraught Hell's Kitchen. He attended St. Mark's parochial school and attended Hunter College for two years, graduating cum laude. His ambition to become a policeman had been sparked by a hero uncle. He began his police career in 1946. He served in World War II in the infantry and attained the rank of major. He worked his way up through the ranks. He won two commendations for meritorious police duty when a detective. Over a period of five years he commanded three different precincts as a captain. He had been commander of all the patrol forces in The Bronx when appointed inspector.

"Inspector Timmons, in 1967 what was your position with the New York Police Department?"

"I was inspector for the Bronx Borough command."

"Did you have an officer Frank Serpico under your command at that time?"

"Yes, I did."

"And did Serpico bring to your attention the fact that a number of police officers in the plainclothes division were involved in a syndicate pad?"

"Objection, hearsay," Colby rasped. "Any conversations with Serpico are inadmissible."

"This is merely background," I retorted.

"Overruled."

"What happened with Serpico?"

"I followed up on his charges by calling for a grand jury investigation."

"Did you have John Tarras come to your office for questioning before the grand jury?"

"Yes, I did." He stroked his cheek with a finger. "The first formal sit-down took place May twenty-third, 1968. I showed him photographs of all the men in my command and asked him to identify those officers to whom he had paid bribes. He gave me names."

"Was Sorrentino's photograph among those you showed him?"

"Yes, as I said, every man in my command."

"What was his response?"

"Well, I don't have my notes from that meeting but I do know he made no statement against Sorrentino."

"What about the grand jury?"

"I can only go by facts that were brought to my attention. At no time did Tarras testify to any payment to Sorrentino in the grand jury hearing."

"Inspector, are you familiar with the past police work of Sorrentino?"

"Yes, I am."

"Isn't it a fact that each precinct had a rating system for its officers based on number of arrests and percentage of convictions?"

"That's right."

"Sorrentino was ranked number one at the 90th Precinct, isn't that true?"

"Yes."

"And number one at the 68th Precinct?"

"Yes."

"And number one in the entire Bronx Borough command?"

"That's right. He was a top police officer."

The summing up for the defense was a significant speech because the prosecution's final address was going to be the last statement of the case, so that whatever points I wanted to make had to be sharply and deeply inscribed in the judge's consciousness, strong enough to resist Colby's later attempts to confute and erase them. I felt tailspins of nerves in my stomach but I brushed them aside by an act of will, getting to my feet for my presentation. I spoke coming out from behind the counsel table and I spoke in a deliberate, calm voice, holding my note pad for when I might need to check on a detail but speaking largely from the outline I had prepared in my mind.

"The testimony of Mildred Tarras deserves not a shred of credibility. She has no percipient knowledge of any of the incidents alleged by her husband. She has tried to foist herself off to this court as a humble housewife, yet her handwriting has been found on hundreds of betting slips suggesting that she was knee-deep in this racket. In the original affidavit she claimed she knew nothing of any payments to Sorrentino, directly contradicting what she has said in this hearing. Like her husband she has shown no hesitancy to commit perjury when it served her interest."

I changed the tone of my voice to give it a bit more edge, turning to John Tarras. "The one thing that is clear is that here is a man whose word is not to be trusted. He is an admitted liar and cheat and perjurer as we have seen with regard to his securing a public defender as an indigent and stating his income for taxes as near the poverty level when he was earning a half million a year and from contradictions throughout his testimony. His memory pattern comes across as the self-serving zigs and zags of a fraud. This man with his prodigious recall of details regarding events of five years ago, giving exact times and places, pinpointing the year and make and color of Sorrentino's car, and painting detailed portraits of men with hand trucks outside of a market, somehow fails to remember which police officer spent fifteen minutes with him at arm's length in a station house bathroom to discuss a bribe. His testimony confounds the basic tenets of common sense and human psychology. If any event should have been indelibly etched in his mind, it would have been that extraordinary situation. Such an offer clashed violently with the flow of previous events. He had been arrested, booked, and charged with a felony, and then, incongruously, in that sequence of events he is secretly yanked into a bathroom to talk about a bribe. This man, who claims to have photographic recall of the tiniest detail, wants us to believe it was a normal lapse in not being able to remember a policeman's face under those circumstances."

I walked back and forth in front of the counsel table, clasping my chin for a pause and gathering a momentum and flow in my thoughts. "I submit, Your Honor, that there never was any bathroom meeting. Mr. Tarras's problem is not that he can't remember a face. His problem is that he forgot what he first said when he made up this whole tale. He thought he had written Sorrentino's name in the affidavit. One does not forget fifteen minutes at arm's length paying off a cop in a bathroom. One can easily forget a lie when one concocts a story. Tarras got his story, not his faces, mixed up."

I glanced down at my note pad to a page I had marked with a paper clip. "Tarras tells of four meetings with Sorrentino. He describes driving around corners and back streets and parking in alleys and riding on highways. Even here there were contradictions, first in the date given for the last rendezvous. In his original statement he gave May fourth as the day, but changed it to May eighth by checking his mind. What probably happened was that he was advised that May fourth was an impossibility. He said in the beginning he only spent minutes with Sorrentino at these meetings but they were later stretched out to hours. He expanded them in subsequent versions, realizing that padding gives more intriguing texture to the story. By embellishing his fraud with layers and tangles and tiers, he was giving it more body and more believability. It was a dictator's axiom that it is easier to fool people if you enlarge the lie. Tarras was going for the big lie.

"At the grand jury, Tarras testified that all the betting action had to be recorded with the syndicate by two P.M. and that he began calling it in by no later than one P.M. daily, and that this was his regular habit. I think we can safely assume that Tarras was giving the right time at his appearance before the grand jury. I think we can safely assume that he knew what his daily procedure was for all the years he had been engaged in this illicit business. I think the facts clearly establish that on May first, 1967 Tarras had called in his betting slips by one P.M. and that when Sorrentino arrived at two-fifteen P.M., he no longer had any cause to copy the slips.

"Inspector Timmons was sure that he had shown Tarras a photograph of Sorrentino during the Serpico investigations and Tarras indicated he had never paid him any money. Again at the grand jury, when he was naming policemen he paid, Tarras said he had never paid Sorrentino. He claims he wanted to hold on to him for protection, but Sorrentino had left the precinct months before the grand jury hearing."

My voice rose dramatically. "Why did Tarras come forward belatedly to make these accusations? After all, he did go through a lot of trouble. He knew he was going to be undergoing a harsh and draining ordeal of grillings by cops and lawyers. He knew he would be losing a lot of time from his family and business. He knew he would be risking self-incrimination. Why did he take these chances? Why did he come forward after all that time? A sudden surge of civic duty!" I turned to stare at a very uncomfortable Tarras and the irony hung grotesquely. "What should be obvious to common sense is that he did not go through this trouble out of civic virtue.

"Tarras couldn't pay off the FBI agents who arrested him for violating the Travels Act and he had already given up the names of the officers he had paid testifying at the grand jury. So his next maneuver was to frame an honest cop, and he could only do that with someone he had previously been with in some connection. Undeniable was the fact that he had been with Sorrentino at the station house and that he did appear with him in court the following morning, so in the context of those legitimate events he slipped in a shady dealing. The fabric of interaction was there to weave in an illicit transaction. He couldn't pull an unknown cop out of the air. He had to pick someone he could place himself near for a considerable period of time as a matter of record. Sorrentino was a target of opportunity and a target of hatred. Sorrentino was the first cop to detect his syndicate activities and the first cop to bring him to trial and get a conviction against him.

"The only reason a man of his character assumes such risks, trouble, and inconvenience is to gain something for himself. The key to Tarras's motivation is self-gain by any ruthless means. We know from federal records that Tarras was in deep trouble with the federal government for violation of the Travels Act, a crime which carries with it a heavy prison penalty. Mr. Tarras was indicted in federal court four days before he suddenly remembered the terrible things my client had done to him. The charges against him were dropped one week later.

"Mr. Tarras says we can't prove the connection, and for once he's correct, Your Honor! We can't prove it. By the very nature of the interaction between Internal Affairs and the federal prosecutor's office, a connection will be impossible to prove! But we shouldn't have to prove it! Why should a policeman be the only member of our society who must prove his innocence? If we give him even the most basic rights that all the rest of society enjoys, then there is no case, Your Honor. Then we have the word of an outstanding officer with an unblemished record against the word of a convicted felon, an admitted liar, and a proven perjurer.

"When I first filed a motion for a new hearing I was told that I was prejudiced. It's true. Tony Sorrentino is my brother and I love him very much and I care that his life has been broken open by this charge." I could feel my voice cracking. I had to fight for composure. "But I appeal to the court not as a brother, but as a lawyer. To examine the evidence that has been revealed. To judge the credibility of the testimony. To perform the final and basic function of this hearing, the accomplishment of simple justice." I felt drained, sitting back in my chair. Anthony reached over and touched my arm, showing his support.

The judge came in with the verdict at 1:45. I could see Anthony next to me bracing himself, his face taut and solemn. We had to prepare ourselves for the worst. The knowledge that the first trial had turned out so unfairly compounded my unease. Did this judge have the guts to stand up for what was right? He spoke evenly, matter-of-factly, selecting his words with careful precision. "And therefore it is the verdict of this court that Anthony Sorrentino is not guilty, and that he will be restored to his position in the New York Police Department in the rank of gold shield detective."

Anthony blinked and his face brightened visibly. My brother Ernie let out an excited screech and when I turned back to him his eyes were lit up with joy and he was flashing the V sign. I felt an exertion drain out of my body and for a few seconds I was numb and rose unsteadily to my feet with my emotions reeling. My eyes met the judge's and I felt a tremendous surge of respect for him. I warmly thanked him, and he nodded back to me, hinting at a satisfaction he felt himself. Over on the other side, Colby was gathering up his papers, putting them in his briefcase and quietly preparing to leave. I no longer harbored any resentment toward him or anyone else in the case, not even the cold, ruthless Internal Affairs agent or the unscrupulous Tarras couple.

Theresa ran into the arms of Anthony and he lifted her up in triumph and they tenderly held each other tight and close while she wept with joy. Sherrill and Mom spontaneously embraced. Ernie went around hugging everybody but the judge. Dad came over to the counsel table, throwing his arms around Anthony, telling him how happy he was for him. Anthony then turned to me with tears in his eyes, fighting for his words. "Joe, what can I say." As he put an arm over my shoulder I kept my eyes on Dad, who was standing in a daze a few feet from us. I could now see he was going to come over to me. I waited expectantly with an excited sense of hope. His face was pensive, his eyes blinking at me. He patted me on the arm. "Nice job. You did a good job as a lawyer." He then turned and headed for the door. Sherrill's eyes were riveted on me. She had been watching what had happened between Dad and me. Her eyes were filling with hurt. For a moment I kept my gaze fixed on my father, who seemed hesitant about leaving yet. I looked over at Sherrill and shrugged, and my tense body seemed to sag, and I felt a little pain in the core of my heart.

"Joe," Dad called back to me.

"What, Dad?" I said, almost feeling like a little boy.

"Joey." Dad came over quickly to hug me.

THE BRONX ZOO

Sparky Lyle & Peter Golenbock

"A kiss-and-tell book, baseball style." —Dick Young, *New York Daily News*

Welcome to the Yankee clubhouse! Come into the locker room. Get the inside scoop! Sparky Lyle—Cy Young Award-winner, ace relief pitcher and ex-Yankee star—calls 'em as he sees 'em. Here are the backroom battles, the grandstand plays, the salary shake-ups and the gossip that's got the sports world burning! "Sparky Lyle fires away with candor and humor."—*New York Times*

A Dell Book $2.50 (10764-4)

At your local bookstore or use this handy coupon for ordering:

Dell	DELL BOOKS	THE BRONX ZOO $2.50 (10764-4)
	P.O. BOX 1000, PINEBROOK, N.J. 07058	

Please send me the above title. I am enclosing $_____
(please add 75¢ per copy to cover postage and handling). Send check or money order—no cash or C.O.D.'s. Please allow up to 8 weeks for shipment.

Mr/Mrs/Miss _____

Address _____

City _____ State/Zip _____

Now a major motion picture from Lorimar-PAC Productions!

The Choirboys

by Joseph Wambaugh

In this blistering exposé, ex-Detective Sergeant Wambaugh reveals what it's like to be a cop today. The Choirboys are ten cops on nightwatch, who congregate in Los Angeles's MacArthur Park after hours for "choir practice." Their experiences are sometimes funny, often shocking, usually tough—and always powerfully real.

"**A brilliant work of fiction.**"—*Los Angeles Times*

"**A master storyteller. Authenticity oozes from this book. Freewheeling and chilling.**"—*Houston Chronicle*

A Dell Book $2.50 (11188-9)

Over 2½ million copies sold!

At your local bookstore or use this handy coupon for ordering:

| **Dell** | **DELL BOOKS**
 P.O. BOX 1000, PINEBROOK, N.J. 07058 | The Choirboys $2.50 (11188-9) |

Please send me the above title. I am enclosing $_____
(please add 75¢ per copy to cover postage and handling). Send check or money order—no cash or C.O.D.'s. Please allow up to 8 weeks for shipment.

Mr/Mrs/Miss_____

Address_____

City_____State/Zip_____

Dell Bestsellers

- ☐ **COMES THE BLIND FURY** by John Saul $2.75 (11428-4)
- ☐ **CLASS REUNION** by Rona Jaffe $2.75 (11408-X)
- ☐ **THE EXILES** by William Stuart Long $2.75 (12369-0)
- ☐ **THE BRONX ZOO** by Sparky Lyle and Peter Golenbock $2.50 (10764-4)
- ☐ **THE PASSING BELLS** by Phillip Rock $2.75 (16837-6)
- ☐ **TO LOVE AGAIN** by Danielle Steel $2.50 (18631-5)
- ☐ **SECOND GENERATION** by Howard Fast $2.75 (17892-4)
- ☐ **EVERGREEN** by Belva Plain $2.75 (13294-0)
- ☐ **CALIFORNIA WOMAN** by Daniel Knapp $2.50 (11035-1)
- ☐ **DAWN WIND** by Christina Savage $2.50 (11792-5)
- ☐ **REGINA'S SONG** by Sharleen Cooper Cohen $2.50 (17414-7)
- ☐ **SABRINA** by Madeleine A. Polland $2.50 (17633-6)
- ☐ **THE ADMIRAL'S DAUGHTER** by Victoria Fyodorova and Haskel Frankel $2.50 (10366-5)
- ☐ **THE LAST DECATHLON** by John Redgate $2.50 (14643-7)
- ☐ **THE PETROGRAD CONSIGNMENT** by Owen Sela $2.50 (16885-6)
- ☐ **EXCALIBUR!** by Gil Kane and John Jakes $2.50 (12291-0)
- ☐ **SHOGUN** by James Clavell $2.95 (17800-2)
- ☐ **MY MOTHER, MY SELF** by Nancy Friday $2.50 (15663-7)
- ☐ **THE IMMIGRANTS** by Howard Fast $2.75 (14175-3)

At your local bookstore or use this handy coupon for ordering:

Dell DELL BOOKS
P.O. BOX 1000, PINEBROOK, N.J. 07058

Please send me the books I have checked above. I am enclosing $_____
(please add 75¢ per copy to cover postage and handling). Send check or money order—no cash or C.O.D.'s. Please allow up to 8 weeks for shipment.

Mr/Mrs/Miss _____

Address _____

City _____ State/Zip _____

"The Hollywood novel by just about the hottest screenwriter around." —*Wall Street Journal*

by William Goldman
author of *Marathon Man* and *Magic*

William Goldman—Academy Award-winning screenwriter of *Butch Cassidy and the Sundance Kid* and *All The President's Men*—has written a shattering, nationally-best-selling novel. He has seen and learned a lot of Hollywood's best-kept secrets. In *Tinsel*, he tells a story only an insider could.

"Scathing, witty, merciless, and a fast enjoyable read. The film colony may squirm, but the rest of us will lap it up."— John Barkham Reviews

"No-punches-pulled slashes at the business. Complete with names named." —*Kirkus Reviews*

A Dell Book $2.75 (18735-4)

At your local bookstore or use this handy coupon for ordering:

Dell	**DELL BOOKS** TINSEL $2.75 (18735-4)
	P.O. BOX 1000, PINEBROOK, N.J. 07058

Please send me the above title. I am enclosing $_____
(please add 75¢ per copy to cover postage and handling). Send check or money order—no cash or C.O.D.'s. Please allow up to 8 weeks for shipment.

Mr/Mrs/Miss_____

Address_____

City_____ State/Zip_____

Comes the Blind Fury

John Saul

Bestselling author of *Cry for the Strangers* and *Suffer the Children*

More than a century ago, a gentle, blind child walked the paths of Paradise Point. Then other children came, teasing and taunting her until she lost her footing on the cliff and plunged into the drowning sea.

Now, 12-year-old Michelle and her family have come to live in that same house—to escape the city pressures, to have a better life.

But the sins of the past do not die. They reach out to embrace the living. Dreams will become nightmares.

Serenity will become terror. There will be no escape.

A Dell Book $2.75 (11428-4)

At your local bookstore or use this handy coupon for ordering:

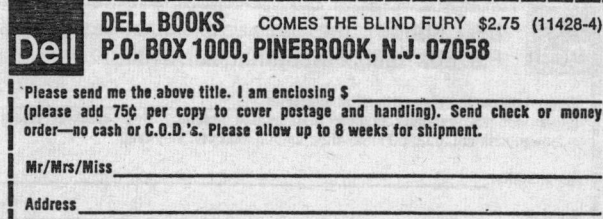

Dell	**DELL BOOKS** COMES THE BLIND FURY $2.75 (11428-4) P.O. BOX 1000, PINEBROOK, N.J. 07058

Please send me the above title. I am enclosing $_____
(please add 75¢ per copy to cover postage and handling). Send check or money order—no cash or C.O.D.'s. Please allow up to 8 weeks for shipment.

Mr/Mrs/Miss_____

Address_____

City_____ State/Zip_____

The unforgettable story of a woman's search for the father she had never known.

THE ADMIRAL'S DAUGHTER
Victoria Fyodorova and Haskel Frankel

It began in Moscow during World War II—a story of secret trysts and midnight arrests. It became the story of a love that leapt the boundaries of fear, of language, of international power and politics to see a beautiful woman reunited with her father at last.

"One of the most thrilling, ingenious and frightening spy stories I've ever read, and all the more powerful because it's true."
—*The Hollywood Reporter*

"A book that you cannot put down."—*New York Post*

A Dell Book $2.50 (10366-5)

At your local bookstore or use this handy coupon for ordering:

Dell | **DELL BOOKS** THE ADMIRAL'S DAUGHTER $2.50 (10366-5)
P.O. BOX 1000, PINEBROOK, N.J. 07058

Please send me the above title. I am enclosing $_____
(please add 75¢ per copy to cover postage and handling). Send check or money order—no cash or C.O.D.'s. Please allow up to 8 weeks for shipment.

Mr/Mrs/Miss_____

Address_____

City_____ State/Zip_____